Small Change

SHEILA ROBERTS

St. Martin's Paperbacks

This is a work of fiction. All of the characters, organizations, and events portrayed in this novel are either products of the author's imagination or are used fictitiously.

SMALL CHANGE

Copyright © 2013 by Sheila Roberts.

For information address St. Martin's Press, 175 Fifth Avenue, New York, NY 10010.

ISBN: 978-1-250-04376-4

Printed in the United States of America

St. Martin's Paperbacks edition / February 2014

St. Martin's Paperbacks are published by St. Martin's Press, 175 Fifth Avenue, New York, NY 10010.

10 9 8 7 6 5 4 3 2 1

p

Acclaim for the novels of Sheila Roberts

"An absolutely wonderful holiday treat, full of warmth and charm and second chances. It's the perfect stocking stuffer." —Kristin Hannah

"This lighthearted and charming read will appeal to fans of Kristin Hannah's magical, light romances and readers who enjoyed Roberts's previous holiday offerings."
—*Library Journal* (starred review)

"Roberts's witty and effervescently funny novel will warm hearts. Realistic characters populate the pages of this captivating story, which is a great escape from the hustle and bustle." —*RT Book Reviews* (Top Pick)

"A fast, fresh, fun and funny story by a major new talent."
—Susan Wiggs, *New York Times* bestselling author

"The funny novel is all about love . . . and friendships. But, most of all, it's about learning to love yourself before you can love anyone else." —*Columbus Dispatch*

"Roberts manages to avoid genre clichés and crafts a heartfelt novel with nuggets of life truths."
—*The Press & Sun Bulletin*

"A beautifully written story that is populated with real and charming people." —*Fresh Fiction*

"Hands-down, this has to be the best Christmas book I have read. The characters are so meticulously developed, I had to double check to see if it really was a work of fiction." —*J. Kaye's Book Blog*

For Myrle,
who taught me the value
of coupons and garage sales.
And for Sam and Selma,
who used a teacher's salary
to prove that it's not
what you make that matters,
it's what you do with it.

Acknowledgments

Thank you so much to all the great people who shared my enthusiasm for this book and helped in so many ways. To the Bainbridge Brain Trust—Susan Wiggs, Elsa Watson, Suzanne Selfors, Anjali Banerjee, and Carol Cassella—for watching over me, to Annette Erickson, the original diva on a dime, who generously shared her moniker with a fictional character, and to Kathy Nordlie, who keeps giving me great recipes like that blackberry cordial. Yum! I'm also indebted to Debbie at Temporarily Yours in Seattle. If I were working as a temp I'd want to work for her. Ruth Ross, you have the eyes of an eagle; thank you for turning them on this manuscript. Of course, huge thanks to my agent, Paige Wheeler, my editor, Rose Hilliard, and the St. Martin's team, who continue to believe in me. You all rock!

Use it up, wear it out, make it do, or do without.
—popular saying during the Great Depression

Now Is the Summer
of Our Discontent

Chapter 1

There it sat, a Cloud Nine queen-sized luxury gold comforter with red ribbon appliqué and metallic embroidery. Forty percent off. It was the last one left. Tiffany Turner had seen it, and so had the other woman.

The woman caught Tiffany looking at it and her eyes narrowed. Tiffany narrowed hers right back. Her competitor was somewhere in her fifties, dressed for comfort in jeans and a sweater, her feet shod in tennis shoes for quick movement—obviously a sale veteran, but Tiffany wasn't intimidated. She was younger. She had the drive, the determination.

It only took one second to start the race. The other woman strode toward the comforter with the confidence that comes with age, her hand stretched toward the prize.

Tiffany chose that moment to look over her competitor's shoulder. Her eyes went wide and she gasped. "Oh, my gosh." Her hands flew to her face in horror.

The other woman turned to see the calamity happening in back of her.

And that was her undoing. In a superhuman leap, Tiffany bagged the comforter just as her competitor turned back. *Score.*

Boy, if looks could kill.

It would be rude to gloat. Tiffany gave an apologetic shrug and murmured, "Sorry."

The woman paid her homage with a reluctant nod. "You're good."

Yes, I am. "Thanks," Tiffany murmured, and left the field of battle for the customer service counter.

As she walked away, she heard the other woman mutter, "Little beast."

Okay, now she'd gloat.

She was still gloating as she drove home from the mall an hour later. She'd not only scored on the comforter, she'd gotten two sets of towels (buy one, get one free), a great top for work, a cute little jacket, a new shirt for Brian, and a pair of patent metallic purple shoes with three-and-a-half-inch heels that were so hot she'd burn the pavement when she walked. With the new dress she'd snagged at thirty percent off (plus another ten percent off for using her department store card), she'd be a walking inferno. Brian would melt when he saw her.

Her husband would also melt if he saw how much she'd spent today, so she had to beat him home. And since he would be back from the office in half an hour, she was now in another race, one that she didn't dare lose. That was the downside of hitting the mall after work. She always had to hurry home to hide her treasures before Brian walked in the door. But she could do it.

Tiffany followed the Abracadabra shopping method: get the bargain and then make it disappear for a while so you could later insist that said bargain had been sitting around the house for ages. She'd learned that one from her mother. Two years before, she had successfully used the Guessing Game method: bring home the bargains, and lull husband into acceptance by having him guess how incredibly little you'd paid for each one.

She'd pull a catch of the day from its bag and say, "Guess how much I paid for this sweater."

He'd say, "Twenty dollars."

"Too high," she'd reply with a smirk.

"Okay. Fifteen."

"Too high."

"Ten."

"Nope. Eight ninety-nine. I'm good."

And she was. As far as Tiffany was concerned, the three sexiest words in the English language were *fifty percent off*. She was a world-class bargain hunter (not surprising, since she'd sat at the feet of an expert—her mom), and she could smell a sale a mile away.

Great as she was at ferreting out a bargain, she wasn't good with credit cards. It hadn't taken Tiffany long to snarl her finances to the point where she and Brian had to use their small, start-a-family savings and Brian's car fund to bail her out.

She'd felt awful about that, not only because she suspected they'd never need that family fund anyway (that suspicion was what led to her first shopping binge), but because Brian had suffered from the fallout of her mismanagement. He'd had his eye on some rusty old beater on the other side of the lake and had been talking about buying and restoring it. The car wound up rusting at someone else's house, thanks to her. Even the money they'd scraped together for her bailout wasn't enough. She'd had to call in the big guns: Daddy. That had probably been harder on Brian than waving good-bye to their savings.

"Tiffy, baby, you should have told me," he said the day the awful truth came out and they sat on the couch, her crying in his arms.

She would have, except she kept thinking she could get control of her runaway credit card bills. It seemed like one minute she only had a couple and the next thing she knew they'd bred and taken over. "I thought I could handle it."

It was a reasonable assumption since they both worked. There was just one problem: their income had never quite managed to keep up with the demands of their life. It still didn't.

She sighed. Brian so didn't understand. All he did was pay the mortgage, utilities, and the car payments. He had no idea how much it really cost to live. First of all, they had to eat. Did he have any idea how much wine cost? Or meat? Even toilet paper wasn't cheap. And they had to have clothes. She couldn't show up at Salon H to do nails in sweats, for heaven's sake. What woman wanted to go to a nail artist who looked like a slob? Food and clothes were the tip of the expense iceberg. Friends and family had birthdays; she couldn't give them IOUs. And she had to buy Christmas presents. And decorations. And hostess gifts. Now it was June and soon there would be picnics at the lake and neighborhood barbecues. A girl could hardly show up empty-handed. Then there were bridal showers to attend, and baby . . . No, no. She wasn't going there.

After the great credit card cleanup the Guessing Game method lost its effectiveness, and she'd had to retire it. Hiding her purchases worked better anyway.

Her bargains weren't the only things she was hiding. In the last year she'd gotten two new credit cards, and they were both well used. Brian might panic if he knew, but there was no need for panic. She'd be okay this time. She'd learned her lesson. In fact, she was going to make a big payment on one of them this week. So, there was no need for Brian not to know about the purchases in her car trunk.

She checked the clock on the dash: 4:50. Brian got off at five. He worked at the Heart Lake Department of Planning and Community Development. It took him exactly six minutes to get from his office to their cul-de-sac in

Heart Lake Estates and another fifty-five seconds to park his car and get to the front door. That gave her seventeen minutes and five seconds to beat him home.

A little voice at the back of her mind whispered, "You wouldn't have to worry about beating your husband home if you were honest with him."

She ignored it and applied more pressure to the gas pedal. She could feel her heart rate picking up as two new voices began to echo in the back of her head.

> BRIAN: *That's a lot of shopping bags. Were you at the mall?*
> TIFFANY: *Yes, but I didn't spend much. This was all on sale.*
> BRIAN: *You had that much cash on you?*
> TIFFANY:

Here the dialogue stopped because she didn't know what script to follow. Should she lie and say, "Yes, actually, I did," or should she say, "Well, I only charged a couple of things."

No, of course, she wouldn't use that last line. She wasn't supposed to be charging anything. She'd promised. But she didn't have enough money to take advantage of the sales. And if she didn't take advantage of the sales, how could she save money? It was a terrible, vicious circle.

She should take it all back. Brian probably wouldn't get that excited about the shoes or the dress anyway. Just show up naked. That was what her friends always joked. Even naked she couldn't explain about the new charge cards. Not these days.

Her best bet was to get home before Brian. She could make it. Her foot pressed down harder. She wouldn't buy anything more all month, and she'd take back the shoes. But the dress—fifty percent off, for heaven's sake.

Just get home and ditch the stuff. Then you can decide what to do. She roared off the exit ramp then turned right onto Cedar Springs Road. Ten more minutes and she'd be in Heart Lake Estates. The finish line was in sight.

Oh, no. What was this behind her? Her stomach fell at the sight of the flashing lights. Noooo. This was so unfair. Yes, she was going fifteen miles over the speed limit, but she had an emergency brewing here. And thirty was too slow. What sicko had decided you could only go thirty on this road anyway? It was probably someone who had no life, nowhere to be, no husband to beat home.

Once again a conversation started at the back of her brain.

BRIAN: *Hey, I beat you home. Where were you?*
TIFFANY: *Just out running some errands.*
BRIAN: *What's that piece of paper in your hand?*
TIFFANY: *Ummmm . . .*

She could not, COULD NOT, get a speeding ticket. They couldn't afford it.

Heart thudding, she watched as the policeman got out of his patrol car. He was big and burly. Big men loved sweet, little blondes with blue eyes. That had to work in her favor. She saw the wedding ring on his finger. Darn. It would have worked more in her favor if he'd been single.

She let down her window and showed him the most pitiful expression she could muster. "I was speeding, I know, but pleeease don't give me a ticket. I haven't had a ticket since I was eighteen." Actually, twenty, but close enough. Parking tickets didn't count. Neither did citations for running stop signs. "I promise I won't speed again. Ever. If I come home with a speeding ticket . . ." And a trunk full of shopping bags. She couldn't even think about it. She might as well throw herself in the lake and be done with it.

The officer regarded her sadly. Good, she'd won his sympathy. She looked back at him with tears in her eyes.

"Lady, you were going twenty miles over the limit. I can't not give you a ticket."

What? What was this? "Oh, God, please." Now she opted to shed the tears. They were wasted sitting around in her eyeballs. "My husband will kill me." How was she going to pay on her credit card if she had to use the money for a stupid speeding ticket?

"Don't worry," said the officer.

"Yes?" He'd had a change of heart. She was saved! Long live blonde.

"They take MasterCard at the courthouse. May I have your driver's license and registration please?"

Tiffany's jaw dropped. "What kind of a sick thing is that to say?"

"License and registration," he prompted.

She fished them out of the glove compartment and handed them over. "I'm so not buying tickets to the policeman's ball." She sniffled.

"We're not doing one this year," he said, and walked back to his car.

This was sick and wrong and unfair. That cop had no heart.

She should have told him she had to go to the bathroom. Then maybe he would have let her go with a warning, maybe even given her a police escort home. A police escort was the only way she'd beat Brian home now.

Tiffany looked at the clock on her dash and ground her teeth. This was a nightmare. She was going to have to return the shoes, the top, the jacket, and the shirt. The dress, too.

"Aren't you forgetting something?" prompted that little voice.

The towels?

"What else?"

Nooooo. And the comforter.

Chapter 2

Brian's old mail Jeep was already parked in the driveway when Tiffany got home. She stuffed the speeding ticket in her purse and left her purchases in the trunk. As she hurried up the front walk she tried to come up with a reason she was late getting home so that she didn't have to use the S word. Brian still didn't need to know about the shopping, especially since she was going to have to take everything back so she could pay for that stupid ticket. Maybe not Brian's shirt. He had to look nice for work. But everything else.

She began to script her arrival.

BRIAN: *What took you so long? I thought you were done at four today.*
TIFFANY: *Something came up.*
BRIAN: *Yeah? What?*
TIFFANY:

Oh, boy. What could she say next? A client, of course—she'd say someone had come into Salon H with a nail emergency just as she was leaving. Brian would buy that. It happened.

She hated lying to him, though. She never lied to him, except about money. Somewhere along their happily-ever-after road, her spending habits had become top secret. Really, there were some things it was better for him not to know. He'd only worry.

Like she was doing right now. For a nanosecond she considered calling her father and asking him to give her the money to pay for her ticket. Her birthday was next month. They could call it an early birthday present. If she had the ticket covered, she could tell Brian why she was late, and in the next breath say, "But don't worry. It's paid for." Sadly, there was no point in calling Daddy. She still remembered his words to her after the great credit card bailout: "Baby girl, this is the last time I'm going to come to your rescue. You're a married woman now, and you need to learn the value of a dollar."

As if she didn't know the value of a dollar. She knew it wasn't worth squat!

She sighed as she slipped in the front door. No sense asking Mom for help, either. Mom never had any money.

Tiffany found Brian already on the back deck. He'd changed into his jeans and was firing up the barbecue to grill hamburgers, their standard fare on the nights he cooked dinner. "You beat me home," she said, stating the obvious, and gave him a quick kiss. "I figured you would. You wouldn't believe the day I had." So far, so good.

"Busy, huh? That's good." Brian sounded more distracted than interested in how her day had gone.

That was normal lately; he had a lot on his mind. But it wasn't sex. The shoes really had been a waste. After two miscarriages, she supposed she couldn't blame him. What was the point?

Love was the point, of course, but sometimes, late at

night, after Brian was dead to the world, she wrote a very dark script:

TIFFANY: *Brian, do you still love me?*
BRIAN: *I don't know. You can't manage money and you can't stay pregnant. What good are you?*

That was always where the script ended because she still hadn't come up with an answer that satisfied her.

"How was your day?" she asked now.

He shrugged.

He used to have plenty to say about work. There was always a contractor who was hounding him, a property owner trying to pass off plans for a garage as plans for a shed, someone unhappy over how long it was taking to get the permit for the addition on her house. But the local building slump was slowing things down at work and spreading insecurity through the office. Brian had mentioned it only once, when he was afraid she was starting to get carried away with her bargain hunting, but it seemed like for the last month, he'd been walking under a dark cloud. She'd ask what was new at the office and he'd say, "Nothing. What's for dinner?" Now he'd gone from "nothing" to a shrug.

"Is everything okay?" Tiffany asked, even though she wasn't sure she wanted to hear the answer.

"I don't know," he said, his voice heavy.

He went back inside the house. She followed him in and watched as he pulled hamburger out of the fridge and began pounding the meat into patties. Okay. So, they weren't talking about her day and they weren't talking about his. What were they going to do?

Make dinner. She washed her hands, then went to the fridge and pulled out onions, lettuce, and a tomato and set them on the counter.

"It's a good thing all the credit cards are paid off," he said.

Meanwhile, back at the fridge, Tiffany almost dropped a jar of pickles.

You'd better tell him about the credit cards now. And the ticket.

Oh, no. This was so not the time to dump that kind of news on her husband, not with the mood he was in. "Is there something you're not telling me?"

"Things are really getting bad at work, Tiffy." Brian gave a piece of meat an extra hard smack.

Getting? They'd already been bad.

"Two people got laid off today."

"Laid off?" she squeaked. They were barely making it now. What would they do if Brian got laid off?

He put the meat patties on a plate. "That's why I'm glad we at least don't have a lot of credit card debt anymore."

She nodded agreement. This was sooooo not the right time to give him any bad news. When would there be a right time? Probably never. What was she going to do?

Brian must have read the panic in her eyes, because he immediately looked regretful. "Hey." He started to hug her, then looked at his meat-greased hands. He washed them, saying over his shoulder, "I didn't mean to scare you."

"I'm not scared," she lied. She could almost see those two credit cards in back of her, grown to monster-sized proportions and leaning over her with giant fangs. Brian dried his hands, then hugged her and she pressed in close.

"It's okay," he said, and kissed her forehead. "We can make it through this. We just have to be careful. You understand?"

She felt her cheeks burning, but she managed to nod.

"You need to know what we're up against. It could get ugly."

It could get ugly if he found out about those charge cards. "I thought you said you didn't want to scare me."

"I don't. I just want you to understand that this is serious."

"I do." It was more serious than he knew.

Rachel Green left her principal's office minus her smile. This was a rotten way to end the school day, not to mention the year. She marched to her empty classroom, mentally chanting, "Why me?" with each step. The answer to that was simple: some gremlin had pasted a Kick Me sign on her backside.

First divorce, now no job—a kick for each cheek.

She'd known teaching fifth grade at Heart Lake Elementary wasn't a permanent position when she'd stepped in to take Ambika Sinj's class after Ambika had gone on maternity leave. But, deep down, Rachel had hoped that once Ambika had her baby she would opt for full-time motherhood. She hadn't.

This school was a great one with an excellent principal and good kids. Rachel didn't blame Ambika for wanting to come back to work, thus depriving her substitute of steady employment for the next year. She blamed the gremlin. Inside her classroom she shook a fist and growled, "You're messing with the wrong woman."

"Steve Martin in drag. Now, that is scary," said a voice from the classroom doorway. "Are you auditioning for a remake of *Planes, Trains and Automobiles*?"

Rachel turned to see Elsa Wilson, a wiry fifty-year-old who taught third grade, regarding her with eyebrows raised. She slumped on her desk. "Don't get too close to me. I'm a bad luck lightning rod."

"Don't tell me, let me guess. Ambika's coming back and you're out of work?"

Rachel nodded. She wanted to cry. Instead, she turned

and began erasing math problems off the whiteboard, ignoring the ache beginning at her temples. "Oh, well. I'll go back to subbing."

Elsa joined her and picked up the other eraser. "Not a bad plan. Between us and the middle school, we'll keep you busy."

But could they keep her busy enough? "I know. It's just . . ." She didn't finish the sentence. She didn't need to. Elsa understood. It was so much easier to come into the same classroom every day and work with the same students, to have your own lesson plans to follow instead of someone else's. Most important, a permanent teaching position meant benefits and a guaranteed salary. Not necessarily a huge salary, but regular. Money was tight even when Rachel was working full time. Once she was reduced to substitute teaching, she'd be vacuum-sealed in debt. Panic grabbed at her ankles. She attempted to kick free. "I'll be fine." At least she'd still have free dental for the kids.

"Of course you will," said Elsa. "You're a survivor."

It was a far cry from being a princess, which was what her parents had raised her to be. When she met Aaron Green the dentist she thought she'd found her prince. First he told her she had a beautiful smile. Then he told her she had a beautiful body. Then, after two kids, two cars, a mortgage, and her fortieth birthday, he'd found another woman and told her good-bye. But not until he'd made sure that much of his money did a disappearing act, probably into some account of his mother's. Just one of the universe's little cosmic jokes. Ha, ha. Almost as funny as finding herself with no steady employment and a student loan to pay off. Now she had a master's degree in education and no job, rather like having a bridal gown and no husband. Oh, bad analogy.

Maybe someday her prince would come. Ha. If he did,

she'd slam the door in his face. She needed another prince like she needed a third boob. She already had her hands full with Aaron, who was as lousy an ex as he once was a husband—always late with his child support payments, but still managing to come up with money for presents for the kids and frequent trips to Pizza Heaven to ensure his status as the favorite parent. She'd been coping with all that, pretty much, but now she'd been set adrift in a leaky raft on a stormy financial sea. *Was* she a survivor?

"You bet I am," she said as much to herself as to Elsa. She'd show Aaron, and his mother (who had never liked her). And she'd show the damned gremlin, too.

Elsa gave her an encouraging hug followed by an invitation to a Sensual Woman spa party. "Just come. You don't have to buy anything. It'll be good for you to get out and have some fun."

"Thanks," Rachel said, but she made no promises. The last thing she wanted to do was go to a home party and spend what little money she had these days on fancy lotions.

Elsa left, and Rachel finished up in the classroom. Then she went to pick up the kids from Aaron's office, where they were getting their semiannual checkups. The sun was shining and the lake was looking especially idyllic, ringed with evergreens and cozy houses. Colorful bundles of blooms erupted from the heart-shaped hanging flower baskets along downtown Lake Way. Late afternoon snackers gathered at tables outside the Sweet Somethings bakery. Funny. It didn't look like the end of the world.

She frowned, listening to the minivan's stumbling motor. It would have to go to the car doctor while she still had a hope of paying for repairs. Maybe she'd let the thing die. Heart Lake was a small town and the kids could bike everywhere. So could she, come to think of it. Great for the thighs, and think of the money she'd save on gas. Go green.

She stopped by the Safeway on her way to pick up a take-and-bake pizza for dinner. No pop, though. Aaron had always been adamant about banning soda pop from the house—bad for the teeth. Allowing Claire and David to drink it would be a small, inexpensive way to enjoy a bit of parental one-upsmanship, but Rachel wasn't about to play that game. Aaron was right about the pop, and when it came to the children, one of them had to be a team player.

Of course, she didn't get by with only purchasing what she'd come in for. By the time she was done, she knew her grocery bill had sneaked up an extra forty dollars. Oh well, she thought fatalistically, they had to eat.

Dan the checker had just finished ringing up her purchases when her friend and next door neighbor, Jessica Sharp, pulled her cart up behind Rachel. Jess was in her early forties. She had short, dark hair, which she kept cut in the latest style, the kind of face that turned heads, and a great, curvy body, which she tended to view as overweight. She drove a red Volkswagen convertible, bought fresh flowers every week, and got her hair and nails done regularly. She didn't work and she didn't worry about money.

At least she never used to. Rachel had sometimes envied her friend's easy life, but not so much now, not with the troubles at her husband's bank, which had gotten bought out by a bigger bank. Her husband's job was in jeopardy and Jess was about to join the end-of-the-world club. Today she was wearing a black, ribbed sleeveless tee, jeans, and red flip-flops decorated with poufy red flowers. She also wore dark circles under her eyes.

"Any news on Michael's job?" asked Rachel.

Jess shook her head. "I used to think no news was good news. Silly me. Waiting is killing us."

"Waiting only starts the dying process," Rachel said glumly. She pointed to the wine bottle in Jess's shopping cart. "If that's for craft night on Friday, you'd better get more. After this week I'll probably inhale an entire bottle single-handed."

"I hear you," said Jess. "And don't worry. I've got something special in mind for Friday. I'll stock up on chocolate, too."

It would take an entire vat of chocolate to raise her endorphin level, Rachel thought as she left the store. She turned onto Deerwood Avenue where Aaron had his dental office. Before he moved in with Misty the lingerie model he brought the kids home after their checkups, but that changed in a hurry. Misty didn't like Aaron coming by the house without her. Misty was smarter than she looked . . . or at least she had good instincts.

The children were already finished with their check-ups and hanging out in the waiting room when Rachel arrived. As always, the place smelled faintly of chemicals. Lately, it seemed to Rachel that it smelled like money, too. This was probably simply her imagination getting fired up by the sight of the expensive new carpet and freshly painted walls. Light green. Between the walls and the turquoise glass window in the door, she always felt like she was underwater when she came in here.

"Hi, Mom," ten-year-old David greeted her. He was a cute boy, with Rachel's long legs. Once he grew into his feet, he'd probably tower over both her and Aaron. The basketball court was already second home to him and he could dart around anyone in his way like he had wings on his feet, but at home he tended to trip over everything. Right now he was smiling and clutching a new game for the Wii Aaron had recently given the kids. "Look what Dad gave me." He rushed to show her, nearly stepping on the toes of a harried-looking businessman in a nearby chair. "Sorry," David muttered as the man frowned and pulled his feet under his chair.

Rachel looked at the expensive prize and smiled around gritted teeth. "That was nice of him." She supposed she should be grateful that at least this time Aaron hadn't given their son some gadget that would require the frequent purchase of batteries.

"Can I go over to his house and play it?"

Of course, Aaron had opted to keep the Wii console at his place even though David and Claire were only over there every other weekend.

"I'll bet you have homework," Rachel said.

David's smile evaporated.

Thank you, Aaron, for making me the meanie. "I tell you what," she said. "You get your homework done, then I'll run you over to Dad's. He can take you to school in the morning."

Now David was beaming. He gave her a kiss and said, "Thanks, Mom. You're the best."

Yes, she was. Aaron was the faux best.

Twelve-year-old Claire sat slumped in a chair and had yet to surface from behind a copy of *People*. She had the same dark coloring as Rachel and big, brown eyes, and she'd inherited Rachel's full lips. But, much to Claire's dismay, she had inherited her father's nose. It was a little long, but it wasn't a bad nose, really. Still, it wasn't a Miley Cyrus nose, which, for Claire, meant it was ugly. Rachel knew her daughter would grow up to be striking, and she assured Claire of that practically on a daily basis, but motherly assurance was a very small shield to carry against peer-driven standards of beauty.

"What did Daddy give you?" Rachel asked her. Why did she ask? Did she really want to know?

Her face still buried behind *People*, Claire produced a gift certificate to The Coffee Stop from her hoodie pocket and held it up.

Her daughter was barely communicating, and behind

that magazine hid a scowly face. Something had put Claire in a funk and Rachel could already guess what it was. The threat of braces, which had been looming on the horizon, had finally materialized. "It looks like several vanilla chai smoothies for you," she said, using her un-fazed mother voice. She stepped up to the reception window where Aaron's young receptionist Liz sat, smiling politely. Polite was the best Liz could give Rachel since the divorce. This hardly came as a surprise. Aaron would, of course, have posed as a long-suffering husband whose wife didn't understand him.

She smiled back just as politely. "Hi, Liz. Can you tell Aaron I'm here?"

"He's finishing with a patient. I'll tell him."

Rachel nodded and sat down in a chair next to her daughter. She gave Claire a playful shoulder nudge. "So, are you reading about me?"

Claire rolled her eyes. "Lame, Mom."

Ah, the love. If she hadn't been twelve, herself, once, she'd have been offended. "How did your checkup go?"

Claire shrugged. "It sucked."

That said it all. "I'm sorry."

"I don't want braces." The words came out, powered by misery. A hand went to Claire's eyes to swipe at fast-forming tears.

"Oh, baby," said Rachel, putting an arm around her. "I know you don't."

"Tell Daddy I don't want them," Claire begged. "My teeth aren't that bad."

"I'll talk to him," Rachel promised, more to make her daughter feel better than because she thought it would do any good. Braces were, after all, the American way.

Claire nodded and wiped away more tears.

Out of the corner of her eye, Rachel could see Aaron approaching. He was forty-four, tall and broad shouldered, with wavy dark hair salted with a hint of gray to make him look both distinguished and trustworthy. He was walking proof that looks were deceiving.

"How about you two go wait in the car?" she suggested to the children. "I'll be there in a minute."

"Okay. Bye, Dad," called David, bouncing out of the room, completely clueless to the unfolding family drama.

Claire stalked out after him without a word to her father.

"She's happy," Rachel observed.

"We really need to get her into braces," he said. "It's time. I can set up a consultation for you with Rencher for next week if you like."

Rachel was aware of Liz, sitting a few feet away from them, pretending to work. "Let's talk." She took Aaron's arm and pulled him out the door onto the second-floor landing. "This is not good timing for me."

He frowned. "Rachel. This is our daughter."

She felt a sudden need to kick him in the shin. "I'm glad you used the word *our*. Does that mean you're going to take care of this expense?"

His frown deepened. "Of course I'll pay my share."

"Your share always seems to be smaller than mine."

Now he stiffened and looked down his nose at her. "Is that so? Need I remind you who got the house?"

"And all the bills to go with it," she retorted sweetly.

"Between what you make and the hefty amount I give you . . ." he began.

"Hefty?" she said with a snort. "Oh, please."

"Rachel, can we stick to the subject?" he suggested in a pained voice.

"I am sticking to the subject. I can't afford braces. I'm not getting hired back next year."

"Oh. I'm sorry."

For a moment he almost had her convinced that he was

sorry for her, but then she remembered whom she was dealing with. Aaron was only sorry because he suspected her problems meant he'd be asked to step up to the plate and help more. When it involved parting with large chunks of money for anything that wasn't his idea and that didn't directly benefit Aaron Green, his heart went into lockdown and his wallet slammed shut.

"We'll work something out," he assured her. "I'll talk to Rencher about setting up a payment plan."

"For who?"

Now he looked very disappointed in her. "That is unfair. I'm paying my part."

"That is debatable."

"Look, I've got to get back inside. My patient's probably numb by now."

"Your patient's not the only one," Rachel said as he started slipping away. She caught him by his sleeve. "One more thing. You saw how upset she is. What about clear braces? Can I at least promise her that?"

He shook his head sadly. "Don't get her hopes up on that. Those aren't as effective for children." He gave her arm a pat before disengaging himself. "You'll handle it."

Sure. No problem.

Back in the car, David was bouncing his basketball off the car ceiling and Claire was plugged in to her iPod and glowering. "Did you talk to Daddy?" she asked.

"Yes. I'm afraid braces have to happen."

"It's not fair," Claire stormed. Meanwhile, the ball kept hitting the ceiling.

"David, if you don't stop immediately, I'm going to give that ball to the Goodwill," Rachel said. It was an empty threat, and they both knew it.

"Sorry, Mom," he said genially. He let the ball fall on the floor, where he began rolling it around with his foot.

That took care of her son. Her daughter was a bigger challenge. Always.

Claire had turned her face and was now pretending to stare out the window. A hand crept up to wipe the corner of her eyes with her sweatshirt.

"Braces aren't so bad anymore," Rachel said gently. "You can get them in all kinds of cool colors."

"I'll be a freak." Claire turned a teary glare on Rachel as if it was her mother's fault that she had tooth issues.

Rachel wanted to say, "You got your messed-up teeth from your messed-up father," but that would hardly be productive, so instead she said, "Sweetie, practically everybody wears braces."

"No, they don't," Claire growled. "I don't want braces. I'm already ugly."

"You are not ugly," Rachel said firmly.

"Aidan thinks you're cute," David offered.

Learning she had the admiration of a ten-year-old's best friend in no way consoled Claire. "No one's talking to you," she snapped.

David shrugged and fell silent.

"Aidan may be the wrong age, but he knows beauty when he sees it," Rachel said.

Claire rolled her eyes and turned back to the window.

Rachel gave up. For the time being, anyway.

After dinner Rachel dropped David off, not bothering to go to the door, and pretended not to see when Misty waved to her from the doorway. After she returned home she went straight to the bonus room off the kitchen that doubled as her office and gathered the pages she'd printed from the Internet safari she'd taken when the children were doing their homework.

Claire had disappeared back into her room, so Rachel went upstairs and knocked on the door. No answer. She opened it a crack and peeked in. It already looked like a teenager room, with teen idol posters on pink walls and clothes scattered on the floor. A lamp shaped like a purse sat on Claire's nightstand and her bedspread, a new one Misty had helped her pick out, was a reversible pink with zebra stripes on the other side. She lay flopped on the bed, facedown, iPod plugged in.

"Knock, knock," called Rachel.

"I don't want to talk."

Actually, Rachel didn't either. She wanted to fill the tub with bubbles and stay there for a million years. But first, she was going to talk and hope her daughter listened. "Just for a minute, 'kay? I have something to show you." Claire reluctantly rolled over onto her side and Rachel sat down next to her. "I know you don't want braces and I don't blame you, but it's better to get them done now. Then you won't have to wear them in high school." At least she hoped not. *Please, God, let that be true.*

Claire's face crumpled and she began to cry. "I'm so ugly."

Rachel took her daughter into her arms. "No, really, you're not. You are going to be so beautiful it's not even funny."

"No, I'm not," Claire sobbed.

"Yes, you are. And the really good news is, you're already beautiful on the inside, and that's the hardest kind of beauty to find."

"You have to say that. You're my mom."

"You think so? Look." Rachel began to lay the pictures of supermodels she'd printed from the Internet out on the bed. There was Gisele Bündchen, Julia Polacsek, Lieke Smets, and Erin O'Connor, who looked like a grownup version of Claire. They all appeared glamorous, exotic, and unique. "Do you know who these women are?"

"No," Claire said grumpily.

"They're international supermodels. Do you notice anything they have in common?"

Claire bit her lip, refusing to state the obvious.

"Here's one more. Recognize her?"

"That's the woman on *What Not to Wear*." Claire's and Rachel's favorite Friday night show. On the weekends Claire was home they always watched it together, even when Claire's best friend, Bethany, was sleeping over.

"Yep. Stacy London."

"But she's pretty," Claire said in a small voice.

"They're all pretty. But they don't all look alike. It's okay to look different. Sometimes different is better."

Claire rolled her eyes.

Rachel gathered the papers into a stack. "Just think about that," she said, and leaned over and kissed her daughter's forehead.

Claire didn't say anything but she nodded.

"And next time we're watching *What Not to Wear* check out Stacy London's nose," Rachel added as she slipped off the bed. She was to the door when her daughter said, "Mom?"

"Yeah?"

Claire managed a tiny smile. "Thanks."

Rachel suddenly felt better than she had all day. She smiled back. "You're welcome," she said, and shut the door feeling pretty pleased with herself.

Until she remembered that in the course of one afternoon she had lost a job and gained a new debt. And somewhere, a little gremlin was laughing.

Chapter 3

In her forty-four years on the planet, Jessica Sharp had learned several important truths: chocolate is good medicine, housework is highly overrated, girlfriends make the best shrinks, and—her latest lesson—job security is an oxymoron, especially if you happened to work for a bank, which her husband did.

"I still have a job," Michael informed her when he came home from work.

Jess was in the kitchen, dumping the chicken salad she'd picked up at Safeway into a bowl. She'd had a bottle of wine standing ready in case they needed to console themselves. Now they'd use it to celebrate. "Thank God," she said with a sigh of relief. They could take their wine out on the deck and enjoy the early June evening and congratulate themselves on how they'd dodged the bullet.

Or not. Michael was not looking thankful.

"There's one small catch," he said. "It's in Ohio."

"O-what?"

"That's where the corporate offices are."

Jess felt suddenly sick. "Open that wine quick." She plopped down on a stool at the kitchen island. "Damn that Washington Federal Loan anyway," she growled as he uncorked the bottle. "As if they haven't screwed us enough already. They turned our stock to junk and our retirement to peanuts. Do they have to shuttle us across the country, too?" Away from family and friends.

"At my level, they do. That's the trade-off." Michael poured a glass of wine and handed it to her.

It was all she could do not to bang her head on the granite countertop, which she'd put in only last year. She took a sip of wine but it tasted bitter. She set down her glass with a sigh.

Michael wasn't drinking either. "I'm sorry, Jess."

She rubbed his arm. "It's not your fault you work for Monsters, Inc. I just hate to move."

She hated the idea of her husband being unemployed even more. She got a sudden image of herself as a bag lady, pushing a shopping cart full of dirty clothes down Lake Way.

That was enough to make her pick up her wineglass again. She had a new thought. "What about Mikey?" Their son had left the nest, but after losing his first job the baby bird had returned, and once more they had another mouth to feed. And that particular mouth gobbled up a lot of food. Jess's grocery bill had doubled since Mikey moved back home.

"He can probably move in with Erica."

"Somehow I can't picture him wanting to live with his older sister." Their daughter had gotten married in February (an event that had cost an arm and two legs) and now lived north of them in a farming community that was turning into a suburb. It didn't offer much for a young, single guy.

"I sure don't see her husband being real excited to have a third wheel," Michael added, obviously remembering his and Jess's own first year of marriage.

They'd shed their clothes at the drop of a smile and

made love in every imaginable location in their little apartment, including on top of the washing machine in the building's communal laundry room. She still remembered diving under a sheet when poor old Mrs. Newcombe came down to check on her clothes.

"He can come with us if he wants," Michael said.

Jess suspected their son would be about as thrilled with moving as she was. "Oh, boy," she muttered.

"There is one other possibility."

Hope blossomed in Jess's heart. "Oh?" Any possibility was better than moving.

"I dropped by Puget Sound National and they might be interested in hiring me."

He'd still be commuting to Seattle to work. Nothing would change. Perfect! "Well, then, call 'em." Now she could enjoy that wine. She grabbed her glass and saluted Michael with it.

"There's one drawback. The position I'm looking at would be less money."

Jess's glass went back on the counter. "How much less?" They had just finished paying off the baby bird's college loans. Another couple of months and the wedding bell blues would be over, too. She'd seen the light at the end of the tunnel. Surely it couldn't be that proverbial train barreling toward her.

"We'd be looking at about a twenty percent pay cut."

"Twenty?" Jess stammered. She took another drink of wine. Suddenly Ohio didn't look quite so bad.

"We could do it," Michael said. "We'd have to tighten our belts."

"Those belts are already on their last notch."

He shrugged. "Or else find a way to bring in more income."

As in her? What marketable skills did she have?

None. Jess had majored in music in college (with a

strong minor in boys and Frisbee), and after three years she'd met Michael and bagged the BA, going instead for a Mrs. degree. Other than singing in a band on weekends— when she was young and hot and still looked like Pat Benatar—and selling craft creations at holiday bazaars, she'd never worked outside the home. She'd never needed to, not when she had Michael, her own personal patron of the arts. But now she needed to. There had to be something she could do to make up that twenty percent. Nothing came to mind, except panic.

Michael looked at her in concern. "Jess? Are you okay?"

"I could get a job," she blurted. *Doing what? What are you thinking?*

Relief flitted across her husband's face, but he valiantly said, "You don't have to. We can make it on less. And, no matter what position I take, my salary will go up eventually."

They'd be dead before eventually. She didn't want to move, but if she wanted to stay, she'd have to pay. "I'm sure I can get something," she said. "If you want to stay here. You do want to stay here, don't you?"

"Of course I do," he said. "Heart Lake is our home."

"Well, then, we'll make it work. See if you can snag that position at Puget Sound National. And I'll . . ." *Oh, boy.*

"Find something," he supplied. "It doesn't have to be full time. We can save a lot of money just by not going out to eat so much."

She nodded and downed the rest of her wine. She had a feeling that, at the rate they were going, what she saved on eating out she'd be spending on booze.

"Don't worry," Michael said, and gave her a kiss. "We'll be fine." The captain of the *Titanic* had probably said those very same words.

* * *

The next morning, Jess decided to make a list of possible jobs. She poured herself a cup of coffee, then grabbed a piece of scratch paper from the kitchen junk drawer and a pen and leaned over the counter, ready to write furiously. The blank page stared at her.

She frowned back at it. "There has to be something you can do," she told herself.

Maybe she should start by writing down her strengths. What was she good at? She still played a mean keyboard.

Like that did any good. Even if she lost twenty pounds in two weeks and got Botox, where would she find a band that would have her? As a band chick she was over the hill and out of the loop. The band thing was hardly steady work anyway.

What else? Crafts. She had a closet full of things she could sell. Except she'd missed Slugfest and there would be no more craft bazaar opportunities until the Fourth of July. Selling crafts was too iffy, anyway—great for making some fun money, but by the time you factored in the cost of the material and renting a booth, hardly profitable enough to earn that necessary extra twenty percent every month.

So, what did that leave? Personality. She was friendly, fun, approachable. Maybe she could get a job as a sales-clerk or a receptionist. She remembered the Help Wanted sign she'd seen hanging in the window of Emma's Quilt Corner, the little shop that Heart Lake residents had saved from extinction the previous Christmas. Jess hadn't gotten around to trying quilting yet, but she could learn. She certainly knew how to cut fabric, and it couldn't be that hard to ring up sales. From what she heard, everyone loved Emma, which meant she'd be great to work for. It could be the perfect part-time job.

Jess checked the clock. Ten a.m. Emma would be open

for business. She called the shop and was greeted by a
cheery voice on the other end of the line. "Hi," Jess said,
making her own voice equally cheery. "I'm calling about
the Help Wanted sign in your window."

"I'm sorry," said the voice, changing from cheery to
sympathetic. "I just filled that position yesterday."

"Oh." A good job was like a good man, hard to find.
But she'd found Michael. She'd find a job. "Well, thanks
anyway." Jess hung up with a sigh and returned to the
piece of paper on the kitchen counter. What else could
she do?

A temp agency, she decided. That would be perfect.
She could earn income but she wouldn't be locked into
anything full time. She got on the computer and looked
up temp agencies in Seattle. She could handle part-time
office work, and if she worked in the city, she and Michael
could commute together.

The first company she found was A-Plus Office Services. *That's me, A-Plus,* she thought, reaching for the
phone.

As it turned out, Ms. A-Plus could fit her in for an interview at one. Could she come in?

Why not? Jess wasn't exactly excited as she hurried to
her closet, but she was determined, which was nearly as
good. Velvet Revolver's version of the song "Money"
began to play in her head. She was going to come
through for Michael, even if it meant chaining herself to
a desk somewhere in the city. She could do it. Millions of
women did it every day. Maybe she'd even get a job as-
signment for the next week. You never knew. It would be
good news to share when Rachel and Tiffany came over
for their monthly craft night.

She encountered a challenge in her closet. Denim jack-
ets, hot pink tops, and various articles of clothing dot-
ted with sequins greeted her. When was the last time

she'd worn a dress? There had to be something here. She flipped hangers along the rack. No, no, no. Noooo. Hmm. Here was a black knit dress, not too low-cut. How about that and her red denim jacket? Red denim was not very dress for success. And black wasn't exactly summery. That decided it. She'd leave for the city right now and detour by Nordstrom's before going on her interview.

At Nordstrom's she managed to find a cream-colored linen suit jacket and pants that fit well but bored her to tears. The price made her want to cry, too. She couldn't believe how much she was paying for boring. She dressed it up with a sleeveless top sporting a great pattern in black and Amalfi blue, perfect colors for a winter. (Jess had had her colors done back in college. With her dark hair—still completely dark, thank you, Wella Color Charm—she was a winter.) The top was no bargain either, but it was worth every penny. This she would wear till it turned to rags.

Small consolation. She had just spent a fortune to audition for a job as a temp. Well, you had to spend money to make money. Unbidden, the lyrics to ABBA's "Money, Money, Money" came to mind.

A-Plus Office Services was in one of the many tall Seattle buildings that looked down on the city's waterfront and its more humble architectural beginnings like the Smith Tower.

Jess had grown up in this city. She'd attended the University of Washington and met Michael at the Blue Moon Tavern. He'd looked like Andy Gibb and, although he couldn't sing a note, he danced like John Travolta. Within a year, they'd managed to fall in love, elope, get pregnant, and celebrate Michael's graduation. Michael had gone on to become a lawyer and she'd worked on turning herself into Mother of the Year—a far more noble occupation than band chick.

Although they'd left the city for the 'burbs, they still drove in on a regular basis to take his mom to dinner at the Waterfront Seafood Grill on Pier 70 or to enjoy Indian food thali style up at Poppy's on Capitol Hill. Visiting the city was great, but Jess wasn't sure how she felt about working there. Seattle had grown far beyond the little big town it had been when she was a girl. And, at an hour each way by freeway, it wasn't exactly a short commute.

She rode the elevator to the twentieth floor and found the A-Plus office in a far corner of the skyscraper office maze. The reception area was small, with a love seat and matching chair upholstered in retro ugly, a fish tank, a blocky coffee table littered with business magazines and, on one side of the wall, a bank of computers. On the other side, at the reception window, sat a twenty-something babe wearing an outfit that looked even more expensive than Jess's, talking on the phone.

"I'll have Mrs. Withers call you as soon as she can," said the girl. She hung up and looked Jess over. "May I help you?"

Jess stepped up to the window. "I have an appointment with Caroline Withers."

The girl nodded. "Have a seat."

Feeling a little like a patient waiting to see the dentist, Jess perched on the couch. It was hard.

She looked over at the computers and felt her pulse rate start to rise. You have a computer, she told herself. *You can type. E-mail counts.* In spite of her positive self-talk, her pulse scooted up another notch. She should get out of here. Was she too old to sell her body on the street?

"Jessica?"

Jess tore her gaze away from the computers and looked up to see a thin woman with shoulder length gray hair, expensively cut, and stylish glasses looking down at her. The woman was dressed entirely in black. Maybe an escapee from New York? Jess thought of all the money she'd spent to avoid wearing black and sighed inwardly.

The woman was studying her, too, her smile polite, professional. "I'm Caroline Withers. Why don't you come into my office and we'll talk."

Talking was good. Jess followed Caroline through a small conference room and into her office. Here the furniture had been upgraded to fake leather. Caroline settled behind a massive desk. "I'm happy you thought of us first," she said, pulling together a pile of forms. "Did you bring a résumé?"

Jess's palms were suddenly damp. "Actually, no."

"Well, you can e-mail it to me later," Caroline said amiably. "What kind of work are you hoping for?"

"What kind?" *The kind that pays?*

"Secretarial, accounting . . ."

"Receptionist," Jess said firmly. "I have great phone skills."

Caroline nodded. "All right. Let's have you fill out some forms."

"Fine," said Jess, forcing the corners of her lips to stay up. Oh, God, she was going to flunk form-filling.

Caroline clipped the papers on a clipboard and handed them to Jess, then she stood and ushered Jess back to the little conference room. "You can fill this out and then we'll get you started on the computer."

The top form was terrifying. A-Plus wanted to know everything about her: educational background, work background, last employer. Jess was pretty sure Bennie at Bennie's Tavern, where her band had played, wouldn't be the right kind of business reference. She should have gotten a job long before this. What had she been thinking?

Twenty minutes later Caroline found her still at the table, hunched over a form with a lot of white space. "Is there a problem?" Caroline asked.

"One small one," said Jess. "I'm afraid I can't give you the kind of references you want." Playing in a band and selling wine cork trivets and beaded jewelry boxes hardly equated to office skills, although Jess was sure she had enough of those to fill in at a front desk somewhere.

"I see," said Caroline slowly.

"But I can type," Jess said quickly. "And I can certainly file and take messages."

"All right, let's put you on a computer and test you," said Caroline.

Test? Jess had never tested well.

The computer hated her. She knew it five minutes after she sat down. Excel was a mystery, and the typing was a nightmare. It was the sweaty palm thing. Her fingers kept slipping to the wrong key. Soon she had both sweaty palms and the beginnings of a headache. She did well on the spelling and grammar test though. That should count for something.

"Well," said Caroline when they met again in her office after the computer torture session, "you can type a little."

Types a little. There was a glowing recommendation. "I think I'd be great with phones," said Jess. *Types a little and great with phones.*

"I think you would, too," Caroline agreed. "How many days a week are you available?"

"Seven."

Caroline smiled at that. "Well, we'd only need you for five."

"Do you think you could use me?" asked Jess.

"I think you could do nicely as a receptionist. Let's have you fill out this card and I'll put together a folder for you."

"A folder?" She was going to get a folder? That had to be good.

"With a booklet that will tell you about our policies and procedures, and a time card, which you'll fill out and submit to us at the end of every work week."

That sounded official. "Great. Thanks."

"It can be hard to reenter the workforce. This is a good way to ease back in. Often companies wind up hiring our temps full time."

"Full time. Really?" echoed Jess, trying to convince both Caroline and herself that she was interested. *Good-bye to staying up late watching TV and sleeping in the next morning. Good-bye to driving north for lunch with Erica. Good-bye to Friday morning tennis with the girls at the Grandview Park tennis courts. Good-bye to volunteering at the food bank.*

It beats saying, "Good-bye, Heart Lake," she reminded herself sternly. And really, it was about time she got a job. The kids were grown and she was no longer needed as a chauffeur, in-house paraeducator, Girl Scout leader, chief cook (she was a rotten cook, anyway), or soccer mom. It was time to do something new with her life.

For a moment her mind wandered to the past and paused at the road not taken, the one she'd been about to go down before love came in the door and her dreams scrammed out the window. How she had wanted to be a star!

She could see herself up there on the stage, adoring fans roaring as she sang and rocked out. Now she was playing a riff on the keyboard. Look at the crowd going wild— women jumping up and down and screaming, men throwing their underwear. Ick.

Her eyes popped open. All right, that was a little too far down the road not taken.

But what about the road she stood at now? Working in an office, answering phones, draining her creative juices to help someone else build his dream or some big corporate monster keep its heart beating—was this really her?

It is now, baby. Welcome to the workforce.

She took her folder and left A-Plus Office Services ready to face a brave, new world.

Chapter 4

It's always good to go into the weekend with something to celebrate. This was another important truth Jessica had learned in her forty-four years on the planet. Celebrating over her possibly successful foray into the job market beat discussing what lay ahead on Michael's job horizon.

He had been more than willing to celebrate her afternoon's success. "Way to go," he said after she'd told him, and gave her a big, smacking kiss. "You're already out there fishing for something. I'm impressed."

"I don't exactly have a fish on the line yet," she reminded him as she ladled canned sauce on their spaghetti.

"But you've baited the hook."

She frowned. "You wouldn't believe how much bait costs."

Both his eyebrows went up.

"I had to buy something I could wear to a job interview. I never realized how noncorporate my wardrobe was."

Michael smiled at that. "You've got a point there. I can't remember the last time I saw anyone in the office wearing sequins or tank tops." She dumped her salad-in-a-bag into a bowl, and he took it to the kitchen table.

She joined him with French bread. "I gave myself permission since I'm investing in my future."

"You are. You have to dress for success," he agreed.

Michael pretty much always agreed with her when it came to spending money because he was a sweet man. In the past money hadn't been an issue in their marriage, but now, between college and wedding debt and a possible period of unemployment, she realized he needed to stop being so agreeable.

"I just hope that investment pays off," she said. It could. Caroline Withers could feel sorry for her.

"You'll get something," Michael said easily. "Try another agency next week."

"Another?" He wanted her to go to another agency and do all that sweating again?

"You probably should. The more temp agencies you have your name with the better, at least if you want to find a foothold in the corporate world."

"I do," she said. Who was she kidding? Michael should be singing Fleetwood Mac's "Tell Me Lies" to her.

"It's like putting out résumés," he continued. "You want to circulate as many as possible so you increase your chances of getting an interview."

"Oh." That made sense, of course.

She thought of having to face that one-hour work commute on a regular basis and shuddered. You don't have to find full-time employment, she reminded herself, something part time will do. Nothing at all would do better. She really wasn't cut out to be an office drone.

Grow up, she told herself sternly. *This is how it works in the real world. Millions of people go to jobs they hate every day.*

Except her husband. He loved his work. So did Rachel Green. So did Tiffany Turner, her other neighbor and craft buddy. Jess sighed.

"Don't worry," Michael said as they settled down with their meal. "I bet you'll have more work than you can handle."

She nodded and managed a smile. Who knew? She might decide she liked office work. She would definitely like a paycheck. She knew that much.

"Where's our son?" Michael asked.

"He went over to the Sticks and Balls to shoot pool with Danny."

Michael frowned. "I hope he spent time job hunting first."

"I'm sure he did," Jess said quickly. Mikey was asleep when she left for the city, but he'd been gone by the time she got home. Surely somewhere in between sleeping and leaving to hang out with his buddy he'd done something other than eat all the leftover chicken she'd been saving for dinner.

"I don't want him sitting around playing games on his computer all day," Michael said sternly, as if Mikey was still twelve and she was, somehow, responsible for his behavior.

"I'm sure he's not."

"Our son really needs to be looking for a job."

"He will," Jess assured Michael. Mikey had a business degree. He shouldn't have trouble finding something. If he looked.

She suddenly understood why her son had been dragging his feet on the job hunting for the last month. It was hard going out there and putting your ego and your future on the line, hoping you'd impress some stranger enough to want to take a chance on you. She really didn't want to do that again, herself.

After dinner Michael went to his computer to check out some business networking sites and Jess drifted to the old baby grand piano she kept in a corner of the living room and vented, pounding the ivories. But hard as she banged, she couldn't stop thinking about the pounding she and Michael were about to take.

Tiffany stopped at Safeway on her way home to pick up a little something to bring to Friday craft night. Jess was hosting this month, and while she always had plenty of goodies, Tiffany never liked to come empty-handed. She found some fresh strawberries that would be wonderful.

There. That took care of the girls. What about dinner? She decided to pick up some odds and ends from the deli. It was a great way to save time.

But not money. Tiffany checked in her wallet. Just as she suspected, she was two dollars short. The woman behind the counter had already put everything in little cartons so Tiffany couldn't very well say, "Put it back." She'd have to use her charge card.

By the time she got home Brian was already there, sitting out on the deck, drinking a Coke. She opened the sliding glass door and poked her head out. "Sorry I'm late. I had to stop at Safeway. Dinner'll be ready in a sec."

"I'm not hungry."

There was something very unsettling about Brian's tone of voice. "Did you have a late lunch or something?" Maybe he'd had bad news at work. With a sick feeling, she sat down opposite him.

He was a hottie, with that beefcake chin and those dimples. Except they only showed when he was smiling, and right now he wasn't smiling. "Tiff, have you been charging things?"

Her heart began to thump wildly. "Why would you ask that?"

"Because I found an unopened package of sheets in a bag under the bed."

Abracadabra sheets. She'd meant to transfer them to

the linen closet and forgot. "What were you doing look-ing under the bed?"

"I was looking for my old running shoes," he said, frowning at her. "What? I'm not supposed to look under the bed?"

"No."

His frown became a scowl.

"I mean, no, that's not what I meant." Oooh, this was not going well.

He looked at her warily. "You've only been using the debit card like we agreed, right? You haven't gotten an-other charge card, have you?"

She could feel her cheeks sizzling under his penetrat-ing gaze. "I . . ." Her mind went blank.

"Oh, God," Brian said faintly. "Tell me you haven't."

She bit her lip.

His lips pressed into a thin, angry line and he left the deck.

"Brian, wait." She followed him through the kitchen. "I can explain."

He walked through the living room.

"Brian, please. It's not much."

He grabbed his car keys from the little table by the front door.

"Where are you going?"

He held up a hand. "I can't talk to you right now, Tiff. I need to go cool down. Okay?"

No, it wasn't okay. "Brian, don't leave. Please."

Tiffany turned on the tears to no avail. Her husband shook his head and went out the door.

Run after him, cried her conscience. *Give him the credit cards and tell him to cut them up.*

She took one step and stopped. *No. I need to let him calm down.*

You just don't want to give up the credit cards.

That was so not true. But it would be stupid to cut them up. Who knew what the future held? They might need those credit cards.

Tiffany shut the door and flopped on the living room couch where she indulged herself in a good cry.

You'd better do something.

And right now there was only one something to do. More bargains had to return to the mall. She hauled her unhappy self into the bedroom and took the sheets out from under the bed. She found the receipt for them in her underwear drawer, where she hid all her charge receipts. She also grabbed the receipt for the body butter she'd stocked up on and fetched one of the two jars from under her bathroom vanity. She could part with one.

But wait. They'd been on sale. It was hardly worth returning body butter she'd eventually need. She put it back under the vanity. The sheets would still go. She'd regret it, she was sure, but she'd take them back. She had to have something to show Brian when he came home.

After much soul searching she also parted with a pair of shoes and a serving platter she'd gotten on sale and had tucked away to give as a wedding present in case someone they knew decided to get married. Her returns assembled, she put the deli dinner in the fridge, grabbed her car keys, and left for the mall. As she got closer with her returns she began to cry again. Her husband was gone who knew where and now the last of her bargains were going. Life sucked.

You're doing the right thing, said her conscience.

"Oh, shut up," she snarled.

Jess shooed Michael out the door to go play poker with his pals down the street and got busy setting out the refreshments for craft night. She and her friends were making wineglass charms and Jess had planned her menu accordingly. She had picked up a couple of bottles of raspberry dessert wine from Bere Vino and truffles from the Chocolate Bar, Heart Lake's favorite chocolateria. Wine and chocolate, perfect.

Next, mood music. She put on a CD she had burned with all of her favorite *American Idol* downloads. Now she was truly ready. Let the crafts begin.

Rachel was the first to arrive. She was tall and willowy, and Jess heartily envied her great legs. If she had legs like that, she'd never waste them on pathetically unshort shorts like the ones Rachel was wearing tonight. Rachel also had on a turquoise colored spring sweater set that was lovely with her dark coloring. Lovely, but not hugely sexy. Rachel had never dressed provocatively, but it seemed to Jess that since her divorce the girl had been sinking into schoolmarm mode, becoming increasingly more conservative. Her long, black hair was now sporting a few fine strands of gray—battle scars, she called them—which she refused to hide under hair color. As far as Jess knew, she hadn't even cut her hair in the last year, preferring instead to catch it in a band at the base of her neck. Her face was a little too long to call her beautiful, but her big, brown eyes were striking and she had a gorgeous smile.

When she had something to smile about. From the look on her face as she walked through the door, Jess could tell that she wasn't going into the weekend with any reason to smile. She'd looked somber when Jess ran into her in the grocery store, but since then, she'd gone from somber to shoot-me-now.

"You look like you need chocolate therapy," Jess said as she led the way to the worktable she'd set up in the family room.

"I need therapy, period," said Rachel.

"Aaron troubles?" Jess guessed. The goodies were laid out on the nearby coffee table. She picked up the plate of truffles and handed it to Rachel.

"This is good for me. What are you and Tiff going to have?"

"That bad, huh?"

Rachel popped a truffle in her mouth, then set the plate back on the coffee table. "Worse. I don't have a job anymore."

Jess sat down on the nearest chair. "Oh, no."

"Oh, yes. But that's not all. Claire needs braces and the Prince of Darkness is being his usual rotten self. I'd stick my head in the oven, except it's electric." She took another truffle.

"What are you going to do?"

"Go back to subbing if I can't find a teaching position. Between the schools in Heart Lake and Lyndale I should be able to pick up enough work. It's just—" She stopped and shook her head.

"That you wanted something permanent," supplied Jess.

"I wanted something to go right," Rachel corrected, eyes flashing. "I swear, the day I met Aaron my life became cursed." She ran a hand through her hair. "All right, that is a major exaggeration, I admit, but I feel like everywhere I look I see bills to pay. I just . . ." Her voice broke.

Jess put the plate of chocolates in her lap and a glass of wine in her hand. "I'm so sorry."

Rachel went for her third chocolate and rinsed it down with a healthy slug of wine. "It's okay. I'll be fine. My mom always says God never closes a door without opening a window."

Rachel's mom was currently busy caring for her husband, who'd had a stroke, and Rachel's deadbeat sister, who had moved home with her two children. Talk about an eternal optimist. But Jess nodded her agreement. "That's a good thought to keep in mind."

"I need a window to open really soon," Rachel said, rubbing her temples.

"I hear you," Jess said with a sigh.

"Oh, geez, listen to me. What's going on with you? Does Michael have a job?"

"If we want to move to Ohio, he does."

Rachel's face lost its color. "You're not moving, are you? Oh, Jess. Please tell me you're not moving. I know it's selfish of me, but if you leave that will be the final straw."

"We're not," Jess assured her. "Michael is looking for something around here. And I'm going to get a job."

"A job?" Rachel looked at her with new interest. "Doing what?"

"Robbing banks," Jess said, deadpan. "I'll start with Washington Federal Loan. They should have plenty now that they've been bought out. Want to drive the getaway van?"

That brought a smile. "Sure. Let's give them something to talk about here on Cupid's Loop. Seriously, what are you going to do?"

"I'm going to see if I can get work as a temp."

Rachel gave a thoughtful nod. "I hear they can keep you busy doing that. I never thought of you as the office type, though." She took in Jess's tight jeans, pink tank top, and pink sequined flip-flops, and added, "I can hardly wait to see what you wear to the office."

"I can do office boring if I have to," Jess said, and plucked a chocolate from the plate. They were disappearing fast. If Tiffany didn't hurry up and get there, she'd miss out. Jess checked her watch. It was now a quarter after seven. Well, Tiffany tended to run late.

But by quarter till eight the chocolate was gone and half of the wine, and there was still no sign of her. Jess went to the living room and looked out the window. She could see Tiffany's Craftsman style house, which sat kitty-corner and across the street of their cul-de-sac. Like all the houses in Heart Lake Estates, it was big, too big for two people really, but Tiffany and Brian had planned to fill it up with babies. So far it was still too big, although Tiffany had done a good job of filling it with home furnishings from Pottery Barn and Crate and Barrel. Her car wasn't in the driveway. Neither was Brain's jeep.

"That is so weird," Jess said, returning to the family room. "Nobody's home."

"I say we start," Rachel said. "She's always late, but this is ridiculous."

"Maybe I'd better call her and see if she's okay."

"She probably found a sale, which means we won't see her until after the mall closes. I don't know where she finds the money for all these bargains," Rachel muttered as Jess went for the phone.

"She got another charge card. Didn't she tell you?"

Rachel's eyes got big. "No. She knew I'd ream her out. And I'm betting she didn't tell Brian, either."

Jess called Tiffany's cell phone, but only got her voice mail. "Hey, where are you? We're ready to start."

"Ready to start? I *am* starting," Rachel said. She seated herself at the worktable and began sorting through the tiny charms, which they would then string along with beads onto little wire hoops to loop around wineglasses. Jess had found everything from multicolored glass fishes to tiny shoes in various styles.

Jess joined her and they worked another ten minutes with still no sign of Tiffany. "Don't you think it's strange that she hasn't showed up yet?" Jess asked. "I just saw her this morning so it's not like she could have forgotten."

"Like I said, she found a sale," Rachel said, slipping a bead next to the charm on her wire.

"I hope everything's okay."

"Of course it is. If it wasn't, we're the first people she'd have called."

They finished their creations and still there was no sign of Tiffany. Jess went to the living room and looked out the window again. The cars were back in the driveway now and a light was on inside. "She's home now."

"Nice of her to let us know she wasn't coming," Rachel said, settling on the couch. "I don't get it. She was the one who wanted to make these."

As she spoke, Tiffany's front door opened and out dashed a petite blonde with a heart-shaped face, wearing designer jeans, a silky pink top, and sky-kissing heels that screamed *designer label*.

"Here she comes," Jess announced.

"Just in time to lick the empty plate," said Rachel, who had devoured the last truffle.

A moment later Tiffany was at the door.

"Where have you been?" Jess asked, letting her in. "We were worried." Then she realized that Tiff's eyes were red and puffy, a sure sign she'd been crying. "What's wrong?"

"Brian found out about the charge cards." Tiffany fell onto the love seat. "It was terrible," she said and burst into tears.

Jess sat down and put an arm around her. "What happened?"

"He, he, he . . ."

"He beat you," guessed Rachel in horrified tones.

"No. He, he, he . . ."

"Oh, my God, he's leaving you!" Rachel cried.

"Noooo." Tiffany wailed. "He took my credit cards. Even after I returned everything."

Rachel stopped looking sympathetic so Jess stepped in. "I'm sorry."

"Well, I'm not," said Rachel. "Tiff, you should be glad Brian took those credit cards. Think of the mess you could have gotten into with them."

"Oh, that's easy for you to say," Tiffany snapped. "You have credit cards."

Rachel's eyes narrowed. "Well, let's trade. You can have my charge cards and I'll take your husband."

This was not good. Jess had two emotional women in her living room going at it and no chocolate left. "Come on, you two," she pleaded. "This isn't like either of you."

Rachel sighed. "Sorry. I'm a little cranky tonight," she muttered.

Tiffany nodded, accepting her apology, but she still looked hurt. An awkward moment passed before Tiff said in a small voice, "You're right to lecture me. I know I'm wrong. It's just that . . ."

"What?" prompted Jess.

"I don't know how to explain it. Somehow it was easier to cope when I could go in the store and buy something on sale. Getting a bargain was like doing a good thing for our family."

She didn't need to explain what she was coping with. Jess had had a miscarriage herself. It was a grief most people didn't understand, a loss met with well meant words like, "Don't worry. You'll get pregnant again." As if losing that life growing in you along with all the hopes and plans for the future meant nothing. She suspected shopping was Tiffany's way of trying to fill the emptiness.

"We're a mess," Rachel said. She went to the family room and returned a moment later with the near empty bottle of wine. She filled a quarter of a glass and handed it to Tiffany. "Sorry. This is all that's left. And we ate all the chocolate, too. We've been consoling ourselves."

Before Tiffany could protest, Jess filled her in on Rachel's lost job and the crisis looming on the horizon for her and Michael.

"Rachel's right," Tiffany said miserably. "We are a mess."

"Only temporarily," said Jess. "Things could always be worse."

"I guess you're right," said Rachel. "Why do we always see the glass as half full?"

"Cuz it is, cuz somebody drank all the wine," said Tiffany, frowning at the glass in her hand.

"Seriously," said Jess. "So we're not rich. Most people aren't. But we've got lots of good things in our lives."

"Mine all went back to the store," Tiffany grumbled.

"Yes, but you've still got your husband," Jess reminded her, "and he loves you. That's huge. Rachel has her kids, I have my family, and we have each other. How many people live on the same block as their best friends? I'll admit, we have some challenges right now, but we're not starving."

"Yet," said Tiffany. "They laid off two people in Brian's department this week. If he gets laid off, I don't know how we're going to make it," she continued, refusing to be sidetracked. "Especially now that I don't have any credit cards."

"I have to admit, I'm scared, too," Rachel confessed in a small voice.

She had a right to be. Her parents weren't swimming in money, and at the moment they had problems of their own. And Jess and Tiffany weren't exactly in a position to help her, other than offering moral support.

But you had to think positive. That was something else Jess had learned in her forty-four years on the planet. "We can't let a little thing like money problems defeat us," she insisted.

"People jumped out of windows in the Thirties over a little thing like money problems," Rachel reminded her.

"Well, you wouldn't have been one of them," Jess told her sternly, "and neither would I, and neither would Tiff."

"You're right," said Rachel. "I'd have pushed Aaron out a window instead and collected his life insurance."

Tiffany giggled at that. But she sobered quickly. "So, what are we going to do?"

"Maybe we should take some kind of money management course," Rachel suggested. "We could probably all stand some improvement in that area."

"Except now I don't have any way to pay for one," grumbled Tiffany.

Rachel frowned. "Good point. Without a job, I can't afford some big, expensive course."

"Me, either," said Jess.

"There has to be something we can do," said Rachel.

They all sat there, the only sound in the room Tiffany's nails clicking against her wineglass as she thought.

"Wait a minute," said Rachel suddenly. "Where's the one place in town where learning is free?"

Jess's face lit with understanding. "Of course! You're a genius."

Tiffany looked from one to the other, confused. "I don't get it. What are you talking about?"

"The library," Rachel explained. "It still doesn't cost anything to check out a book. I'll bet we can find dozens of books on managing money."

"Why not? Let's go tomorrow morning," Jess suggested.

Tiffany looked pained. "I can't go. I have three clients coming in to get their nails done tomorrow morning."

"We'll find something for you," Rachel promised.

"It better be something on how to get through credit card withdrawal," muttered Tiffany.

Chapter 5

The library proved to be a treasure trove of free information. The shelves in the finance section offered a wide selection of books from finance gurus like Dave Ramsey, Suze Orman, and Robert Kiyosaki, and Rachel and Jess loaded up.

"It looks like you two are going to be busy," observed Lucy the librarian as she checked out their books. She picked up one. "*Budgets for Babes*. This looks good."

"Well, good for us, anyway," said Jess. "We're babes," she added with a wink, making Lucy smile.

"While we're here let's check out the Friends of the Library book sale," suggested Rachel.

So after they'd stowed their borrowed books in Jess's car, they went to the lower level of the small building where two rooms had been set aside for the library's popular monthly fund-raiser. It seemed half of Heart Lake had decided to check out the sale. Senior citizens looked through gardening tomes and cookbooks while moms and preschoolers raided the picture book section. Several women had gathered at the women's fiction and romance section and were pulling down paperbacks by their favorite authors.

"We're going to die from lack of oxygen," moaned Rachel as she and Jess swam through the crowd toward the finance corner.

"But we'll die with a book in our hands," Jess said as she squeezed between two walls of people.

The woman in front of them smiled over her shoulder at Jess. "What are you looking for?"

"A miracle," said Rachel.

"We need to get our financial act together," Jess elaborated.

"Don't we all," said an older man with a grizzled chin and tufts of gray hair growing out of his ears. "At the rate my savings are disappearing I'm going to be spending the rest of my retirement flipping burgers at Crazy Eric's."

Rachel pulled a hardback off a top shelf. "Here's a good one."

Jess read over her shoulder. *"Your Magic Money Makeover."*

The man gave a snort. "They make it sound so easy."

"I guess that's the way to sell books," said Jess.

"Who would buy a book titled *Welcome to Your Life: It Sucks*?" put in Rachel.

"Believe me, ladies," said the older man, "there's no magic formula."

"Tiff will be sorry to hear that," cracked Rachel. She opened the book and began reading the chapter titles. 'Making Debt Disappear: The Trick to Budgeting.'"

Jess read over her shoulder, "'Pulling Extra Money Out of Your Sleeve.' Oh, I need that one."

"Me, too," said Rachel. "'Who Are You: Learn Your Money Type.' Ha! That one's easy. I already know my money type: broke."

"My money type would probably be clueless," Jess said, reaching for a book.

Rachel shut hers. "I think I'll get this. It looks interesting."

"This one has my name on it," said Jess, showing Rachel her find, *Weathering Tough Times.*

"That one has all our names on it." Rachel pulled another book off the shelf titled *Diva on a Dime.* "Here's the perfect one for Tiffany." She turned the book so Jess could read the title.

Jess gave a snort. "She'll love it."

"Let's go show her," said Rachel.

Salon H was a small salon, with only three chairs and Tiffany's manicure/pedicure station. Like all the business establishments in town, hearts were the theme. The mirrors had been specially made to look like artsy hearts, and several glass-blown red, orange, and purple hearts made by a local artist hung in the window. There was always a candle burning on the reception desk—a valiant effort to combat the usual hair salon smell of potions and treatments—and always women chatting in the comfy wingback chairs in the reception area, drinking espresso that Jody the receptionist had made for them.

Tiffany was in the middle of painting Maude Schuller's nails cotton candy pink when Jess and Rachel walked in with their finds.

"It's important to learn to manage your money," said Maude, assuming she was part of the conversation. "The problem with your generation is that you girls don't know the value of a dollar."

Tiffany rolled her eyes. "Yeah, we do, Maude. It doesn't have any value."

"That's for sure," said Cara, the stylist on duty, who was busy giving a zitty teenage girl a hot new hair look. Today Cara's hair was maroon. Six months earlier it had been raven's-wing black with blue highlights. "You know how much cigarettes cost these days? Not that you should smoke," she quickly added for her client's benefit.

"A dollar still has value when you know how to stretch it," Maude insisted. "I was always careful with my money. That's why I can afford to come here and get my nails done. If you're not careful when you're young, you wind up sorry when you're old. I have friends who have to get their food from the food bank because they were foolish when they were younger."

"I'm going to live with my children anyway," said Rachel with a grin. "Payback."

Maude shook her head in reprimand, making her loose jowls jiggle. She waggled a pink-tipped finger at Rachel. "You joke now, but when you're there, it's not funny."

Rachel suddenly didn't look amused.

"Let's see those books," said Tiffany weakly.

"We got one specially with you in mind," Rachel told her, and dug the book out of her plastic bag.

Tiffany read the cover and actually smiled. "*Diva on a Dime*? I like the diva part."

"We knew you would," said Rachel. "So start reading. You can give us a book report next month when we meet at my place."

"We never did decide what we want to make," said Jess.

"Something cheap," said Rachel.

"Nothing is cheap," said Tiffany with a sigh.

"You girls," Maude said in disgust. "When I was young we made all kinds of things on the cheap: bath salts, friendship tea, Amish friendship bread."

Tiffany made a face. "Amish what?"

Maude frowned at her. "It's delicious. I have recipes for all those things. I'll give them to you if you like."

"Uh, sure. Thanks," said Tiffany, looking anything but thankful.

"People don't know how to be self-sufficient anymore," Maude said with a frown.

"Hey, I'm self-sufficient," said Cara, highly offended.

"Oh, I don't mean as far as work goes," said Maude. "I mean knowing how to grow and preserve your own food and sew your own clothes."

"I can buy clothes cheaper on sale at the mall," insisted Tiffany.

Maude ignored her. "We made our cakes and casseroles from scratch, not out of a box. And we made our own syrups and jams. I can tell you, there is nothing like homemade huckleberry jam." She looked in the direction of the teenager and lowered her voice. "I even have a recipe for blackberry cordial."

"Cordial, what's that?" asked Tiffany.

"Booze," Rachel explained.

"Now that's something I wouldn't mind learning how to make," Jess said with a smile. "We'll take it."

"If you girls like, I'll also give you some of my rhubarb to plant," Maude offered. "You can make all kinds of things from rhubarb."

"Free food? We'll take it," said Rachel. "And any other recipes you want to share. Maybe I'll do an Internet search and find a bunch of recipes we can make out of all this free food we're going to scrounge. As soon as school's out I'm going to have nothing to do but job hunt and worry anyway."

"You girls," Maude began with another shake of her faux strawberry blonde head.

"Had better be going," Jess said, edging away.

"See you later," Rachel added, following her.

Once they were outside, Jess turned to Rachel. "That woman creeps me out. She's like the ghost of Finance Future, all gloom and doom."

"And free rhubarb," Rachel reminded her. "Don't forget the free rhubarb."

"I can guarantee you it won't be free," said Jess. "We'll have to pay by listening to more charming tales of all her friends who whooped it up instead of saving and are now eating dog food. That hits a little too close to the bone for me."

"She did paint a grim picture," Rachel agreed. "I sure don't want to end up a broke old lady."

"Well, we're not there yet. We still have time to get our act together," Jess assured them both.

"I'm not wasting any," said Rachel. "I'm going to start reading my book tonight. With the kids at Aaron's I don't have anything else to do anyway."

"You need a man," Jess told her.

"Like I need cancer. I'll stick with my book and a good glass of wine."

Jess didn't push it. She couldn't blame Rachel for being in no hurry to add a new man to her life. Maybe someday she'd be willing to risk her heart again, but probably not anytime soon. It was too bad, really. It was hard to cope with hard times even when you had the support of a good husband. Jess couldn't imagine being in Rachel's shoes and having to do it all alone.

Except she wasn't alone. She had her friends. They'd get through this all somehow. Together.

Tiffany sent Maude on her way with shiny, pink fingernails and checked the salon clock. She still had fifteen minutes before her next client, so after cleaning up she plopped down in her chair and began to thumb through her new book.

If you're reading this book, let me congratulate you on your excellent taste, wrote Rebecca Worth, the author. *You are obviously a woman who is creative, and a little creativity is all you really need to live a fabulous life.*

That and a credit card, thought Tiffany.

Stay with me through these pages and I'll give you all kinds of tips for squeezing every bit of fun and glamour out of a dollar that you possibly can. I am living proof that any woman can live like a diva on a dime.

Tiffany was up for that. She flipped through the pages to the chapter titled "Looking Great for Next to Nothing." *Consignment stores are the way to go,* claimed Rebecca. *Did you know that you can outfit yourself in designer clothes for secondhand prices?*

As if.

Cara had finished with her teenage hair makeover now and the girl waltzed out the door, obviously feeling like a million bucks. The girl had paid more than a dime for that haircut. If you wanted to look really good, you had to be willing to spend money.

What did this diva chick look like? Tiffany turned to the back of the book and checked out the author photo. Okay, she had to admit the woman looked pretty glam, but if the diva on a dime had really gotten those clothes at a consignment store Tiffany would eat her acrylic nails.

She flipped back to the chapter and read on. *Everything I'm wearing in my photo on the back of this book I got at consignment stores . . . right down to my bra—Victoria's Secret, I'll have you know.*

Shut up. Tiffany studied the picture again, giving a lock of her blonde hair a thoughtful twirl. This woman had to be right around the corner from the New York garment district. You wouldn't find anything like that around Heart Lake.

Tiffany read on. *Get your nails and hair done at vo-tech schools for a song,* said the diva on a dime.

Tiffany dropped the book like it was a hot potato. If

women listened to that kind of advice and went to vocational schools they would be missing out on getting topnotch beauty care. And she and Cara would be standing at the freeway exit, begging for money.

Tiffany didn't want to read on, but morbid curiosity got the best of her and she picked the book up again and turned the page. The first thing she saw was the heading "The Truth About Tiaras." That got her attention.

Most jewelry stores have a huge markup. It can run as high as one hundred percent. You'll save a bundle if you buy your jewelry from direct importers or wholesalers who don't have the high overhead. Okay, now that was valuable information. *Negotiate,* advised the diva. *A jewelry store may not be able to match the price you found at, say, a wholesale site on the Internet, but trust me, they can come down some.*

Tiffany probably wasn't going to be able to afford any new bling until she was ninety-nine, if then, but this was good information all the same. Okay, maybe there was something to this diva on a dime stuff. Tiffany's next client came through the door, so she had to set the book aside. As she did, she couldn't help wondering if some jeweler somewhere was reading a copy of this book and having the same reaction she'd had over the thought of discount manicures.

She heaved a sigh. Tough times affected everyone, both businesses trying to keep their doors open and people trying to keep a roof over their heads. A girl did what a girl had to do, including finding affordable beauty treatments. Still, she was glad there was no vo-tech school near Heart Lake.

No wholesale jewelers, either. That was probably just as well.

Chapter 6

Saturday night Rachel got comfy in her sweats and T-shirt. Then she dipped into her hidden stash of Hershey's kisses, and settled on the couch with her secret guilty pleasure: a romance novel.

She'd been a loyal reader since she'd picked up her first paperback in college, but when things went south with Aaron, she had taken all her romance novels to the Goodwill. Dumb. She'd had some first edition hardbacks in there that were probably worth something now. At the time, though, she hadn't cared. The last thing she'd wanted to read about was some pretend woman's happy ending with her perfect man. The perfect man didn't exist, except in fiction. And guess who made up those perfect men? Women, probably women who wished they could find such a thing as a perfect man.

But when she'd passed the romance paperbacks at the library she hadn't been able to stop herself from adding a couple to her pile of finance books. Maybe pretend wasn't so bad. Maybe reading about love and happy endings was good for the soul and gave a girl hope. With school (and her job) about to end, she could use a little hope.

She popped a chocolate in her mouth and opened the book.

Destiny Vane knew she had found her soul mate when she first saw Auguste Baiser. He was darkly handsome with sensual lips, a chiseled chin, and powerful arms, and he was helping an old woman across the dirty streets of Paris.

Rachel snuggled down deeper among the sofa pillows. Auguste Baiser, would, of course, turn out to have other body parts as powerful as his arms, and after many ups and downs (no pun intended), many tears and terrors, Destiny and Auguste would walk off into the French sunset hand in hand. In the book, this would take months. At the rate Rachel read, it would take until Sunday afternoon.

Which it did. She gobbled the story down like candy, even though this particular book was one big cliché after another. But so what? Her real life was a cliché.

She was done and ready to return to the real world by the time the children came through the door from spending the weekend with their father and Misty the lingerie model. Rachel was slipping peanut butter cookies onto a cooling rack when the door opened and the sound of voices and a bouncing basketball echoed through the house, announcing that her babies were back.

David bounded into the kitchen first. "Cookies!" His basketball landed on the floor and dribbled away and he scooped up two, juggling the hot goodies in his hand.

Rachel smiled. She couldn't run out and buy her son the latest Wii game, but cookies worked almost as well. "Did you have fun with your father?" she asked, keeping her voice conversational. Of course, he had fun. Fun was all the kids ever had with Aaron. No homework ever got done, no chores. Aaron's house was Fun Land. Sigh.

David had already stuffed half a cookie into his mouth. "Yeah," he said, spitting crumbs.

Normally Rachel would correct him for talking with his mouth full. Not now, though, not when he'd just returned from being with the other woman.

"Except Misty can't cook."

Her son, who was basically a support system for a stomach, always said this when he came home, and she always kept the same thought to herself: Aaron didn't marry Misty for her cooking skills.

Now Claire was in the kitchen, too. She was smiling, which meant Misty had done something cool with her, something where money was no object. It only took a second to guess what. Claire was wearing a new necklace and earrings.

"You look like you had fun. What did you do?" asked Rachel, working hard to sound like a good sport. *Let me guess. Does it start with an S?*

"We went to the mall," said Claire.

Big surprise. Clothes were Misty's life. How nice to have the perfect body for clothes, and for attracting someone else's husband. How nice to have money to spend on clothes, not only for yourself but to use to buy the affections of someone else's daughter, as well. How nice. Where was the Kick Me sign for Misty's backside?

Okay, enough. Misty might have been able to steal Rachel's husband, but she'd never be able to steal her children. Kids couldn't be bought. They saw right through feeble attempts like trips to the mall, at least that was what Rachel's mother was always saying. She sure hoped her mother was right.

"Guess what," said Claire, still smiling. "Misty had braces when she was my age."

"And look how she turned out," Rachel said, finishing her daughter's thought. She'd had braces, too, and had

told Claire that. It hadn't done a thing to encourage her.
But then Rachel wasn't a model.

"I still wish I didn't have to get them, but I guess it will
be okay," said Claire, helping herself to a cookie.

All right. She still hated Misty, but she could at least
be glad that Claire had come home, not simply resigned
to her fate, but feeling better about it. "It will be okay,"
Rachel said, and gave Claire a one-armed hug. "It always
is. Isn't it?" she added, rumpling David's hair.

"Yep," he said, and took two more cookies.

"That is enough cookies for you," she told him, deciding she needed to get back in mother mode. "You'll spoil
your appetite for dinner."

"I'm not hungry," said Claire. "We went to Pizza
Heaven."

Oh, well, Rachel told herself. Misty couldn't bake. So
there.

Still, the possession of baking skills didn't seem like
much of an upper hand when compared to trips to the
mall and Pizza Heaven and looking gorgeous enough to
inspire a preteen to accept the necessity of getting braces.
Children didn't care how long you were in labor with them
or how much you sacrificed to keep them in the same
house they'd always lived in. They didn't tell themselves
that someday they'd thank you for making them eat their
vegetables, do their homework, and practice good hy-
giene. Children, when faced with a choice between boring old Mom and the Pied Piper in drag, always chose the
Pied Piper. Her mother was wrong. Children could be
bought.

Where was she going with all this? How much nega-
tivity could a woman pack in one brain? No more already,
she told herself, and tried hard for the rest of the evening
to be upbeat and positive. And in the process of being
upbeat and positive she consumed six peanut butter

cookies. Maybe she really did need therapy. Or another romance novel. She decided on the romance novel.

The next morning Rachel woke up determined to be optimistic. She was tough and resilient. She would be fine. She'd gotten kicked, but she wasn't down. She and her children still had a roof over their heads and she had a steady paycheck for a little while longer. If she couldn't find a full-time teaching position for fall, she'd sub. Or she'd clean houses. Or she'd sneak over to Aaron's, steal Misty's lingerie, and sell them on eBay. Snort.

"What are you laughing about?"

Rachel turned from where she stood toasting bagels to find her daughter looking at her like she was crazy.

"Nothing. I just thought of something funny, that's all."

Claire shrugged. She helped herself to a bagel and started slathering jam on it. "Can I hang out downtown after school with Bethany?"

"I know that Coffee Stop gift card is burning a hole in your pocket," Rachel teased. "I guess, for a couple of hours."

"Ummm, can I have some money?"

"You spent all your allowance?"

"Pleeease?" Claire begged, dodging the question.

Rachel noticed her daughter was wearing the new necklace and earrings she'd gotten at the mall with Misty. The woman poured money on Claire like it was water and Rachel was bickering over a few dollars? "I have a ten in my wallet. You can have that."

"Thank you, Mommy! You're the best mom in the world." All smiles, Claire gave Rachel a kiss on the cheek and bounded out of the kitchen.

Ten dollars was a small price to pay for being the best mom in the world. Or was it? What was she teaching her daughter about money? Her head suddenly hurt.

* * *

Jess had called in to A-Plus Office Services first thing in the morning and learned that they had nothing for her. Michael was right; she had to cast her net further. So, back to the city she went and signed up with Solutions, Inc.

"You don't have a lot of experience," said Ms. Solutions Inc., offering an empathetic expression to soften the harsh reality.

"You're right, I don't," Jess agreed. But how hard could it be to sit at a desk and push those blinking lights on a telephone? And she knew the alphabet, for crying out loud. She could handle filing.

"We mostly get requests for data entry. It would help if you knew Excel. But we'll keep a watch and call you when something comes up that we think is a good fit for you."

Jess nodded and left the office with a strong suspicion that she wouldn't be hearing from Solutions, Inc. *You need a Plan B.*

On her way home she passed Heart Lake High, and catching sight of the school tennis courts suddenly inspired her. Now there was something she could do: teach tennis. She played doubles every Friday, spring, summer, and fall. She knew her way around a racquet. It had only taken her twenty years of playing to reach an intermediate level of excellence, but nobody had to know she was nothing more than a jock wannabe. It was like dying your hair—don't ask, don't tell.

As soon as she got in the house she called her friend Mary Lou, the head of the Heart Lake Park and Recreation sports department and offered her services for the upcoming summer program.

"I wish you'd called about a week earlier," said Mary Lou. "I hired my last instructor on Friday."

It figured.

"But we just lost a kinder gym teacher. I could use some help there."

"Kinder gym, like in gymnastics?" Tennis was one thing, this was quite another. "I don't think so. I can't even do a decent somersault," Jess confessed.

"They call them forward rolls," Mary Lou corrected. "You really don't need to know as much as you think you do."

"I must have to be certified or something. Otherwise, what happens if some poor kid gets hurt on my watch?"

"Trust me. You don't have to be a gymnast to teach kinder gym," Mary Lou assured her. "Anyway, you're not exactly teaching at a level that involves injuries."

"But if someone did get hurt?" worried Jess.

"That's why we have insurance. Look, I'll train you myself. Okay? Come in and help me with my morning classes this week. That way you could start teaching when the new session begins."

As in she'd be hired? Just like that? It paid to have connections.

"Okay," Jess decided. It beat waiting by the phone, hoping to hear from temp agencies.

"Great! You'll love this," Mary Lou enthused. "The kids are so cute. That's why I still teach a couple of classes. I love it."

You can do this, Jess told herself as she hung up. How hard could it be to teach little kindergartners and preschoolers to hop around on a mat?

Not that hard, she decided the next day, watching Mary Lou in action at the old junior high gym where classes were held. All the kinder gym pupils were really young so it was mostly fun and games and an introduction to the basics of gymnastics with lots of stretching at the beginning. "Stand on your tippy-toes," Mary Lou said, demonstrating. "Reach for the ceiling."

All the little gymnasts (mostly girls in pink leotards) stood on tiptoe on cute, little baby fat legs. Jess fit right in with her hot pink tee. She stood, too, on legs that also had fat, the grown-up variety.

After stretching they worked on skill-building while parents sat in folding metal chairs on the far end of the gym and smiled at their future Olympians, oblivious to the smell of eau de sweat that perfumed the air. Mary Lou made it all look easy.

"See?" she said later as they waved good-bye to the last set of parents and children. "You can do this."

"What if somebody asks me to demonstrate?" Jess worried.

"I'll work with you this week and teach you the basics, like how to do a forward roll and mount the beam . . ."

"Wait a minute," Jess interrupted, "as in balance beam? They learn that in kinder gym?"

"Well, we have a grade school class we need you to help with, too. But don't worry. You'll only be an assistant. Gene the gymnastics coach will be the instructor."

Still. Mounting a beam? What else was she going to have to help with? Someone was whimpering and Jess realized that someone was her.

"You'll be fine," Mary Lou assured her.

"Are you sure you don't need another tennis instructor?" asked Jess.

"We might later this summer, but not now. What I really need is a kinder gym teacher." Mary Lou cocked an eyebrow.

Jess thought of the office assignments she wasn't getting and could almost hear the old Beatle's song "Money" playing at the back of her brain like a soundtrack. "Okay. Teach me a forward roll."

Mary Lou beamed. "All right. You do it exactly like we tell the kids: tuck and roll." She turned herself into a tight ball and rolled across the mat, then bounced back up like a spring. "See? Nothing to it."

Right. The last time Jess had been able to curl up that tightly was in the womb with her thumb in her mouth. She took a deep breath, then squatted on the mat and tried to turn herself into a ball. All the blood rushed to her head as she bent over and she suddenly felt sick. The thought of what she looked like from behind made her even sicker.

Mary Lou was next to her now, coaching her. "Tuck a little more."

Easy for her to say. She didn't have to figure out where to tuck a couple of 38Ds. Jess made a superhuman effort, rallying every muscle in her body to help fold her into something that would roll. The sound of ripping fabric echoed through the gym.

"Please tell me that wasn't my pants," Jess groaned and started to straighten up.

"Never mind. They're already split so you may as well keep going," said Mary Lou, and proceeded to turn Jess into a pretzel.

Now Jess could barely breathe, but she managed to protest, "Hey, I'm not made of elastic."

"Stretch more and you will be. Come on now, roll."

Rolling was preferable to getting smothered by her own boobs. Jess let gravity take over and started forward. She was doing great until her nose made contact with something hard. Her knee, of course. She saw stars and rolled over onto her side, landing like a beached whale. "Oooh, my dose." She reached a tentative hand to her nose and discovered it was bleeding. Great. Mary Lou could trot her out when she wanted to show the kids what not to do.

Her friend handed her a tissue. "Are you okay?"

In the space of ten seconds she'd managed to split her pants and give herself a nosebleed. Oh, yeah. She was great, a real natural. She flopped back on the mat, pinching her nose. "Fide."

"Maybe you really aren't cut out for this," mused Mary Lou.

Oh, no. She'd already washed out as a temp. She'd be darned if she'd flunk forward rolls. "I can do this," she insisted. "Let's try it again."

Half an hour later she limped to her car while all the muscles in her body cried, "Pain, pain, pain."

"Oh, shut up," she told them. "No pain, no gain."

And she had gained something today. She was now a Park Department employee. She wasn't going to make a fortune at this, but at least she'd be making something. And, at this point, something was better than nothing. She only hoped she didn't spend all her paycheck on aspirin and muscle cream.

Tiffany had driven straight home from work on Saturday. No bargain-hunting detours. (What was the point without a credit card?) She didn't even so much as stop at the grocery store. Not only had she spent no money, she'd acquired a free book on how to live great on next to nothing. She could already hear how the conversation with her husband would go.

> BRIAN: *You didn't so much as stop at the grocery store? That's amazing. And what's this, a book on saving money?*
> TIFFANY (looking modest): *I didn't pay anything for it. I'm going to save us so much money from now on, you won't believe it.*
> BRIAN: *I'm proud of you, Tiffy.*

But the conversation did not go as planned.

"*Diva on a Dime,* huh?" he said, stopping work on the

Jeep and wiping his hands on a rag. "You really think you can do that?"

"I'm going to try," she said.

"The diva part won't be a problem," he said, frowning at the book. "You already work that pretty good."

"What's that supposed to mean?"

"I mean, we don't need half the stuff you bring home. This book looks like one more way to get you to spend money." He took it and flipped through the pages, landing on the chapter that dealt with how to save on jewelry. He began reading, growing a frown in the process.

"Those are good tips," Tiffany insisted. "Give it back. You're getting it all greasy."

"Yeah, well, an even better tip is don't buy the stuff in the first place," he said, handing over the book.

"I wasn't going to," she said. "I'm trying, Brian. I'm really trying. Anyway, Jess and Rachel found me this book at the library, so it didn't cost us a thing."

Of course, he hugged her and said he was sorry, but things were a little strained after that. Oh, they pretended everything was all right. They spent the evening with friends, playing Wii. Then they came home and went to bed and he kissed her good night.

And that was all. There it was, proof that everything wasn't all right (as if she'd needed any proof!). It hadn't been so long ago that on a Saturday night Brian would have been all over her. And she'd have been all over him, too, and not only on a Saturday. Friday and Sunday and Tuesday and Wednesday, and sometimes, even Thursday. After her second miscarriage, sex had dwindled down to the weekends. Now Brian was claiming he was stressed, but she knew, deep down, he was losing interest. How could he not be? She was a malfunctioning baby machine and he wanted kids. They both did. Or maybe he still hadn't really forgiven her for getting those credit cards and he was punishing her.

On Sunday, Brian watched a baseball game on TV and she read her book. It was all very cozy on the surface. The only thing missing was the cozy feeling. On Monday, life went back to the weekday routine with one exception: things were not right between them. She could feel it. Brian kissed her good-bye when he left for work and hello when he came home again, and he helped her with the dishes after dinner. But then he wandered outside and hung out across the street with their neighbor, who was restoring an old car.

Tiffany watched out the window. Hanging out under the neighbor's car hood was as close as Brian could get to his dream of having something old to play with, and it was her fault. Sigh.

Tuesday she got him to watch a chick flick on TV with her, but it didn't inspire him to do anything more than kiss her good night, and by Wednesday, the emptiness deep inside her that had opened up after her second miscarriage was back. She'd managed over the last few months to fill it with all her bargains, keeping herself happy with shots of shopping vaccine, but there was no vaccine now, and worse still her marriage needed a wonder drug.

On Wednesday she attempted to nurse it back to health by pulling out candles and her best Victoria's Secret bargain and making margaritas. She managed to lure Brian into a wild bout of sex on the living room couch, but it didn't lead to any real intimacy, no spooning, no whispering in her ear how much he loved her—not that he had to do that every time, but this time, after he'd been so mad the week before about her spending, it would have been reassuring.

Instead, he said, "Wow, babe, you did me in," and wandered off for a shower.

Wow, babe, you did me in. Well, that was . . . not the same as *I love you.*

"I love you," she called after him. All she heard in response was the water running. He probably hadn't heard her. She should go after him, tell him she loved him, pour out her fears, and promise that in exchange for his love, she would never again sabotage them with her reckless spending. Instead, she poured herself another margarita.

When he came out she asked, "Can we do something together tonight? It doesn't have to cost a lot of money."

"Like what?" He dropped his towel and began pulling his clothes back on.

"I don't know." She picked up the towel and hugged it to her. "Something romantic."

He looked at her with a perplexed smile. "We just did."

"Something more," she said. "I know! Let's go to The Family Inn and see what we can get for five dollars."

He frowned. "Five dollars, ten dollars, twenty dollars—Tiffy, it all adds up. We really need to get into the habit of cutting back. You know that."

All week she'd been trying so hard. She'd just wanted to reward herself with a little treat—dessert someplace inexpensive, or sharing a cup of hot chocolate and holding hands with her husband across the table. Was that really going to break them?

He pulled her to him. *Good,* she thought as he kissed her. He got it. He ended the kiss and grinned down at her. "I've got a better idea." He picked up the TV remote and handed it to her. "This doesn't cost a thing. I'm going to work on the Jeep, so the remote's all yours tonight. I bet one of your reality shows is on." With that he gave her a peck on the forehead and then left her alone and unsatisfied.

She went through the next day at work with a smile pasted on her face, watching other women parade through the salon, flaunting their credit cards at the cash register.

No one paid by check or with cash. The whole world ran on credit and she'd been knocked out of the race. It was like being the only woman at a dance with no date.

She thought back to Black Friday when she and Brian had their big fight. She'd told Jess and Rachel that Brian had taken her credit cards. It was true. No, he hadn't yanked them out of her hands or grabbed her wallet from her and removed them. Instead, he'd emotionally black-mailed her into giving them up, telling her she wasn't be-ing a team player, that she hadn't been honest with him. He'd insisted they had to get rid of the credit cards. Those credit cards were going to ruin their marriage. Well, now she had no credit cards and she wasn't seeing much of an improvement in the marriage department. That showed where spending nothing got you.

By the time she left Salon H she had a good head of angry steam propelling her out the door, and the last thing she wanted to do was go home to Brian. She still had her tip money in her pocket. Suddenly she was possessed by a need to buy . . . something, anything. It took over, moving her hands on the steering wheel, guiding the car toward the mall. Then it drove her from the mall parking lot into the nearest department store where she found, miracle of mir-acles, the same shoes she'd gotten the week before and had to return, back on the rack and waiting for her, and still marked down. She had just enough money to buy them. . . .

If there was no sales tax. She frowned at the money on the counter.

"If you open up a credit card account you get ten per-cent off," said the clerk.

"I have an account," Tiffany muttered glumly. Much good it did her when her credit cards were cut in tiny pieces and buried in the garbage. "I don't have my card."

"We can look up your card number," the clerk said brightly.

Good idea. She'd only be spending a dollar more than what she already had sitting on the counter. What was one more little dollar on the account? "Okay," said Tiffany.

On the way out of the store, she saw a clearance rack at the back corner of the Juniors department. She'd just take a minute and look. Oh, that top. It was only $8.99. She'd make that much in tips tomorrow. As she marched to the service counter a new script played out in her head, one that completely justified her behavior.

BRIAN: *This is not the way to be a team player.*
TIFFANY: *Neither is refusing to go on a date with your wife when all she was asking to spend was five measly dollars.*
BRIAN:

Ha! Nothing to say.

Still, when she got home she left her purchases in the trunk. Not that she had anything to hide, really. She'd only spent her own tip money. Well, today's and tomorrow's, but that was beside the point. The point was she was in control of her spending.

She went inside and found Brian in the kitchen, stuffing sandwiches and wine coolers into a big grocery bag. "What are you doing?"

"Getting ready to take you out to dinner," he said.

She looked inside the grocery bag. In addition to sandwiches he'd packed a couple of snack-sized packages of chips and two bottles of her favorite coffee drink. And what was this? She pulled up a Hershey's chocolate bar and looked questioningly at him.

"I had a dollar in my wallet," he said with a smile. He took the candy bar from her and dropped it back in the bag. "You ready?"

"Where are we going?"

"Someplace romantic," he assured her.

Someplace romantic. There was hope after all.

They climbed into the Jeep and he drove her to the public park on the lake. Taking his bag of goodies and a blanket, he led her down to the far edge of the lake and spread out the blanket on the grass. "I know it's not a restaurant," he said, "but will it do?"

It would more than do. This was a perfect diva on a dime, romantic date. Why hadn't she thought of it? "Yes," she said, and put her arms around his neck and kissed him. "This is even better than going out."

"I'm sorry I'm being a hard-ass," he murmured, nuzzling her neck. "I don't want you to be miserable, Tiffy. Sometimes I wish I was rich. Then you could buy all the bargains you want."

Lack of riches hadn't exactly stopped her. She thought guiltily of the purchases hiding in her car trunk. Buying them had made her feel really good when she got them, but now she felt like a woman who had eaten too many cookies.

"I don't need to be rich," she assured Brian and kissed him, vowing to cancel her credit cards the next day. All she needed was to keep the empty spot filled. Not an easy task, that, for the empty spot inside of her was like a hungry piggy bank, always crying for more. And what it wanted most she wasn't sure she'd ever be able to give it. "Brian, I'll do better, I promise," she said, her voice quavering.

"Me, too," he said, and they kissed again.

Then they enjoyed their meal while watching the evening sunlight dance on the water. People were at the park, throwing Frisbees. They could hear the *thwunk* of a tennis ball as a couple played singles over on the tennis courts. The sound of laughter drifted in to them from somewhere out on the lake, mixing with their own happiness. Now, this was cozy.

Tiffany had just finished her half of the chocolate bar and sighed happily when Brian cleared his throat. "This probably isn't the best time to tell you this," he said, "but you need to know. Starting next Monday I have to take two weeks off unpaid."

"No pay?" she squeaked.

"I'm not the only one," Brian said. "We're all taking turns, hoping nobody else will have to get laid off."

Two weeks off with no pay. The shoes would have to go back. Again.

And she would have to do better. For real this time. She found herself wishing she had someone to help her, like an AA sponsor, or even a support group. Wait a minute. She had one in her own backyard.

Chapter 7

School was over, for the kids at least. The teachers had a few more days of postschool cleanup left, but they weren't waiting to celebrate. Everyone was going to Elsa Wilson's spa party. And it looked like that included Rachel. The last thing she wanted to do was spend money, but it was hard to turn Elsa down, especially when she knew that both Rachel's children were going to be off with friends, celebrating the end of school and leaving their mother alone. Excuses were hard to find when your coworkers knew you had no life.

So now here she sat in Elsa's living room, surrounded by other broke teachers who were all spending money they didn't have to help Elsa get a free spa basket full of expensive creams and lotions. Elsa's house was a ramshackle older home, but it was on the lake, and her living room framed a view of shimmering blue water. Rachel tried to use it to distract herself while Chere the Sensual Woman told them all the reasons why they needed to spend a fortune on body butters, perfumes, and candles. Every woman but Rachel bought a bottle of Magnetique, which Chere assured them would make each of them irresistible to the opposite sex.

Rachel settled for a candle that Chere said was designed to inspire romance whenever they lit it. Rachel didn't know about that, but she loved the exotic floral scent it was sending from the refreshment table. Anyway, she had to buy something. Elsa would be disappointed if she didn't.

And there went twenty-some more dollars. As she wrote her check Rachel tried to console herself with the knowledge that she had done her part to make Elsa's party a success. To have a friend you had to be a friend.

Maybe she couldn't afford to have friends.

It was Jess's first day of flying solo and she had three classes. She looked at the eight little girls and the one boy who was already all over the mat like an escaped slinky and thought, *I can handle this.*

If she couldn't, Brenda Bletznik would tell the whole neighborhood. Why, oh why, thought Jess, did I get stuck with the daughter of the biggest mouth in Heart Lake in my class? *Never mind,* she told herself. *You can do a forward roll. You are queen of the gym.*

Still, the queen of the gym took as long as possible with taking attendance.

But soon, every little future Olympian was accounted for and she had to begin. "All right. We have to stretch all our muscles really good so they'll be happy," she said. Her muscles would probably never be happy again but oh, well.

The students looked at her eagerly, expectantly, as if she was a gymnastics goddess and mimicked her every move. The parents smiled benignly. So far, so good.

"Now we're going to play follow the leader. Do what I do." She demonstrated, showing off her new sashay skills. "Can you do that? Follow me."

Around the gym they went, Jess sashaying for all she was worth, arms held gracefully to the side like a ballerina. She checked over her shoulder. They were all following her like so many baby ducks. "You're doing great," she called. The children smiled. The parents watching smiled. She smiled.

And then something sneaked in front of her foot, something big and thick and pain inducing.

Down she went like a whale doing a belly flop, her startled "Oomph" ricocheting off the walls of the gym, and probably floating out the door for half of Heart Lake to hear. All her students stopped in mid-sashay to stare. Out of the corner of her eye she could see the incredulous gaping of the parents seated on the edge of the gym and Brenda Bletznik eagerly leaning forward in her seat, taking in every detail. She clambered to her feet and turned to see what had caught her so unaware. The stupid practice beam—why hadn't she noticed someone had moved it?

"Are you all right?" called Brenda.

"I'm fine," she replied with a game smile. It was a lie. Her ankle was on fire and so was her toe, just like her face.

"We'd better move this balance beam a little bit." If she wasn't in so much pain, she'd have kicked it. "We don't want anyone else to trip, do we?" Not that anyone else would. She was the only klutz in the room. She picked up one end of the thing and heaved it out of the way. It fell with a satisfying *whump*, but the satisfaction only lasted long enough for Jess to remember that she'd have to move it back on the mat for the kids later. She returned to where her students stood gaping, limping as she went. *Ow, ow, ow.* She looked down. Her ankle was already swelling.

"Okay, everyone," she said weakly, "we're going to sit

down and stretch for a minute." And while her little dears stretched, she crawled to the phone and called Mary Lou. "Can you come down here? I think I need help."

She also needed Advil, ice, a doctor visit, and an Ace bandage. So far the queen of the gym was not having a very successful reign.

Chapter 8

Warm air caressed Jess's face as she limped out her front door on Friday to go meet with Rachel and Tiffany. It wasn't their usual craft night. This get-together was at Tiff's request.

The sky was blue, almost every flower bed in Cupid's Loop was in full, fragrant bloom and somewhere a robin was singing. It was, in short, a beautiful evening. The only thing marring it was Jess's uncertain future, she thought miserably as she made her way next door to Rachel's two-story colonial.

She diverted her eyes when she passed her little red Volkswagen convertible, not wanting to see the For Sale sign in the window.

"You love that car. Are you sure?" Michael had asked her before finalizing the ad on Craigslist.

She'd steeled herself and said, "Yes. We don't need the car payments." Her finance book had reminded her what pioneers crossing the desert learned when faced with a choice between keeping their possessions and surviving: lighten the load. She wanted to survive. Someday, down the road, she'd get another little red convertible. Meanwhile they had Michael's car and the truck, which was free and clear. How many vehicles did two people need, anyway?

"I feel awful, babe," he'd said, like it was, somehow, his fault that she was being responsible and shedding financial deadweight.

She'd wrapped her arms around him, kissing him on the cheek. "Well, don't. It's only a car. And if we find a buyer it will be one less headache."

At least that was her story, and she was stickin' to it.

Her feet disappeared in Rachel's shaggy grass as she crossed the lawn. Gardening wasn't Rachel's favorite chore and she had trouble keeping up with the rest of the block when it came to yard maintenance. Of course, it was nothing compared to the house on the other side of Rachel, which had been in foreclosure. That was fast becoming the neighborhood eyesore—not good for property values.

A large grocery bag sat on Rachel's front porch with some kind of dirt-encrusted plant bulbs inside. Maybe Rachel was about to change her ways and get in touch with her inner gardener.

Jess knocked on the door, and then let herself in. Rachel and Tiffany were already in the formal living room with glasses of iced tea.

"What happened to your foot?" asked Rachel.

"Occupational hazard," said Jess. At the rate she was going she was going to have to find a new occupation before she killed herself. "What's with the bag on the front porch?" she asked, accepting an iced tea from Rachel.

"It's rhubarb," said Tiffany. "Maude brought it to the salon today. We're supposed to split it three ways."

"Never turn down free food. That's my new motto," put in Rachel.

"Speaking of free things," said Tiffany, "that's actually why I wanted to meet tonight. I want us to start being a money group."

"What does that mean exactly?" asked Rachel.

"I'm not sure," said Tiff. "I thought if we met every week and talked about what we were learning from all those books you got at the library it would . . ." She stopped and gave a little shrug. "I don't know. Keep us on track."

"That might not be a bad idea," Rachel mused.

"And maybe you guys can help me not spend money," Tiffany said. She gnawed her lip, making Jess and Rachel exchange concerned glances. "My *Diva on a Dime* book is great, but she's not exactly around when I'm having a money problem. I need something like AA that we could do here in our own neighborhood. I mean, Rachel, you're going to have to be on a budget, and Jess, if you don't move . . ."

"We'll be on the street," Jess finished glumly. Okay, that was overstating it. They'd have her little paycheck and Michael's unemployment. But they weren't exactly going to be rolling in dough, and it was going to be a challenge to pay the mortgage and the bills on their new and unimproved income. "Why, oh why didn't we save more when we were making good money?" she lamented.

"The same reason I never squirreled away a nest egg," Rachel said, with a shrug. "I thought I was doing fine."

The three women fell silent. A faint *kaboom* echoed from the TV room as something blew up in the movie David and his friends were watching.

"It's not too late," Tiffany finally said. "We can help each other. We've got the books. How about instead of doing crafts once a month we meet once a week and work on budgets and find ways to save money?"

"Design our own money class?" asked Rachel.

"And support group," added Tiffany.

"All right," Rachel said decisively. "I don't think any of us is going to inherit a million dollars in the next few months, so we'd better do what we can with what we've got."

"Since you're the teacher, you can lead it," said Tiffany. "Okay?"

"Me? I don't teach economics, you know. I teach grade-schoolers," Rachel protested.

"Perfect," said Tiff, undeterred by her reluctance. "That means you won't make it too hard." Rachel still hesitated, so she added, "You don't have to be an expert, just keep us organized and on track."

Rachel heaved a resigned sigh. "Okay. I'll see if I can pull something together for our first meeting."

"Awesome!" cried Tiff happily.

"Goody," said Jess grumpily. It had been hard putting her car up for sale. Somehow, in light of what was happening here, she suspected that, like the pioneers, she still had a lot of desert to cross.

The next Friday the three women reconvened at Rachel's house.

Jess's portion of the evening was fun as she had brought the ingredients for homemade bath salts, providing them with an inexpensive craft.

Rachel's contribution didn't go over quite as well. "Your spending personality?" Both of Jess's eyebrows rocketed up as she read the questionnaire Rachel handed her. "I don't know if I want to know mine."

Rachel sneaked a look at Tiffany. Tiff was curled up in an easy chair, twirling a lock of blonde hair and scowling at the paper. "You guys wanted to do this. Remember?"

"I didn't want to do *this*," retorted Tiffany.

"Look, we've all got leaky financial boats. If we're

going to get to that golden shore of solvency we need two things: a better paddle, as in ways to bring in more income, and a way to plug the leaks."

"I think right now I should work at finding a better paddle," said Jess. "I've already got my car up for sale so that will plug a major leak."

"Oh, your cute little car," mourned Tiffany. "Gosh, that's so sad."

"No, that's smart," Rachel approved. "But look. If we don't get a handle on why we spend, we're bound to keep springing leaks. At least that's what one of my books said."

"That makes sense," Jess admitted grudgingly. "It sounds like about as much fun as a mammogram, but let's do it."

"We can start with me," Rachel offered. "I'm a guilt spender."

"How do you know that?" asked Tiffany.

Rachel could feel her cheeks growing warm. "Because that's what motivates where a lot of my money goes. Both Claire and David get an allowance, but every time they want money for something I give it to them."

"Maybe you don't give them big enough allowances," suggested Tiffany.

Rachel shook her head. "That's not it. Deep down, I think I've known for a long time that I'm trying to buy my children's love."

"They already love you," Tiffany said.

Rachel found it suddenly hard to look at her friends. "I know they do, but I want them to love me more than Aaron. Pretty sick, huh? I mean, he is their father. But he's such a bastard. Somehow, it doesn't seem fair that he gets the same amount of love. So I've let myself get sucked into this sick bidding war that I can't possibly win."

Tiffany heaved a sympathetic sigh.

"Someday he'll get what he deserves," Jess predicted,

and belted a pithy line from Jo Dee Messina's "Lesson in Leavin'."

"Meanwhile, he's Mr. Popularity and I'm Meanie Mom," said Rachel. "And I'm really going to be Meanie Mom when I break the news to them that we can't afford to go anywhere this summer."

"We've got a great lake right here. Do you really need to go somewhere?" asked Jess. "How about planning a staycation?"

"Hmmm. I've read about those," said Rachel. "But I never thought of trying one before."

"I know what the diva on a dime would do," piped Tiffany. "She'd make staying home like a camp and do beading and baking and fun stuff like that. I could come over and give free pedicures to Claire and her friends. We could have a girls' spa day."

"I like it," Rachel said with a nod. "That takes care of Claire. Any suggestions on what can I do for David?"

"Let him camp out in a tent in the backyard and he'll be happy," Jess assured her. "I'll even throw in a few tennis lessons with Aunt Jess."

Rachel found herself smiling. She could do this. She'd save money over the summer and go into fall with a healthy bank account, which would be a good thing considering the lack of teaching positions posted on the school district's Web site. She suddenly remembered the looming orthodontist bills. Well, semihealthy.

"Look at that," Jess was saying, "you've already saved a small fortune by not going on vacation. You can hunker down and pay the bills."

"I need to find a way to bring in more money though," said Rachel. She tapped her chin with her pencil. "Maybe I can find some parents who would be willing to pay me for tutoring."

"You could do a get-ready-for-school program in August," suggested Jess. "I'd have been all over that when Mikey was little."

Rachel nodded and made a note to herself. "I like it. Okay, that takes care of me. Who wants to go next?"

Her friends fell quiet.

"You know, this doesn't work like in the classroom where you just keep your head down and hope the teacher doesn't call on you. We all have to take turns."

"Okay, I'll go next," said Jess in a resigned tone.

As they talked about Jess's expenditures, it was easy to see Jess did a good job of rationalizing whatever she spent.

"But I don't normally do that," Jess excused herself. "I mean the work wardrobe—I had to have that. And we can't go in and see Mike's mom and not take her out to dinner."

"Why not?" asked Rachel. "You could bring her something."

"You know I don't cook," Jess replied.

"The diva on a dime says you save a fortune by making food from scratch," said Tiffany.

That went over like a failed soufflé.

"It's a great way to be creative," said Rachel.

"You can't be creative in everything," argued Jess.

"She's a rationalizer," Tiffany said as she doodled on her paper. "Write that down," she added.

Jess frowned and wrote.

And then it was Tiffany's turn under the microscope. "I already know," she said in a small voice. "I'm a retail therapy shopper."

With a little sob, she confessed her latest relapse. Soon she was spilling everything, from her other spending relapse to her concern that she couldn't give Brian the family they both wanted.

"Don't give up," said Jess, handing her a tissue. "Look at me. I had a miscarriage, but now I have two great kids."

Tiffany nodded and blew her nose. She smiled at Jess, trying to convey that she'd be fine.

Maybe they all would, because by the end of the evening Jess was smiling and Tiffany was looking determined. And Rachel was pumped. "Here's to small changes," she said.

"They'd better make a big difference fast," added Jess grimly.

On Monday Rachel took Claire to Dr. Rencher for a consultation and took her first step toward change. Braces were definitely in order. "Then let's get started," she said to him after they'd finished the consult. "Bill Aaron. He's taking care of this."

She left the office with a smile. Before yesterday she'd have sucked it up and paid her share (which, knowing Aaron, would have wound up being three-quarters of the bill). Not today. She had a new attitude.

And somewhere, a little gremlin was cowering.

Every Day,
in Every Way,
We're Getting
Better and Better

Chapter 9

"It's going to take forever to pay off my credit cards," Tiffany complained to Cara at the salon.

"So speed up the process," said Cara as she swept a pile of hair from the floor. "Girl, you got a fortune in clothes hanging in your closet. Sell 'em on eBay."

Tiffany looked at Cara as if she had suggested Tiffany cut off an arm.

"You can make money doing that. My sister in California is."

"What's she selling?" asked Tiffany.

"Stuff she finds at garage sales. Last year she got all kinds of cool junk: Victoria's Secret powder, knockoff purses, Gucci sandals."

Tiffany's eyes bugged. "Serious?"

"Oh, yeah."

Gucci sandals at a garage sale—now, that was worth looking into.

"I'm thinking I might start an eBay business," she said to Rachel later that day. "Want to hit some garage sales this Saturday?"

Rachel nodded thoughtfully. "You know, I haven't been to a garage sale in years. Sure, I'll ride shotgun." She studied Tiffany a moment. "You're not a morning person. You do know you have to get up early if you're going to get the bargains, right? A lot of these start at eight."

Tiffany set her jaw like a soldier preparing for battle. "I shop the Thanksgiving sales. I can do this. I'll be at your place at seven-thirty."

True to her word, Tiffany was on Rachel's front porch at 7:28 on Saturday morning, clad in a top, jeans, and flip-flops. "Caffeine," she mumbled. "We've got to hit The Coffee Stop."

"Oh, no we don't," Rachel corrected her. She brought Tiffany in the house and poured her a cup of coffee. Then she squirted in some chocolate syrup. "A poor woman's mocha," she said, handing it to Tiffany. "No dribbling our money away anymore. Right?"

Tiffany grunted and took a sip, then looked surprised. "You know, this isn't bad." After consuming half the mug Tiffany's brain joined the party. "This is going to be fun," she said as Rachel's minivan coughed its way down the street. She stopped talking and listened. "What is wrong with this thing?"

"Nothing that a good mechanic who wants to work for free can't fix," said Rachel with a shrug.

"Maybe we should take my car," Tiffany suggested. "It's newer."

"Don't be a snob," teased Rachel. "This one is free and clear."

"Yeah, but will it get us where we want to go?"

"Of course."

"Well, it better," Tiff said, and downed the last of her mocha. "I've got twenty-five dollars to spend. I hope I can find something with it. I have to prove to Brian that this can work."

"I take it he's not excited about your moneymaking scheme," Rachel observed.

"He thinks I've found a new way to spend money. But you have to spend money to make money. Jess said that," Tiffany added.

"A lot of people have said that," Rachel informed her. "Let's hope they're right."

Tiffany proved to be a garage sale power shopper. She had an eye for finding valuable trinkets and she was fast. She found a Lenox figurine for five dollars and beat a senior citizen to a jazzy, pink rhinestone clock.

Rachel felt the woman's scowl like a laser beam. Tiff was oblivious.

"Wow," said Rachel, as they drove away. "You don't mess around."

"This is business," said Tiffany. She tapped the little clock thoughtfully. "But I may keep this." Rachel frowned at her and she added, "Or not."

Soon they were almost out of money and time, as Tiffany had appointments at the salon. "Okay, one more," said Rachel, "then we'll go home. This should be a good one. It's right on the lake."

She was right. She could tell even as they pulled up. The house was relatively new and not only was the garage open for business, the owners had spread some wares along the driveway, too. "Treasure Island," Rachel predicted with a grin.

"I hope so," said Tiffany. She was practically salivating.

The same older woman whom Tiffany had beaten out of the clock earlier was climbing out of her car when they pulled up. At the sight of Tiffany, she began to speed-walk down the driveway.

"Oh, no you don't," growled Tiffany, leaping out of the minivan before it had even stopped.

"What are you doing?" Rachel protested. But it was too late. Tiff was already gone with the wind. Rachel sighed and parked. This could get ugly.

Sure enough, Tiffany and her older competitor were now actually racing . . . until Tiff slipped and went down. "Ooooh!"

Every head turned. Actually, every female head turned. The few men present had already noticed her.

"What did you step on?" Rachel asked, coming alongside her.

Tiffany inspected the bottom of her flip-flop and scrunched her face like she'd just seen something truly grisly. "Dog poop," she squealed, completely unaware that her competitor was now strolling triumphantly into the garage.

The owner of the house hurried up to her. "Are you okay?"

"It's on my foot. Eeeew!" Now Tiffany was shaking her hands like they'd been contaminated, too. She kicked her foot in an attempt to fling off the offending mess.

"Oh," the woman groaned. "Our neighbors have a dog. I'm so sorry."

"Not as sorry as I am," Tiffany said, her face screwed up in disgust.

"Here," offered the woman. "We can hose it off. Follow me."

Tiffany limped after her, "eeewing" all the way.

She was still shuddering and "eewing" when she and Rachel got back in the minivan. "I am never doing that again," she announced.

Rachel was surprised to see Tiff throw in the towel so quickly. She'd had great success herself, finding a name-brand top she knew Claire would love and several romance novels. This kind of shopping wouldn't break the budget. "That was a short-lived business."

Tiffany looked at her like she had said something crazy. "I'm not bagging garage sales."

"Then what are you talking about?"

Tiffany lifted her foot. "I'm never wearing these. You've got to dress for the job." They were about to drive off when she caught sight of the older woman leaving with a Tex-Mex–style pitcher. She gasped and pointed. "Crate and Barrel."

The woman smirked as she walked past.

"From now on I'm wearing running shoes," Tiffany muttered. "And I'm staying off the grass."

Chapter 10

After stowing away her garage sale finds, Rachel started on some much needed house cleaning. She was washing windows when she heard a lawn mower fire up next door. It was a sound no one had heard over there for a long time, and she peered out the family room window for a closer view. Sure enough, someone was mowing the lawn. Whoa. That was some someone.

She squirted more glass cleaner and quickly rubbed the window for a clearer view.

Holy Danielle Steel, but he was gorgeous. She took in the slim hips encased in Levis, the T-shirt stretched across broad pecs, and the arm muscles rippling under caramel colored skin and swallowed hard. This man could be a cover model. Why was he wasting time mowing lawns? Was there room in the budget for her to hire him to come mow hers?

Of course not. Darn.

The sun was out and the weather was balmy, making it a perfect day for weeding flower beds. Maybe she would just go out and pull a few weeds. Except she didn't have a thing to wear.

The man next door was now doing the side yard, giving her a clear view of raven black hair and straight black eyebrows, gorgeous brown eyes. And that strong, square jaw that practically screamed, "Touch me." Would he like a drink of water? Was he hungry? Was he married? She craned her neck, trying to zoom in on his ring finger.

"Mom, what are you doing?"

Rachel gave a start and the bottle of window cleaner dropped from her weak hand. "Claire." She picked up the bottle.

Her daughter looked at her like she had slipped a cog. Maybe she had. Ever since her library visit her brain had been operating under the influence of romance novels. From now on she was sticking to her finance books. "Did you need something?" she asked. She needed something, and she wasn't going to find it in any finance tome.

"Can you take Bethany and me to a movie?"

Rachel turned her back on the view out the window. "Is your room clean?"

Claire nodded emphatically. "Yes."

"And you have money left from your allowance?"

Emphatic turned into hopeful. "Could I have five dollars?"

"Sweetie, I can't keep bailing you out every time you blow through your allowance. That's why it's called an allowance. You know, so much allowed for spending every week?"

Claire frowned. "You don't give me enough."

Her daughter could find Rachel's guilt button blindfolded. She gave up. "All right." Still, nickled and dimed and dollared to death—this was no way to save money. "I tell you what," Rachel added. "I'll give you five dollars today, but that's the end of the line for the gravy train. Starting next week, we'll sit down together and work out a budget for your allowance. And when the fun money is gone, it's gone. No more bailouts. I am not the government. Got it?"

Claire nodded. "Got it."

"Good."

Of course, she probably didn't get it at all, Rachel thought as they walked to the car. How could she? She was only twelve. And at twelve why should she have to face the stark realities of life? Those came along soon enough.

Out of the corner of her eye Rachel was aware of Señor Gorgeous mowing the lawn. He was probably married. Or gay. Because that was one of those stark realities of life every woman over twenty-five had to face. Good men didn't grow on trees. And they sure didn't show up next door, mowing the lawn.

Still, that didn't mean she couldn't be neighborly. When she got home she'd offer him a glass of water. She surreptitiously checked out his truck, looking for the name of the lawn guy. The truck was an older model, white and beat up. She didn't see a lot of equipment or yard refuse in the truck bed, but maybe this was his first job of the day.

Picking up Bethany took some time since her mom wanted to chitchat. And then there were the usual arrangements to be made regarding the rest of the girls' day. "I can pick them up, and Claire's more than welcome to stay for dinner," Bethany's mother offered.

David was already off at a friend's house and wouldn't be back until after dinner. Rachel would have the whole day to . . . weed. She should have had the whole weekend, but Aaron had canceled his time with the children, claiming something had come up. Translation: Misty had gotten new lingerie. Something had come up all right.

"Mom?"

Rachel pulled herself back into the moment. "What?"

"Can I?" Claire asked eagerly.

Rachel pretended to consider. "I think we can make that. Thanks, Alice. Well, we'd better hurry," she added, moving the girls up the front walk. "We don't want you to miss the movie."

Halfway to the theater Claire said nervously, "Uh, Mom, you're going kind of fast."

Rachel looked down at the speedometer and was surprised to see she was ten miles over the limit. She took her foot off the gas pedal. "Good catch. Thanks." Speeding. She never sped.

She dropped the girls at the theater with all the usual admonitions. "Wait right in front of the theater for Bethany's mom, and don't talk to strangers."

"We know, Mom," said Claire in long-suffering tones, and shut the minivan door. "Don't speed."

"Of course not," Rachel said, highly incensed, and then sped off.

But by the time she got home the white truck was gone and so was Señor Gorgeous.

Fine. She didn't want to weed anyway.

With the temptation removed from her field of vision, her common sense returned. What were you thinking? she scolded herself. *You need a man like a diabetic needs a Twinkie.*

She sighed as the realization hit her. Just because a woman developed a problem with sugar, it didn't mean she lost her taste for sweet things. It sure looked like Rachel hadn't.

You are pathetic, she told herself. Maybe she needed a little aversion therapy. She took a moment to revisit the pain Aaron had inflicted on her in the past year and a half.

What gardener?

Chapter 11

Jess came home from her afternoon nail appointment—
which was probably another spending leak, but Tiff needed
the business—to the sound of voices, loud, angry male
voices. *Oh, no.* She followed the noise to the kitchen,
where Michael and their son stood nose to nose, faces red,
neck muscles bulging. In spite of the age difference, they
looked so much alike it was scary. Same hunky profiles,
same lanky build, same stubborn set to the jaw.

"Hey, if you don't want me here I'm gone," Mikey
yelled.

"Fine. If you want to be a bum, go live like a bum,"
Michael yelled back.

The anger in the room came at her heart like a knife.
Michael and Mikey had had their father-son clashes,
but never like this. They were a family; they worked
through things. This was wrong and out of control, and she
wanted to cry as much as they obviously wanted to fight.

Mikey marched toward the kitchen door but Jess
blocked it. "What are you two doing?"

"I'm out of here," Mikey announced, and pushed past
her. Behind his angry bravado, she could see her son was
close to tears.

She shot a punitive glare at her husband, and then chased after Mikey. He was already in the living room when she caught him by the arm. "Mikey, honey, this is no way to settle things."

"I'm done, Mom. I've been trying, but he doesn't believe me."

She wasn't sure she did either, which made her feel ashamed of herself. What kind of mother didn't believe her son? "He's just concerned."

Mikey's eyes flashed. "Yeah, I can see that. So what if I haven't had any interviews? I've been on the Net looking every day." He nodded toward the kitchen. "I don't see him going on any interviews."

Now Michael was in the living room, too. Mikey stiffened at the sight of him, and Jess worried he would bolt. He and Michael hadn't fought like this since Mikey sneaked out with the car when he was fifteen. Even that war had ended quickly. Their son had always been a good kid. Okay, more interested in playing computer games than doing homework. Even in college he'd skated by the first couple of years. But he'd buckled down and finished and gotten a job, and everything had been going so well. Until he lost the job. And now he was poised to storm off in a rage and go live . . . good God, where would he live, in his car?

Michael came up to their son and laid a hand on his shoulder. "Son, I'm sorry I lost my temper with you."

Mikey's jaw was tight and his lips clamped together. He managed a nod.

"I just need to know you're trying, that's all."

"I *am*, Dad," Mikey insisted, and his voice broke. "You can't blame me that there's nothing out there."

Michael opened his mouth to speak. Many years of marriage had turned Jess psychic, and she knew whatever came out of that mouth would be a fresh salvo for a new battle. "You'll find something," she assured her son.

He frowned and nodded. "I gotta go." He bent over and gave Jess a kiss on the cheek and then slipped out the front door.

Jess staggered over to the couch and fell on it. "Good God." She frowned at Michael, who had taken the chair opposite her. "What did you say to him, anyway?"

Michael looked at her as if she'd accused him some unspeakable crime. "What did *I* say? How about asking what he did to make *me* mad?"

"All right. What did he do?"

"Well, he finally got up at eleven. Do you know what time he came in last night?"

"Do I need to know what time he came in last night? He's over eighteen, Michael."

"He came in at two a.m., the same time he came in Wednesday and Thursday night."

"How would you know that? We were asleep."

"Well, I wasn't," Michael said grumpily.

"What were you doing awake?"

Now Michael turned wary. "I couldn't sleep."

Of course. "You were up worrying." She frowned at him. "You keep saying not to worry and then you stay up all night and do just that. Then you explode at our son."

"Our son is a man now," Michael said, frowning right back. "He can't dodge the fact that he's unemployed anymore than I can. He needs to be really working at looking for a job. Now, how hard do you think he's working if he's out screwing around with his buddies all night and sleeping the day away?"

Michael's voice was going up in volume. "Why are you yelling at me?" Jess protested.

He fell back against the chair cushions and dragged his fingers through his hair. "Sorry. I don't mean to yell. I don't want to yell at anybody, but Mike has got to get serious. We can't all be unemployed."

"Hey, I'm not unemployed," Jess protested. It wasn't much, but she was trying.

"You know what I mean, Jess. All I want is for him to try a little harder," Michael continued. "Why does he have to take that so personally?"

Jess shrugged. "Because he's a man?" She came over and squeezed into the chair with Michael.

"That's exactly why I want him to set some goals," Michael said sternly. "He needs to log in as much time looking for a job as he would working a job. Now, are you going to tell him that or am I?"

She could already envision another shouting match. "I'll take care of it," she promised. Though how she had no idea. Hopefully, something would come to her. "But give me a little time."

"Define a little time."

"Longer than you want?" She slid a hand up his cheek and gave him a kiss.

He closed his eyes with a sigh.

"It'll work out," she murmured. One way or another, she was going to make sure of it.

It took a couple of days of mulling for her to realize that her baby bird needed motivation. Michael was right. Mikey was having a hard time mastering the art of job hunting. Maybe that was because he'd gotten his first job so easily. Michael had had a friend in HR who'd pulled a couple of strings on Mikey's behalf. His job had practically fallen in his lap. Now he was sitting under the employment tree, wondering why he couldn't reach any plum position. Someone was going to have to teach him the importance of finding a ladder and climbing up to get what he wanted. Jess knew this called for something more important than firsthand experience and wisdom. It called for sneakiness and manipulation.

On Monday she came home from hopping around the

mats in the overheated, smelly gym, to find her son raiding the fridge. "I could use a sandwich," she said, dumping her purse on the kitchen counter.

He nodded, and went to work building her a super turkey sandwich with everything from green peppers to avocado.

"You put together a mean sandwich," she said with a smile as he set the creation in front of her. "Maybe you're wasted in the corporate world. Maybe you should become a chef."

He shook his head. "I think you have to go to school for that."

"Maybe." She took a bite. "Good stuff," she managed around a mouthful of sandwich. She swallowed. "You know, I've been thinking."

Mikey looked at her suspiciously.

He had the prettiest eyes. The boy could be a model; there was an idea. Except that kind of work was about as steady as being a musician. "I think right now you are having a crisis."

"Well, duh, Mom." He frowned and poured himself a glass of milk.

"I'll take one, too," said Jess, and he took another glass from the cupboard. "But, lucky for you, I have a solution to your crisis."

"You found me a job?" He pushed the glass her direction.

"Don't be sarcastic. And yes, I've found you an interim job." She grabbed a piece of paper from her little pile of scratch paper and started making a list.

"No shit? Where?"

"Here," she said brightly.

"Here?" He looked at her like she'd suffered a brain malfunction.

"It's the pits having nothing to do," Jess continued,

unfazed. "You feel like you have no purpose. So, until you find something, you'll be working for me, Mommy Dearest."

He didn't look at all thrilled with his new boss. "Doing what?"

She shoved the paper at him. "All kinds of things. Most people like a job with variety, so I'm going to make sure we vary your job description from week to week.

He picked up the paper and looked at it. "Clean garage."

"Dad really doesn't have time. It's a mess."

"Weed flower beds?" He looked slightly sick.

"I'm working. I don't have the time."

"Paint house?" Now he was staring at her in shock.

"Well, you know we didn't get it done last year and paint doesn't last forever."

"Mom, you expect me to do all this in one week?"

She took the list from his suddenly limp hand and examined it. "Okay, you can do the garage next week. That will work better anyway. After you clean the garage you can do a dump run. Oh, and I'll need you to take some things to the Goodwill for me."

"How much am I getting paid for all this?"

"Paid?" She looked at him as if he had just spoken to her in a foreign language.

His eyebrows shot up clear to his hairline. "I'm not getting paid?"

"Of course you are."

He looked relieved.

"You're getting free rent and all the food you can eat."

He frowned. "Funny, Mom."

"Mikey, I'm not being funny," she said, letting her smile slip away. "I'm being serious. I understand that you're looking for a job, but until you find one this will be a good way for you to feel good about yourself and help us out, too. We could have some tough times ahead of us. It's important that we pull together as a family. Since you're not working for someone else, you may as well work for me."

"But you don't pay," Mikey protested.

"Correction. I don't pay what you want. But what I pay beats getting nothing and sleeping in your car. Until you find something, I'm the best game in town." If that didn't motivate him to turn over every rock for a new game, nothing would. She downed her milk and picked up the plate with her sandwich. "This sandwich is really good. I think I'll have you cook some meals for me, too."

"I don't like to cook," he protested.

"Me, either," she said, and left her baby bird standing at the counter gaping in shock.

Chapter 12

Brian was at Rachel's house Friday evening before either his wife or Jess arrived, working on Rachel's minivan.

"I see you found a way to get your car fixed," Jess said to Rachel as she walked in.

"All the thing needed was some spark plug wires," said Rachel. "Brian's saving me a fortune. Of course, I offered to pay him but he wouldn't take anything other than cookies."

"Bartering cookies for car repairs. Somebody sure got the good end of that deal. So, where's Tiff? I thought she'd be here by now," Jess said, handing over a bottle of white wine. "I ran into her at Safeway and she was all excited about some big surprise she'd bought for us."

"Oh, no. She's spending money again?"

"In a way. She told me to bring three dollars to cover my share of whatever this is, and some gardening gloves. I left them on the porch along with a pair for you and a couple of spades."

"Gee, thanks," said Rachel. "Whatever she got, it had better be edible."

Jess pointed out the living room window. "Speak of the devil."

Rachel looked to see Tiffany coming up the walk, balancing a large cardboard container full of plants. Whatever was in the box was making it tippy. Brian was under the minivan's hood, oblivious.

"She's going to drop them," said Jess, hurrying for the door.

They got to Tiffany just before she dumped the entire contents on the front walk. "Thanks, guys," she said. "That was a close one."

"Are those strawberries?" asked Rachel.

Tiffany nodded. "Kathy at the Trellis gave me a great deal. We can put them in our flower beds along with the rhubarb."

"Strawberry and rhubarb pie," said Rachel, her taste buds thinking ahead. "For that I'll garden. Let's get started."

"Strawberry season around here is just about over, isn't it?" asked Jess as they trooped outside to start with Rachel's flower beds.

"Maybe that's why I got a deal," Tiffany said with a frown as she pulled on her gloves.

"Not to worry," said Jess. "Strawberry plants spring up every year. We'll consider this an investment in our food supply for next summer."

"Homemade strawberry jam. Yum," said Tiff. She was beaming again and obviously proud of her bargain find.

They had to pull a few weeds to make room for the new plants, but the evening sun was warm. The hum of a lawn mower drifted to them from down the street. It felt so idyllic. Not to mention satisfying, thought Rachel as she watered the new addition to her landscaping.

"We'll have jam from these next summer," she predicted as they moved on to Jess's yard.

"Too bad it's too late for this year," said Tiff, still disappointed with her bargain.

"We can still pick berries," said Rachel. "My friend Elsa was just telling me that she's got tons of raspberries, more than she knows what to do with. I think they'll be ready soon."

That made Tiff smile. "So we will get jam this summer."

"Tons," said Rachel. "After the raspberries the black-berries will be ripe." Rachel remembered her mother's homemade blackberry pies. The thought of home-baked goodies and a cupboard stocked with good things for winter really had her fired up now. "Then September the huckleberries should be ready to pick," she continued, warming to her theme. "Green Mountain is only five min-utes from here and I hear there are tons of wild huckle-berries there. By the time we're done we can have lots of jam and liqueurs, not just for our families, but to give away as Christmas presents."

Green Mountain was no Mount Rainier. It was really more of a foothill with no place to go, but it was the closest thing Heart Lake had to wilderness. DNR land, it consisted of woods, various wildflowers and shrubs, and trails, which made it popular with hikers and nature en-thusiasts. Although Rachel wasn't much of a nature girl, she was willing to adapt if it meant free food.

"I heard there are bears up there," Tiffany said.

"They're more afraid of you than you are of them," Rachel assured her. She hoped she was right. She'd heard that . . . somewhere.

"Unless they have a cub," said Jess dubiously.

"I don't like going out in the woods," Tiffany said.

"We should at least give it a try," Rachel urged.

Jess shrugged. "I'm all for stocking the pantry, espe-cially now that I've got a live-in cook." Tiffany stopped planting to stare at her and Jess grinned and said, "My son. He still doesn't have a job so I've put him to work for me. Until he finds employment he is my slave."

Rachel high-fived her. "I saw him out there today, painting the house. Way to go."

"It's getting done slowly," Jess said. "He's been pretty busy sending out résumés all week."

"Sounds like things are improving at your house," said Rachel.

"They'd be improving more if my husband found a job," Jess said with a sigh. "Sometimes I wonder if we should have said yes to Ohio."

"Don't even wonder," Rachel said sternly.

Jess sighed. "If Michael can't find anything, we are in deep doo-doo. We sure aren't going to make it on what I'm bringing in. Anybody know of any employment ops for a forty-something woman who plays the piano and does crafts?"

"Piano lessons?" suggested Rachel.

Jess rolled her eyes. "Oh, dear God, please no."

"Piano teachers make good money," Rachel pointed out.

"They should. It's torture to try and teach kids who don't want to learn." Jess heaved an elaborate sigh. "If I was thirty, I'd start a band."

"You still could," said Rachel, but Jess shook her head. "Okay, this will do it for me. Let's plant the rest at Tiff's place."

"You should help me with my eBay business," said Tiffany as they crossed the street with the last of the strawberries. "My clock went for fifty-one dollars," she bragged. "And the figurine for thirty-eight."

"Wow," said Rachel. "I'm impressed.

"So is Brian," said Tiffany.

"At this rate you'll have your charge cards paid off in no time," Jess told her.

Tiffany nodded. "Except when the money comes I'm going to reinvest it in my business."

Rachel wasn't so sure about that idea. "All of it?"

"I have to have things to sell," Tiffany said.

That was hard to argue with, so the friends moved on to Rachel. "Claire and Bethany are so excited about Girl Camp," she said once they'd settled back in her living room. "We start right after the Fourth. You know," she added thoughtfully, "I bet I can get them to help us pick raspberries. We can all learn how to make jam together."

The phone rang but Rachel ignored it. Other than her mother, the people who called her most were right here with her, which meant it would be for Claire. Sure enough, a couple of moments later she heard an excited squeal from her daughter.

"Somebody called with hot news," Jess observed. "Which means there's probably a boy involved."

A moment later, Claire was bounding into the living room, phone in hand. "It's Daddy."

A call from Daddy was cause for squealing? Only if . . . Rachel took the phone with a sick feeling. "Hi, Aaron. What's up?"

"Well, we're making some vacation plans over here."

And I'm about to outdo you. Rachel braced herself. "And?"

"My parents really want to see the kids."

His parents lived in New York, glamour capital of the world. Rachel quickly gave herself a good mother speech. *The children need to see their grandparents, and you can't deprive them of time with their father.*

Her competitive mother side immediately chimed in. *He's doing it again. He's buying their affection, the bastard.*

"We thought while we're at it we might as well take a quick jaunt down to Disneyland."

"Because it was right on the way? Please. I see." Girl Camp shriveled and died under the mighty shadow of Disneyland.

"Rachel, before you raise any objections, let me remind

you that the children live with you," Aaron said in his condescending Aaron voice.

"Yes, they do," she said, forcing her voice to stay even and her features neutral. *I get to be the main caretaker and you get to pretend you care.* She was aware of her daughter hovering, her face a study in excitement and worry. Of course Rachel had to say yes, but not before she got a few things off her chest. She left the room, not wanting to spill her bitterness in front of her daughter.

Behind her, she could hear Claire's unhappy voice. "She's going to say no."

"When are you planning to take this trip?"

"Actually I'd like to leave right before the Fourth."

Rachel shut herself in the bathroom.

"We want to get to Disneyland for the fireworks display."

New York, Disneyland. He could afford all kinds of expensive junkets, but he fought her tooth and nail over things like orthodontist bills. Fireworks. Well, she was about to show him some fireworks. She turned on the bathtub faucet full force to use as cover. "You are such an incredible bastard," she hissed.

"Because I'm involved with my children? What have you been smoking?"

"Oh, don't pretend you don't know what I'm talking about. I'm barely scraping by here, and do you help me at all?"

"Yes," he said in perfect time with her *no.* "Who is footing the bill for the orthodontist? Cute move, by the way."

"Oh, my heart is bleeding."

"Can we please stick to the subject?" Aaron said in a pained voice.

"I am sticking to the subject," she snarled. "Don't think I don't know what you're trying to do. You're trying to buy our children's affection. Fine time to be worrying about their affections, by the way, after you split up the family."

"You're the one who wanted a divorce."

"You're the one who had the affair and made me!"

"Rachel, we can't go back."

She slumped on the side of the tub and rubbed her aching forehead. He was right, much as she hated to admit it. "Okay. Just take them."

"I can only be gone for two weeks, but my parents want them to stay for the whole month. They don't get to see them very often."

"That's all well and good, but when is Claire supposed to get her braces?"

"As soon as she comes back," said Aaron. "Waiting a few more weeks won't hurt, Rach."

Rach. When was the last time he'd called her Rach? Of course he would now, evoking memories of happier times. "Fine." Her former in-laws would spoil the kids even more than her ex. But they were still her children's grandparents. She couldn't begrudge them time together.

"Until the end of the month then," she said. "I want them back in August though. And if you're going to California, you have to promise to give them a couple of days in San Francisco with my mom." What the heck? She might as well work a deal.

"I don't know if there'll be time," Aaron hedged.

"You make time, Aaron," she growled. "I'm not letting them go if you don't."

He heaved a long-suffering sigh. "All right."

It was a small victory, but size didn't matter. "Good," she said, and turned off the water. "I'll tell Mom to expect you. And I want to see the tickets and the itinerary before you go."

"You can trust me," he said, sounding offended.

What a joke. "That's the deal, Aaron. Good-bye." She came out of the bathroom to find Claire lingering in the hall, looking hopeful. "Yes, you're going," she said, and forced herself to smile as she handed back the phone.

Claire took it with a squeal and hugged her fiercely. "Thank you, thank you. You're the best mom in the whole world." She ran down the hall, squealing all the way. The price for being the best mom in the whole world kept going up.

Chapter 13

The Fourth of July weekend was garage sale heaven, which made up for the week of hell Tiffany had endured with Brian being home and grumpy. She returned from her bargain safari on the third laden with treasures to add to the piles of goodies she already had sitting in various shipping boxes in the spare room that served as Brian's home office. Not only had she taken over his office, she'd pretty much taken over the dining room, too, using her glass top dining room table as a staging area where she took pictures of her goodies before putting them up for sale.

"Good God, did you hit every house in Heart Lake?" Brian complained as he helped her lug her finds into the house.

"Just about," she said.

A saltshaker shaped like a rabbit fell off the top of his pile and bounced on the carpet.

"Be careful," Tiffany said, bending over to pick it up. "That's Fitz and Floyd."

He set a pile of lingerie and plates on the table. A black nightgown caught his attention. "You're selling this?" He sounded disappointed.

" 'Maybe," she said slyly. "Or I might keep it."

"Keep it."

Heaven knew their sex life could use a boost. She moved the nightgown off the to-be-sold pile.

With raised eyebrows, he held up a Christmas plate. "Who's going to buy this in July?"

She took it from him and set it back down on the table. "No one, silly. But it will sell like crazy in November."

"Speaking of selling, what's been happening to the money from the stuff you already sold? I thought that was going to go to pay down the credit cards."

Tiffany added a pink quartz beaded necklace to her keeper pile. Now that she thought of it, the necklace probably wouldn't sell anyway. "I'm going to. But I have to build my business first."

Brian looked at all the items spilled across the table. "Uh, I think you've got enough to sell between this and all the junk in my office. There's barely room for me in there now."

"It's not junk. And yes, once these go, I'm going to have a big, fat wad of money."

Well, hopefully. Some of her items had been sitting around like eBay wallflowers, with no bids and no watchers. She wasn't going to tell Brian that, though. He'd say she was wasting money they didn't have and tell her to quit, and she had no intention of quitting. Even with the wallflowers this was a great way to earn money. She got as big a buzz watching her bids go up as she got when she was bargain hunting. And, talk about bargains—she'd found some great things for herself on eBay. That probably had something to do with why she wasn't turning a profit more quickly. But she was saving a fortune staying out of the stores. Talk about willpower.

Brian shook his head. "If you ask me, this looks like one more way to get deeper in debt."

"What is that supposed to mean?" she demanded. Here she'd found a creative way to earn extra money and he was dissing it.

"How much of the money you've made has gone to pay down those credit cards?"

"I'm getting them paid down," she hedged.

He raised an eyebrow.

"I am!"

Brian just shook his head and walked away.

"Where are you going?" she called after him. "I thought we were going to the car show."

"You go," he called over his shoulder. "I'm not in the mood."

"Fine," she snapped. "And I'm not in the mood to keep the nightgown."

"Whatever," came his disembodied voice.

Tiffany threw the nightgown on the to-be-sold pile. Her husband was an ingrate and it would be a long time before he saw her in anything sexy.

Chapter 14

Claire and David were having a great time in California. They'd done Disneyland and now were seeing the sights in San Francisco. "But they miss you," Rachel's mother assured her when Rachel called to check in on Tuesday.

"They told you that?" Rachel asked, amazed.

"They didn't need to. I could tell."

Good, old Mom. "In other words, they're too busy having fun to miss me. I hope they're behaving."

"They're practically perfect. You've done a wonderful job with them. Thank God they live with you and not that horrible creature." It was hard to know which horrible creature Mom meant until she added, "May her breasts fall off."

"Well, I'd like to say Aaron is getting what he deserves, but he's too happy."

"What goes around comes around," said Mom. "So don't you worry. The children aren't up yet, but I'll have them check in later."

"No, don't do that. I don't want to be one of those needy mothers. Just give them an extra kiss for me."

"I will. But I'll also have them call. Meanwhile, don't

waste this time to yourself. Go out and have a little fun already."

"Don't worry, I am," Rachel assured her. She'd had a little fun on the Fourth. And yesterday? Hmmm. Did tutoring Cara's daughter count?

Rachel said good-bye to her mother, then made herself a cup of coffee before going online to see if any teaching positions had miraculously appeared on the school district's Web site. No miracles there. She heaved a sigh. Her job situation, or rather lack of job situation was, to put it mildly, disheartening. "That which doesn't kill me makes me stronger," she quoted to herself. Which meant, at the rate she was going, she could take down Arnold Schwarzenegger.

She ventured a look out her window but here was no sign of her own personal Mario Lopez today. Sigh.

She'd seen him in the crowd at the lake when she went with Jess and Michael to watch the fireworks on the Fourth. He had stood talking with two other men and a couple of Latina women, his hands stuffed in his back pockets. Those women had been drop-dead beautiful and she'd wondered if he was with one of them. Surely not; otherwise his hands wouldn't have been in his pockets. He must have felt her gaze on him because he'd turned his head and looked right into her eyes.

She'd felt a Roman candle–sized zing from her chest to her panties. Embarrassed over having been caught ogling, she'd quickly found a new direction to look, but it had been impossible to stop from sneaking another peak when she thought he wasn't watching.

It had also been impossible to resist imagining them sitting together on a blanket, her tucked safely against him with his arms around her. That had been a nice fantasy to put under her pillow for sweet dreams, but it was daylight now. Time to come back to the real world. She turned her back on the nonview and went to her office to dig into her finance book and come up with ideas for how to save more money.

The more she worked the more inspired she became. In fact, she became so inspired she decided to start a blog. Why not chronicle what was happening with her and Jess and Tiff? After an hour of fingers flying over the keyboard she had her first entry on her new blog site, which she had titled Small Change, Big Difference. "Feel free to join the small change club," she finished. "Let's start a movement." She smiled. She was now the mother of a movement. It was probably easier than being the mother of children.

Speaking of motherhood, why hadn't her children called? Her mother was too smart to take her at her word and let them off the hook. She'd make Claire and David report in.

As if on cue, the phone rang. "Hi, Mom," sang Claire.

"Hi, sweetie. Are you having fun?"

"Yeah. Grandma taught me how to make dumplings. And Misty took me to Chinatown."

Naturally, Misty would make sure they shopped till they dropped wherever they were. Rachel felt her eyes turning green. "Did you get anything?"

"I got you a charm," Claire said, proud of her thoughtfulness.

"That was sweet. Thanks. What else?"

"I got a cool necklace with a fish for me and Bethany."

"Bethany and me," Rachel corrected automatically.

"Bethany and me," said Claire in a tone of voice that told Rachel her daughter was rolling her eyes.

"So, what else?"

"That's all. Next we go to New York."

"Well, I'm glad you're having fun," Rachel said. *You*

are, she told herself. The kids were having a great summer adventure after all and she didn't have to pay for it. Really, that was a win-win situation. She sighed. Another cup of coffee would make her feel like more of a winner.

On her way to the kitchen her eyes strayed to the window again. This time she was rewarded with a glimpse of a paint can and a fine male posterior all wrapped up in denim going up a ladder. She casually drifted over for a better look. Señor Gorgeous was back. This would be a good day to weed. Did she have any cute weeding clothes?

Deciding to channel her inner Jess, she dug out a sleeveless red top (it wasn't as hot as Jess's style, but it at least had a scooped neck and hinted that she had breasts) and the shortest pair of shorts she could find. Sadly, they fell into the same lukewarm category as the top. Mom shorts. And they were white—great color for working in the dirt. Who was she kidding? She wasn't planning on doing much work. She was only going to go out long enough to smile and offer a neighborly glass of water to a thirsty working man. She cuffed her shorts to show off some leg, applied some red lipstick, and stepped out the door.

She could certainly be out here all day and never run out of things to do, she thought as she walked through her backyard. Her flower beds were a mess. Probably the only neighborhood eyesore bigger than hers was the house next door, and that was quickly changing. First the lawn, now a fresh coat of paint in a new color—somebody was clearly putting some money into that place.

She casually strolled around to the side of her house. The hunk was at the top of the ladder over there, not more than ten feet away and swinging that paintbrush like he meant it. And he was shirtless—gloriously, lusciously shirtless. She licked her lips. Everyone who lived on the lake talked about their fabulous view, but right now she couldn't think of any view she'd rather enjoy.

He was much too busy to notice her, but he couldn't stay up there forever. He'd have to come down some time. When he did, she'd say a friendly hello. She casually dropped her foam gardening pad on the ground then knelt daintily in front of the side flower bed—at an angle so she could keep sneaking peeks at those rippling back muscles.

You're being ridiculous, she scolded herself. What was she doing out here, channeling Danielle Steel? The last thing she needed was another man in her life, breaking her heart.

In disgust, she picked up her gardening pad and started back around the house.

"Hot day, isn't it?" called a voice.

She turned and looked over her shoulder to see Señor Gorgeous stepping off the ladder.

Maybe she wasn't done gardening after all. "It is," she agreed. What the heck? There was no point in being rude. "Could I offer you a glass of water?"

One of those dark eyebrows rose cynically, making her wonder what she'd said wrong. "Sure. Why not?"

She nodded and walked into the house, the picture of sophistication, until she tripped over the front porch step. She forced herself not to look back to check if he'd seen. Hopefully, he'd been busy with his brushes.

In the kitchen she filled a glass with ice and took a cube to rub on her neck and cool down. This attitude (not to mention the accompanying behavior) was beyond silly for a woman who didn't need a man in her life. She filled the glass with water and hurried out of the house. *You don't have to fall in love with him. You can use him for your own selfish pleasure. Get in touch with your inner Misty.*

But once in front of the stranger she couldn't seem

to get in touch with her vocal cords, let alone her inner Misty.

She held out the glass with a brain as blank as a new whiteboard.

"Thanks," he said with a nod and took it.

She watched as he tossed down half the contents. Even his throat was gorgeous. "I live next door." Had she just said that? Of all the inane . . . She cleared her throat. "My name's Rachel." She held out her hand.

"Chad Alvarez," he said, taking it.

Her mouth suddenly felt dry. She should have brought out some water for herself. *Never mind the water. Think of something to say!* "It's nice to see this place getting fixed up. Do you know who bought it?"

"As a matter of fact, I do."

"Do they have children?"

He shook his head. "Afraid not. The owner's single."

"Oh. Is he going to live in it?"

"He's going to rent it out. As soon as he finishes painting it."

She nodded. As soon as he . . . "He? You?"

His smile was mildly mocking. "Yeah. He me."

"I thought . . ." She stumbled to a stop.

The eyebrow went up again. "That I was the hired help?" He finished off the rest of the water, then handed back the glass. "Thanks for the drink."

"I guess you didn't need it since you could just go inside and get one anytime you want."

"It was a nice thought."

"I get those sometimes. When I bother to think." She managed an embarrassed smile.

He smiled back. "I appreciate the neighborly gesture."

She managed a one-shouldered shrug. "What are neighbors for? I guess I'll get back to my weeding." *And go swallow my tongue.*

"Weeding can be thirsty work," he observed. "Maybe I should bring you some lemonade later."

"Lemonade definitely tops water," she said.

He nodded. "I'll be ready for a break after I finish this side of the house. You can tell me about the neighborhood."

She noticed he didn't say anything about telling him about herself. Maybe he figured he'd learned enough about her already. *Horny woman who hits on helpless manual laborers.* Pathetic.

But later, when they sat on her front porch, drinking bottles of Mike's Hard Lemonade, he did show an interest in her. "So, you have children?"

"Two. They're with their father and his girlfriend for a few weeks." *And I'm all alone in this big, old house. Subtle, Rachel. Very subtle.* "How about you? Oh, yeah. Single. No children. And you do your own painting?"

He smiled. "I like to do my own maintenance work. It keeps me in shape."

"And what beautiful shape you're in." Oh, no. Had she really just said that out loud? She looked into her half-empty bottle. "What's in here, truth serum?"

He chuckled. "It's refreshing to meet a woman who says what she thinks."

"Especially when she thinks nice things about you?"

"Even when she doesn't."

"Do women ever think things about you that aren't nice?"

"They've been known to."

Of course. He was probably one of those love 'em and leave 'em types. Aaron: the Latino version. So, they'd make some more small talk, finish their lemonade, and then she'd retreat into the house to the safety of a novel where happy endings were guaranteed.

"What do you do besides make over houses?" she asked.

"Real estate."

"So I guess you heard about this house from someone at your real estate office."

"Something like that," he agreed.

He must have sunk his fortune into the place and was now trying to make a go of it. "Kind of a gamble, isn't it?"

"Life's a gamble," he said, and took a swig of lemonade.

"Well, I admire anyone who's out there trying," Rachel said.

"What about you? Are you out there trying?"

"The best I can. I'm a teacher, learning how to live on next to nothing."

"How are the lessons coming?"

"Not bad," she said with a thoughtful nod.

"Yeah?" he prompted.

She still had some lemonade left. The sun was warm. There was really no hurry to hole up inside the house like a mole. She leaned back on her elbows and told him about what she was doing with Jess and Tiffany, finishing with the blog she was starting.

"I admire a woman who's willing to work for what she wants. Some women would be out there looking for a rich man to take care of them."

Rachel gave a cynical snort. "Like we have a lot of those in Heart Lake."

"Wealth is overrated anyway," Chad said, pushing up from the porch step where he'd been sprawled.

"So I hear. But I'm coming to suspect that most of the people who say that sort of thing don't have to live on a budget."

"Everyone lives on a budget, even rich people."

"Define live." She shook her head. "Don't mind me. I'm just your typical bitter divorcée."

He didn't say anything to that. Instead, he downed the last of his drink. "Well, I'd better get back to my painting."

"Thanks for the lemonade."

"Sure," he said. Then he turned and walked back to his house.

As she watched him go she wished she'd asked if he had any more lemonade. Except now that he knew she was a bitter divorcée he probably wouldn't give her another drink even if she paid for it. *Way to impress a man, Rachel. Whine. It's so attractive.* Oh, what did she care anyway?

She hauled herself inside the house—it was too hot to work outside anymore—and started pulling together some more information for her next meeting with Jess and Tiff. That kept her busy for the next hour. Now what? Sitting inside the house with Chad Alvarez next door was like camping next to a diamond mine.

She found herself suddenly feeling restless, weighing her desire to peep against the mortification she'd feel if he caught her. Jess was back from her job at the gym. Maybe she wanted some company.

Chad was nowhere in sight when Rachel came out. He'd probably moved his ladder to another side of the house. That was just as well. Out of sight, out of mind.

He was so out of mind that the first thing she said when she stepped inside Jess's door was, "I met the new neighbor."

"Really? Was she over there and I missed it?"

"He," Rachel corrected, "and he's a total hunk. He looks like Mario Lopez, only better."

Jess's eyes got big. "No way."

"Way," said Rachel, following her into the family room. On the other side of the sliding glass door stood

Jess's son Michael, shirtless and wearing old cutoff jeans, busy painting the side of the house. "I see you're keeping your slave busy," she teased.

"It's part of Mikey's unemployment package. Work in exchange for free room and board."

"I can tell he's pleased with the deal," said Rachel, noting Mikey's somber expression.

A corner of Jess's mouth slipped up and she sang the last line from "Summertime Blues." She went to the kitchen and opened the refrigerator, pulling out a pitcher of iced tea. "By the time he's done with Mom's Work Release Program he'll be at Crazy Eric's, begging them to let him flip burgers."

"You're a real motivator," Rachel teased.

"I try," said Jess. She gave Rachel a glass and settled on the sofa next to her with a sigh. "I feel sorry for him, really. Life was going great until he got the rug pulled out from under him."

"It happens," said Rachel, thinking of her own life.

"Boy, does it." Jess heaved a sigh. "But, back to the main subject. Tell me about Mario."

"His name is Chad Alvarez and he bought the house as an investment."

"Never mind that part. Is he single?"

"As a matter of fact, yes." Rachel held up a hand. "But before you start singing, let me tell you nothing's going to happen."

"How do you know?"

"Because I can't bring myself to use him."

"Oh, try."

Rachel gave a rueful smile. "Too late for that. I think I scared him away."

"You've talked to him?"

"Oh, yeah. First I mistook him for the gardener. Then I told him I was a bitter divorcée."

Jess leaned back against the couch cushions. "Wow, girl, you really know how to make an impression."

"I don't want a man, anyway."

"Correction. You don't want a man like Aaron," Jess said. "You don't really want to lock up your heart, do you? That leaves you a lot of years of lonely."

"I'm not lonely. I've got my children."

"Who will grow up and leave you. Theoretically," Jess added, frowning at the figure moving around outside.

"And I have my girlfriends."

Jess propped a foot with frosty pink toenails on the coffee table. "There are some things we can't do for you."

Rachel stared into her empty glass. "I guess I'm not ready."

"Not every man is going to send you to the Heartbreak Hotel," Jess said gently. "You can't lose your faith in people."

"I haven't lost my faith in people, just men."

"You haven't been divorced that long. Give yourself some time. Your mojo will come back," Jess predicted. "You have to keep reminding yourself that not every man is an Aaron. Look at mine. Look at Brian. And take another look at your new neighbor. You never know. God could be rewarding you for all the suffering you went through. So, if this man asks you out, go."

"Like I said—"

"I know, I know, you don't want a man. But if you don't get out and live a little you *will* become a bitter divorcée, so don't be stupid."

With those pithy instructions, Jess sent Rachel back across the street to be available in case Mario Lopez the Second knocked on her door.

He didn't. She knew he wouldn't. She watched from the living room window as he loaded up his ladder and paint cans. "I don't need a man," she repeated, turning back to her book. "I've got Danielle Steel."

But then, out of the corner of her eye, she saw him walking across the lawn toward her front door. Her hormones rose from the dead and that awakened her heart, which began to flutter around in her chest. Oh, stop, she told them both.

The doorbell rang and her heart went berserk. She forced herself to walk to the door. *He probably wants to . . .* What could he possibly want? She took a deep breath and opened the door.

"Hot day out," he observed.

Obviously. He had a nice sheen going on that gorgeous caramel skin. "It is," Rachel agreed. "Would you like a glass of water?"

He smiled, appreciating her humor. "No, I was thinking more like a drink. If you don't have anything going on this evening."

Of course she had something going. She had a book to read. And she probably should clip her toenails. "I think I can fit you in."

"How about at the lake?"

"They serve drinks at the lake?"

"I do. I thought you might like a picnic."

Of course, the man was in hock up to his eyeballs. He wouldn't exactly be a big spender. But that was okay with Rachel. She'd done the man-with-money thing. She'd rather have a man with heart.

"You know, that sounds like fun."

"How about meeting me at the public dock at six?" he suggested.

"I could do that."

He nodded like they'd accomplished something, then smiled at her and left for his truck.

She let out a calming breath as she watched him walk

away and her heart settled from a gallop to a trot. A picnic at the lake with the most gorgeous man she'd ever met. "What was I thinking?"

She shut the door, ran to the phone, and called Jess. "I've got a date."

"All right! Way to work it," Jess approved.

"What was I thinking? Do you know how long it's been since I've gone out with a man?"

"It'll all come back to you," Jess assured her. "Like riding a bicycle."

Rachel tried not to think of all the times she'd fallen off her bike as a child. Well, too late now. She'd accepted so she had to go. After all, she wanted to be on good terms with the new neighbor.

Very good terms, added her hormones.

Chapter 15

Tiffany was on her way home from the salon when the call came through. "Rachel has a date," said Jess, her voice filled with urgency.

"Oh, my gosh. With who?"

"With the gorgeous guy who bought the house next door."

"Oh, no," said Tiffany. "She doesn't have anything to wear."

"Tell me about it. We need to do a wardrobe consult."

"Wardrobe consult? She needs a whole makeover. What time is her date?" asked Tiffany.

"In an hour."

"Oh, my gosh! I'll be right there. Don't let her leave the house." Tiffany pushed her foot down on the pedal and prayed that no cop would be within striking distance.

Almost everything from Rachel's closet now lay on her bed. They were nice clothes, purchased back when she'd had some money to blow. Looking at them now, though, nothing seemed worthy of a date with a gorgeous man. She frowned at the sweater sets, slacks, and jeans. The weather was too hot for jeans, which was too bad, because she would have looked great in those. It looked like the white mom shorts were the best she could do, and they weren't doing much. *This is who you are,* she reminded herself. *Anyway, it's only a picnic at the park. No big deal.*

Why the heck didn't she have hotter taste in clothes?!

"I'm here," Jess called from the foot of the stairs.

"Come on up," Rachel called back. At least Jess could help her pick out something from this mess she'd pulled out of the closet.

Jess blew into the room, her head hardly visible behind a mountain of clothing that winked with sequins. She was barely through the door when a glittery black flip-flop hopped off the top of the pile and landed on Rachel's cream-colored carpet. "Have no fear. Your personal wardrobe consultant is here to save the day."

"You realize none of that is going to fit," Rachel said. "And my feet are a whole size bigger than yours."

"These are big on me," said Jess. "They might fit, and if they do then at least your feet will look hot."

Rachel rolled her eyes. "Which will really only benefit me if this man has a foot fetish. This is silly." It was ridiculous to try and package herself as something she wasn't, and she definitely wasn't a sequins and glitter kind of woman.

"You have to put your best foot forward," Jess insisted. She held out a red top with a scooped neck. "Try this on. Brunettes always look great in red, and men love red."

Rachel slipped it on. The scoop scooped down to her nipples.

Jess looked momentarily perplexed. "Oh."

"I don't have enough chest to fill out the fabric," Rachel said. She shook her head. "None of your tops are going to fit."

"Hello," called a new voice from downstairs.

"The rest of the makeover crew?" Rachel inquired.

"You need help," Jess explained.

Now they could hear Tiffany running up the stairs. She burst breathlessly into the room and announced, "I came as soon as I could." She, too, had her arms full of clothes." Her mouth dropped at the sight of Jess's baggy top. "Oh, my gosh. This is worse than I thought."

"Don't bother. Those are obviously not going to fit either."

"They might," Tiffany said. "My boobs aren't as big as Jess's."

"Nobody's boobs are as big as Jess's," said Rachel, pulling off the top.

"Thanks," Jess said grumpily, and plopped on Rachel's bed.

"I only say that with the purest envy," Rachel informed her.

"Here," said Tiffany holding out a pale blue camisole and a top to go over it. "Try this."

Rachel heaved a long-suffering sigh, but obeyed. "I don't know why we're worrying about what I'm wearing. This isn't going to go anywhere anyway." She didn't even know why she was going other than the fact that Chad Alvarez was gorgeous and the kids were gone and she'd been reading too many romance novels lately.

"You never know," said Tiffany. "It could."

"It should," added Jess.

They both studied her. Rachel looked down at herself. Tiffany's offering was certainly an improvement over Jess's. At least the girls were covered. "It doesn't look bad."

"You know, I don't think that's your color," Tiffany said. She produced a black ribbed sleeveless top. "Try this. I was going to sell it in a lot on eBay."

"I can't take your eBay merchandise," Rachel protested.

"Sure, you can. I'll sell it after you've worn it."

Rachel put on the top.

Jess nodded approvingly. "Now, that looks good. But what is she going to wear for shorts?" She held up the mom shorts Rachel had worn earlier and frowned. "Is this really the best you can do? My God, with legs like that you're wearing things like this. You should be ashamed."

"If my wardrobe is so bad, how come neither one of you said anything before now?" Rachel demanded.

"Duh," said Tiffany. "You didn't have a date with a hot guy." She pulled a pair of shorts from her pile of clothes. "Try these."

"You're a petite. No way am I going to fit in those," said Rachel.

"Just try them and see."

Rachel struggled into the shorts. Of course, they were too small. "My crotch is numb."

Jess nodded approvingly. "Tight shorts are a good look for you. You need to start showing off your assets."

"My assets are about to split these shorts at the seams," said Rachel.

"You look great," Tiffany assured her.

"I won't look great if my face turns purple," Rachel said, peeling them off. "I can barely breathe." She reached for her own shorts, making Tiffany shake her head in disgust.

Tiffany picked up Jess's flip-flops and held them out. "At least put these on."

"Those are not me," said Rachel crossing her arms over her chest.

"I hope those ugly things I saw you in on the Fourth aren't you," said Jess in disgust as she cuffed up the shorts. She shook her head. "I swear. How long have you been watching *What Not to Wear*? You haven't learned a thing."

"I have, too," Rachel insisted.

Jess took the flip-flops and shoved them at her. "Put them on."

"They're going to be too small," Rachel predicted, but she obliged.

Jess and Tiffany both checked out her feet. Both sighed.

"Told you," muttered Rachel.

"Well, you can't wear those ugly sandals of yours." Tiffany said it with such finality that Rachel couldn't help but believe her.

"I don't have anything else." Suddenly, that seemed downright tragic.

"Then Jess's flip-flops will have to do until we can get you a consignment shop makeover," said Tiffany.

That decided, they did a hair consult, refusing to let Rachel gather her hair in a ponytail. Then they made sure she put on gobs of mascara and lipstick and finally sent her out the door, assuring her that she looked date-ready.

"Have fun," said Jess. "And try to be a little mysterious. That's always good on a first date."

"And don't act like a teacher," added Tiff.

"What does a teacher act like?"

"Smart."

"You two sound like time travelers from the Fifties," Rachel said in disgust.

"You so have to call us when you get back and tell us how it went," Tiffany finished, unrepentant.

"I will," Rachel promised. Then, feeling a little like a high-school girl getting sent off to the prom by proud parents, she climbed into her minivan and left for the lake.

Chad was already waiting for her at the dock, holding a canvas Safeway grocery bag that bulged with goodies. He stood talking with the man who ran the boat rentals,

a grizzled senior citizen wearing a baseball cap, plaid
Bermuda shorts, and a Hawaiian print shirt. Chad was
the picture of virility in his cutoff jeans and shirt, which
hung open over the kind of chest that simply cried out for
a month on a calendar. And he was wearing a plain pair
of guy-sized flip-flops. Obviously, anyone who was anyone wore the things. Why hadn't she bought any?

"Hi," he greeted her. "How about a cruise?" He motioned to the row of swan-shaped paddleboats moored
behind him.

"A cruise?" she repeated stupidly. Every time she
looked at this man her brain cells short-circuited. She
made an effort to mentally recharge. "What girl doesn't
like a cruise?"

"I guess we're good to go," Chad said to the man. He
walked to the nearest boat and deposited his bag of goodies, then climbed in after. The thing bounced in response
like an oversized rubber duck.

It had taken Rachel most of her teen years to learn to
manage her long legs. Even now, as an adult, she'd been
known to trip over a root or two when hiking. The little
bobbing boat looked like a recipe for disaster. "Where's
the land version of this?"

He smiled and held out a hand to help her in. "These
are impossible to tip."

She took a deep breath, grabbed his hand, and hopped
into the boat. It rocked and she lost her balance, tipping into
her Sir Galahad and sending him backward. They both
landed on one of the turquoise plastic seats with an
"oomph," her stretched out on him like a clumsy lap dancer.

"Sorry," she said, scrambling off, her face flaming.

"Don't be sorry on my account," he said with a smile.

The old man slipped the boat from its moorings. "You
two have fun."

"We will," Chad said, and smiled at Rachel.

"If I can keep from crushing you," she added, placing her feet on the pedals.

"Believe me, I didn't mind." He started pedaling. She followed suit, and the little boat eased away from the dock, the paddles *clack-clack*ing as they went.

This was getting off to a Lucy Ricardo start. Rachel decided to steer them in a more sophisticated direction, beginning with some witty banter. "Do you always take girls on a cruise on the first date?" Wait, was this a date? Maybe that hadn't been such a witty thing to say.

"Only the ones who I know will appreciate it."

All right, it was a date. The sun was shining, the lake was sapphire blue, and someone—oh, what a someone!—had deemed her date-worthy. *Take that, Aaron!* She enjoyed a full moment of self-satisfaction before wondering what to say next. Maybe, by not talking, she was coming off as mysterious.

Or maybe she was coming across as a brain-dead woman who didn't have anything to say.

"So, are you staying around here while you fix up the house?" she asked. Hardly brilliant, but a good conversation starter.

"I've got a friend with a place on the lake."

Nice to have friends like that. She waited a moment for him to say more about his lake friends but he didn't, so she started in a new conversational direction. "When do you think I'll have some new renters next door?"

"Maybe by the end of summer. I'm going to spruce the place up on the inside a little, and it will take some time to find good renters. I'm pretty particular."

"You've done this before?" She'd thought this was his first investment.

"A couple of times," he said. Now they were out in the middle of the lake. Someone on the far end was water-skiing. He pointed to the skier. "Do you do that?"

"Only when I have a death wish," she said. "We went to Lake Chelan a couple of summers ago. The kids and my husband—ex"—she corrected herself quickly. Why was she mentioning him anyway?!—"did some water-skiing."

"And you didn't?"

"It took a long time to get a license to operate these things on the sidewalk," she said, sticking out her legs. "I wasn't sure how well they'd work on water."

He gave them an admiring look. "It would be a shame to damage something so fine. But you never know. You might be good at water-skiing."

She could feel herself blushing like a kid at the compliment. "Maybe. I've never broken anything though"—except her heart—"and I wouldn't want to start now."

"Sometimes you just have to take a risk. Otherwise you miss out on the thrills."

He stopped pedaling, so she did, too, and watched as he picked up his canvas bag and pulled out a bottle of wine and two plastic glasses. He gave her the glasses to hold while he grabbed a wine opener and went to work. "I hope you like pinot grigio."

"Love it," she said, and held out the glasses so he could pour. Next came a baguette.

"A loaf of bread, a jug of wine?" she teased.

He grinned. "Something like that. Except I added cheese and grapes."

It was a veritable feast, but Rachel found she couldn't eat much. She had too many butterflies dancing around in her stomach to leave much room for anything else. So she sipped her wine and listened as Chad told her about growing up in eastern Washington, picking apples in the fall and cherries in the summer to pay for his college education.

"A degree in business, that's got to be good to have during hard economic times," she said.

He freshened their wineglasses. "I think the best thing to have during hard times is a lot of common sense, a good work ethic, and a certain amount of distrust."

"Distrust?" Now, that was strange. Or not. Although Chad hadn't told her his age, he looked like he had a couple of years on her, which gave him plenty of time to develop a history and a wary attitude.

"If you don't protect what you have, you'll lose it," he said. "It's as simple as that."

She studied him. "Isn't that a little cynical?"

"No, it's smart. Did you trust your husband?"

Heat raced across her cheeks and she took a healthy slug of wine before answering. "Yes."

He shrugged as if to say, "See?"

"Not everyone is like my ex," Rachel said.

"When it comes to money, most people are like your ex. I believe in being careful because you never know."

"I take it you learned that from personal experience?"

"I have an ex, like you," he admitted.

Hence the healthy sense of distrust. Had the ex taken him to the proverbial cleaners? Was that why they were on the lake in a paddleboat instead of in an expensive restaurant? Not that Rachel cared. A man who appreciated the simple things in life was more her style now.

"I suppose the only way to protect yourself from heartbreak is to become a hermit," she mused.

"I don't think I'm ready to do that," he said. "Women are like fine wine. A man could live without them, but who wants to?" He smiled at her, making her heart do a flip, and they touched wineglasses.

"I don't want be used," she blurted. She looked into her half-empty glass. *Way to be mysterious, Rachel. No more truth serum for you.*

"Me, either," he said. "So it looks like we're on the same page."

What did he mean by that? Was he looking for a serious relationship or simply friendship? And if all he wanted was friendship, did he want to be friends with benefits? Maybe she should have said, "Define *use*." But he was offering her grapes now and asking her how long she'd lived in Heart Lake, and the moment had passed. And, anyway, they were simply enjoying a paddleboat on the lake and drinking some wine. Nobody was making a commitment here.

Except her heart, which was already running way ahead of her brain, looking for the rose petal road to happily-ever-after.

Chapter 16

The longer Rachel and Chad sat in the paddleboat, bobbing on the lake, the more perfect he became. That little gremlin must have been off on vacation somewhere, or else the universe had decided it was her turn to get something good.

They talked about movies. Of course, being male, he loved anything with action and great special effects, but he also enjoyed films that were thoughtful and funny—just like she did. They talked about books. Chad enjoyed reading, and not just Tom Clancy. He was a big fan of the classics, especially Alexandre Dumas's *The Count of Monte Cristo*.

They moved on to other topics, the conversation flowing easily as they pedaled leisurely along. This was what had been missing with Aaron for a long, long time. In fact, had she ever felt this connected to Aaron? Oh, she'd been dazzled by his Prince Charming behavior when they first met. And they'd certainly found enough to keep them happy as they planned their wedding, honeymooned, and then reproduced. But somewhere along the way conversations had become routine and sex had happened by appointment and wound up feeling obligatory. No wonder Misty had looked so attractive to Aaron.

"That was a big sigh," Chad observed.

Oh, no. Had she actually sighed? "I was thinking about my marriage and how easily we drifted into . . . nothing. I've been blaming him all this time but, well, it does take two, doesn't it?"

"Not always," said Chad with a frown. "Don't beat yourself up."

She hadn't been. The one she'd preferred to beat on all this time had been Aaron. Well, it was a brand-new day, and there was no sense wasting it mulling over the past.

She smiled at Chad. "This has been perfect."

He smiled back. "Yes it has." As they made their way back to the dock, he added, "We need to have drinks again. Or maybe dinner."

"I know the perfect place," said Rachel.

"Yeah?"

"My house. Next time you're over working on your place I'll feed you."

"A home-cooked meal, that sounds good."

And so, just like that, she had another date with a gorgeous man. She could hardly wait to tell Jess and Tiff.

A perfect man, a perfect date, a perfect day.

It would have remained so, too, if she hadn't decided to hop off the paddleboat and help moor the thing. At the time, the decision had made perfect sense. Her side was now closest to the dock. But just when she was congratulating herself on her grace, one of her Cinderella-sized flip-flops did a slip-slop and she lost her footing and went down. Not on the dock, which would have been humiliating enough, but into the water, with an undignified screech that turned to "urghlugggg" once she went below the surface.

She came up spluttering and barely able to see through

a wall of wet hair. She made a clumsy grab for the two pairs of hands reaching for her and was caught and hauled back up to dry land.

"Well, there, missy, that was quite a feat," said the same old man who had launched them.

Feat. Feet! Hers were now bare. "My flip-flops!" Or, rather, Jess's.

There they went, slowly drifting away.

She'd barely spoken before Chad slipped into the water and swam for them with Olympic star grace. Meanwhile, she stood on the dock, shivering and feeling like the world's biggest dingbat.

She knew she was blushing from her neck to her forehead. She tried to ignore it as he pulled himself back up on the dock with as much grace as he'd showed when he went in. The man looked good dry, but he looked incredible wet, with his hair and skin glistening. Rachel's mind did a quick leap from lake to shower and her blush got hotter when he took her ankle and lifted her foot. The hand to body contact made it next to impossible to climb out of that mental shower.

She watched as he slipped a flip-flop back on her foot, praying all the time, *Please don't notice that my foot's too big.*

Either her prayer worked or Chad was very gallant. He kept his mouth shut as he worked.

"Thanks," she murmured after he'd finished. "I'm sorry you got wet."

"It felt good," he said, and retrieved the wine bottle and the canvas bag from the boat.

"You'd better get home and get out of those wet clothes," said the old man, and slipped a wink in Chad's direction.

Chad was a gentleman and didn't wink back. He gave the man the leftover wine, then walked Rachel to her minivan and opened the door for her. "Sorry you fell in. I hope that didn't ruin the day."

"Impossible," she said, her gaze drifting to his lips.

He leaned an elbow on the minivan and smiled at her. "Good." Then, before she could say anything, he kissed her. She felt it from her lips to her toes and everywhere in between. It produced so much heat she was surprised to find that her clothes were still wet when they'd finished.

"Thank you," she murmured, not even sure which she was thanking him for, the boat ride on the lake or the kiss or for looking so hot in wet clothes.

"I'll see you soon," he said and stepped back, allowing her to fumble her way into the driver's seat. Once she was in he shut the door. "Try not to catch pneumonia. I don't want to wait forever for that dinner."

And she didn't want to wait long for another kiss. She nodded, then started the car and backed out of the parking space, trying to wipe the goofy smile off her face and look mysterious, even though, after falling in the lake, it was too late for that.

Mom was right. Whenever one door shut another opened. She'd have to step further inside before she knew if this was someplace she really wanted to be, but from what she could see it sure looked like it. After the heartbreak of her divorce, of seeing her husband leave her for another woman, she'd never envisioned herself with a man again, hadn't thought it was possible she'd ever be able to trust someone. Maybe, just maybe it was possible.

As soon as she got home and changed she called Jess. But she only got voice mail, which was odd since both Jess and Michael's cars were in the driveway. "Where are you? I'm dying to tell you about my romantic adventures," she said. Oh, heck. Why wait for Jess to call back? She'd just run over there.

Jess's windows were open and Rachel heard the racket

before she even got off her front porch. Jess was pounding on the piano, something classical and furious, and it accompanied angry male voices. This was, obviously, not a good time to talk. Disappointment at not being able to share was instantly swallowed by concern for her friend as she ducked back inside her house. Life on Cupid's Loop these days was like living on some giant seesaw. When one of them was going up the other was going down. If only they could all go up together.

Jess finally couldn't take it anymore. The two men in her life had had their moments over the years. She never knew if that was a father-son thing or simply a man thing. Most of the time she tried to stay out of the middle of their man clashes and let them work out their own relationship issues, which they always did. But this latest argument wasn't anywhere near getting worked out and the yelling was escalating to such a fever pitch that she was sure one of the neighbors would wind up calling the police.

She left the piano for the kitchen, where both the Sharp men had been going at it. Michael's expression was a study in parental anger and frustration as he scolded his son. "You're just being lazy!" he accused, one hand beating the air. "Get off your butt, grow up, and be a man, for God's sake."

Mikey was a statue of stone and fire, glaring at his father. "Thanks for understanding, Dad." His voice broke and he whirled and marched out of the kitchen.

"Mikey, wait," Jess pleaded.

He shook his head and brushed past her.

She glared at her other half. "Go after him."

Michael shook his head. "Not this time, Jess. He needed to hear that. If he wants to throw a tantrum, let him."

"Oh, for God's sake," she said in disgust. She ran to the front door, hoping to catch Mikey, but of course she

was too late. She got there in time to see his old Chevy
roar off.

She marched back to the kitchen where Michael was
pouring himself a glass of iced tea. "He's gone."

"He'll be back," said Michael, his voice hard. "You
can't beat free room and board."

"That was a mean thing to say."

"It's the truth, Jess."

Jess glared at him. "Well, right now he needs free room
and board."

"Right now he needs to grow up."

Of course, Mikey needed to grow up, but he also
needed their love and understanding and support. In the
good times and the bad. "You didn't have to be so hard on
him." She opened the dishwasher and yanked out the top
rack. For a moment she debated between putting the
dishes away and throwing them at her husband. No sense
ruining good dishes. She turned her back on him and
went to work.

Michael sighed. "We're not doing him any favors letting him hang out at home and turn into a bum."

"Everyone needs a favor once in a while," Jess said,
slamming a mug on the cupboard shelf. "Would you want
me riding you about getting a job?"

Michael's brows dipped. "You're not comparing me to
our son, I hope. I'm looking, Jess. What's he doing?" He
didn't wait for an answer. Instead, he took his drink and
went to the family room. Back turned to her, he grabbed
the remote and shot on the TV.

Jess shoved the rest of the dishes into the cupboard.
One of her favorite mugs had gotten cracked. With a scowl,
she tossed it in the garbage then let her anger propel her
back into the living room. She sat down at the piano once
more and began to bang. What was happening to them?

They'd always been a happy family, a close-knit family. Now were a few financial troubles going to make them unravel completely? It sure looked that way. She banged harder and began to cry.

She cried off and on most of the night, and when her son still hadn't come home at two in the morning she cried some more. She tried his cell phone but only got his voice mail. "Mikey, just call and let me know you're okay," she begged.

But he didn't.

He's asleep, she told herself, *that's why he's not calling back.*

But where was he sleeping, in his car? With a friend, of course, she assured herself. He was fine. Even if he wasn't there was nothing she could do. She had no idea where he was and he wasn't answering his cell.

She finally went to bed around three, where she tossed and turned. At some point she slept, but then she dreamed her son was huddled inside a dirty sleeping bag on a downtown street in Seattle, a few clothes parked next to him in an old grocery cart. She awoke with a sob. It was nearly six, useless to try and sleep now that she was freshly keyed up. Next to her, Michael, the tough love king, lay snoring. She felt a sudden urge to hit him. Instead, she got up, padded down to the kitchen, and made coffee.

Michael came down at six-thirty.

"Mikey never came home," Jess greeted him with a punitive frown.

"He's fine, Jess. He's probably sacked out at one of his buddies'."

"You need to call him," Jess said, handing over a mug of coffee.

Michael shook his head, before taking a sip. "Not this time."

"Michael. Our son didn't come home."

"Our son is a big boy now. If he chooses not to come home that's his business."

Her eyes filled with tears and she turned her back on her husband. All this misery to prove a point—Michael should be ashamed of himself.

"Jess," he said softly, "I know this is hard. But you're not a man and there are some things you don't understand."

"Well, then, thank God I'm not a man," Jess snapped. "This is how people end up not speaking for years."

"We'll be speaking," Michael assured her. He kissed her on the cheek, took his mug, and left for work.

It was his last week. After this no one in the family would be working but her. She closed her eyes and had a sudden vision of all three of them lined up on that city street in their sleeping bags.

"Oh, stop," she told herself. What a silly, unrealistic thought.

But the possibility of her husband and son growing increasingly estranged was not unrealistic. It fell like a stone into her heart. She went upstairs to shower and get dressed, hoping Mikey would call before she left to teach kinder gym. Otherwise, it was going to be a long, hard day, maybe the first of many.

Her son finally eased her anxiety, reporting in that afternoon just as she was settling down to watch Dr. Phil counsel people whose lives were worse than hers.

"Mikey, I've been so worried. Where are you?"

"I'm staying at Danny's," he said, his voice stiff.

"For how long?"

"Till I get a job. Dan's mom says I can stay here as long as I want."

Jess's heart cracked and she felt suddenly sick. They'd said that, too, and then Michael had changed the rules.

"Look, Mom, I gotta go," said Mikey, his voice taut.

Jess sighed. "Okay. I love you."

"I love you, too," he assured her, and then he was gone, leaving Jess with nothing but a dial tone and a heavy heart.

She went to her piano and played Greig's "Piano Concerto in A minor" then moved on to Shostakovich.

Banging the keys helped her work out some of her sadness and anger, but she still had plenty left over when she was done. It kept her in the clutches of a bad mood the rest of the day and she was still feeling grumpy when she arrived at Rachel's house late that afternoon to take her friend shopping.

Rachel took one look at her and demanded, "All right, what's wrong?"

"Other than wanting to kill my husband? Nothing," Jess replied.

Rachel gave her an empathetic look. "You two are the closest thing I know to a perfect couple. You're not going to go bursting my bubble, are you?"

"Wouldn't dream of it," Jess said, and managed a smile.

"What wouldn't you dream of?" asked Tiffany, who was now in the open doorway.

"Never mind," said Rachel, sensing Jess didn't want to talk about her problems on the home front.

Rachel was right. Jess didn't want to talk about it, not with her girlfriends, not even with her husband. Especially not with her husband. He would be lucky if she ever talked to him again.

Chapter 17

"Have you got your money?" Tiffany asked Rachel before they set out on their bargain shopping safari.

Rachel held up a twenty-dollar bill. "I do."

"Twenty dollars?" That was what Rachel was spending on a new single-and-ready-to-mingle wardrobe? Tiffany was good but she wasn't that good.

"This is all I'm going to spend," Rachel announced. "Anyway, I am who am, and anyone I date may as well know it up front."

"Absolutely," said Jess, "but you can still be who you are and have some hotter clothes." She linked arms with Rachel and led her out the front door, adding, "Remember, there's nothing wrong with self-improvement."

Tiffany smiled and followed them out. Jess was one smart woman.

Bargain Boutique was a fairly new business, located in Valentine Square in what used to be a jewelry store. Bonnie, who ran the consignment store, was as tall as Rachel. She was now a regular at Salon H, always coming in to get her nails done, maintain her blondeness, or add hair extensions. Tiffany had alerted her that they would be arriving with a bargain makeover in tow. She'd described

Rachel in great detail and now Bonnie stood ready with an assortment of clothes for Rachel to try on.

"Just like at Nordstrom's," Tiffany explained.

"Only more affordable," added Bonnie.

"I hope so," said Rachel. "I've got a whole twenty to blow."

Bonnie shot a look at Tiffany as to ask if Rachel thought she could work miracles there at Bargain Boutique and Tiffany managed a little shrug. She moved over to the clothes Bonnie had set aside and started sorting through them. "Since we've only got twenty to spend, that's out. And forget the jeans."

"I already have jeans anyway," added Rachel. She drifted over to a rack and began moving clothes. She pulled off a yellow sweater set and held it up for Jess to see. "This is pretty."

Jess snatched it from her and hung it back up. "Not on you."

Rachel pouted. "Why not?"

"It will turn your skin sallow," said Tiffany, pulling out a knit navy top. She paired it with a hot pink sweater, then handed them to Rachel, along with a sleeveless black satin top. "Here. Try these on."

Still pouting, Rachel took the items and stepped into the dressing room at the far corner of the shop.

Meanwhile, Tiffany kept sorting through the clothes. "Yay! You did have some hot shorts."

Bonnie held up a halter top with a floral pattern in varying shades of red. "I thought this would look good on her, too."

Tiffany checked the price. It was only seven dollars. "Absolutely."

"Oh, yeah," agreed Jess. "That goes in the keeper pile."

Tiffany turned to see that Rachel had stepped out of the dressing room to model the black top. Combined with her long, dark hair it turned her into a goddess of sleek. Well, as long as you ignored the bits of gray in her hair and the fact that she was wearing those ugly tennis shoes with her jeans. She struck a pose. "What do you guys think?"

"Perfect," Tiffany approved. "Add some silver jewelry and a pencil skirt and it will be totally hot."

"Or she could wear it with her jeans and some cute shoes," added Jess, drifting over to the counter to sort through a basket of jewelry.

Rachel nodded decisively. "I'm getting it. That's ten dollars. I have ten left to spend."

Tiffany looked at the floral top and frowned. "I guess we'll have to put this back."

"I'll get it for her," offered Jess. She held up a sterling silver cuff bracelet. "And this."

"No, you won't," Rachel called from the dressing room.

"Yes, I will," Jess insisted. "We're not out of money yet."

Rachel stepped back out, modeling the navy top and pink sweater. "That looks great," Tiffany approved.

Rachel nodded. "I'll take it. And that's the end of my money so I'm done."

Tiffany took the white shorts over to her. "Try these on. They're only five dollars. If they fit I'll buy them for you."

"Then we need to get her some decent sandals," said Jess.

"I'm afraid I can't help you there," said Bonnie.

"That's okay," said Tiffany. "There's a great discount shoe store over in the mall. Don't worry," she added, knowing Rachel was firm on not spending any more money. "I'll take care of it."

Both Rachel and Jess looked at her like she'd fessed up to planning a bank robbery. "I don't think going anywhere near the mall is a good idea," said Rachel.

"I have some tip money. And I've got eBay money coming in at the end of the week, too."

"Which you're supposed to be using to pay off your credit cards," Rachel reminded her.

"It's okay. I can handle it."

"So can I," Rachel said decidedly. She snatched the shorts from Tiffany without even bothering to try them on and marched to the counter. "I'll write a check for all this, then use my cash to buy sandals. Will you take a check?"

"Sure," Bonnie said, looking guiltily from one woman to the other like it was, somehow, her fault Rachel was spending more than she intended. "By the way, Tiffany told me about how you're helping each other with saving money. I think it's a great idea."

"Well, we're trying," said Rachel.

"Think of all the money we just saved," Tiffany told her, feeling immensely pleased with how much she was accomplishing for her friend on so little.

"I'm still not sure about the mall," Jess worried as they left Bargain Boutique.

"I'll be fine. If I even touch anything, you guys pull me away," said Tiffany.

"Gladly," said Rachel. "We don't want Brian to murder you and bury you in the backyard. Which he'll probably do if he sees you coming home with anything more."

Rachel's words jogged Tiffany's memory. She suddenly had a vision of a small pile of packages sitting on the porch. She'd bought a few little bargains on eBay. It was nothing much, but Brian might not understand if he saw them. She checked her watch. Could she make it to the shoe store and then home before Brian got there? She was sure going to try.

Jess was still putting on her seat belt when Tiffany roared off down the street. "Whoa," she protested. "Where's the fire?"

"I still have children to raise," Rachel added as they squealed around a corner. "And you can't afford another speeding ticket."

Tiffany wasn't sure she could afford another fight with Brian, either, but she slowed down to a semireasonable speed.

The Shoe Bin was Rachel's favorite discount shoe store. "We'll find the best bargains here," she said as they walked in.

Jess got stalled in front of a display of flashy flip-flops. Rachel stopped, too, but Tiffany pulled her away. "Come on. They'll have those on the aisle anyway."

By now Jess had caught up with them and was carrying a delicate silver sandal. "How about this?"

"That would go great with my new silver bracelet," said Rachel, reaching for it.

Jess jerked it away. "I meant for me."

"Here they are in your size," said Tiffany, pulling out a box. "Try them on."

Rachel pulled off her tennis shoes and socks, and Tiffany snagged a couple of cut-up nylons for her feet. She slipped on the sandals.

"Oh, yes," approved Jess. "Those with jeans and your new top and that silver bracelet and you're lookin' like something."

They did look great. "Perfect," Tiffany approved. She sneaked a look at her watch. If they left right now . . .

Jess was reaching for another box. "Hey, try these on."

"Those silver ones are perfect," said Tiffany.

"I like these, too," said Rachel, reaching for the next pair of sandals.

She tried them on. She walked up and down the aisle in them. Then she tried on the silver sandals again. "I don't know."

"Buy both," suggested Tiffany. *Then we can get out of here.*

"No. I only have money for one." Rachel stood for a moment, looking at both boxes.

"Then live it up," said Jess. "Go for the silver."

Rachel smiled and nodded. "I think I will."

"See. You can wear fabulous shoes and still be you," Jess teased as they moved to the cash register.

"Maybe there's more to me than I realized," Rachel admitted.

Tiffany tried not to pace as the clerk rang up her friend's purchase. She strolled over to a display by the door. Ooooh, those heels were cute. And they were on sale. She picked one up.

And felt a hand on her arm. "Oh, no. No purchases for you, little lady," said Jess. She took the shoe out of Tiffany's hand and returned it to the display. "But I tell you what. I'll buy you a blended coffee drink before we go."

Go. They had to go. "Umm, can I pass? I forgot, I need to get home right away."

Jess looked surprised, but she nodded and said, "Sure."

"Okay, I'm done," Rachel announced, joining them.

Good. Maybe, if she drove just a little over the speed limit, she could still beat Brian home.

No such luck. His Jeep was already parked in the driveway when she pulled in. Maybe the packages hadn't come. She didn't see any on the porch. She let out her breath. Saved.

"This was great," Rachel was saying. "I'm now a beauty on a budget."

"You mean diva on a dime," teased Jess, grinning at Tiffany.

"That, too." Rachel hugged them both. "Thanks, you two."

"No problem," said Tiffany, who was already breathing easier. Since her packages hadn't arrived there would be no problem at home. Thank God.

But there was a problem at home. She slipped inside the door to see a tiny tower of boxes on the entryway floor. Uh-oh.

Brian wasn't going to be interested in hearing about these bargains, even though one was a book on how to make money selling on eBay and another was a postal scale she could use to weigh her merchandise at home. Those, at least, were justifiable. It was going to be harder to explain the Pottery Barn pitcher she'd gotten for a song—until she had pay shipping—or the Juicy Couture tote bag she'd snagged. Suddenly, as if she was psychic, she could hear the conversation between her and Brian.

> BRIAN: *Don't tell me you needed all that stuff.*
> TIFFANY: *I did. Really.*
> BRIAN: *Yeah? What did you need that green bag for?*
> TIFFANY: *To carry all my stuff when I'm at garage sales.*
> BRIAN: *You're joking, right?*

Tiffany suddenly felt like she did when she ate too much sugar, all full and barfy and disgusted with herself. She could have used an old bag or even a grocery bag. Why hadn't she thought of that when she was bidding on the Juicy Couture one? Her heart began pounding painfully against her chest. What was she going to do? What could she say? *Come on, brain. Think!*

"I can't," replied her brain. Who could blame it? Bidding fever, like gold fever, had no rational explanation.

She wanted to run away. Instead, she called, "I'm home," trying to make her voice sound normal.

She got no answer. Oh, this was so not good.

"Bri?" She went through the living room and into the kitchen. She found him under the sink, repairing the leak she'd been after him to fix for the last two weeks. "Oh, you're fixing the sink. Thanks!" Brian was home and happily puttering. All was well.

But he didn't say anything. No "You're welcome." Not even a "Where have you been?"

She tried another conversation starter. "You beat me home." Well, duh. She hurried on. "We were giving Rachel a makeover at Bargain Boutique."

He came out from under the sink and set his wrench on the counter. He kept his back to her as he dried his hands on a rag. "And what did you buy there?"

His voice sounded like steel. She pulled out a kitchen bar stool and sat down because her legs suddenly felt as incapable of helping her as her brain. "Nothing."

"No money left?"

Now he turned and looked at her. Tiffany felt suddenly cold and rubbed her arms. "I . . ." Her brain refused to supply her with any words, forcing her to stop there.

"You. Yeah, that about sums it up, Tiff. It's all about you. That's who you were thinking about when you bought all that crap in the hall. It sure wasn't us. It sure wasn't about helping us get out of debt, was it?"

"Brian." Again, she couldn't seem to get anything else out although her heart was crying, "Please don't be mad. Please give me another chance. Please love me through this even though I know I don't deserve it."

"I'm moving out."

"What?" *Oh, please tell me I'm dreaming this.* "Brian, no. Don't leave me."

"I think we need some time apart. I just . . ." He shook his head, his jaw suddenly clenched.

"Just what?" She could barely get the words out.

"I can't stay here and watch you do this. It's like being married to an addict who won't go for help."

"I'm working on this," she said, her voice pleading. She was. Yes, she had a little slip once in a while, but she was really trying. Why couldn't he see that?

He heaved a sigh and shook his head. Then he took his wrench and started for the garage.

"Where are you going?" she protested. His home was here. With her.

"To put this away."

"I mean after."

"I don't know yet. I'll let you know."

She followed him and stood in the doorway, watching as he carefully hung his wrench back in place on the garage wall where he kept his tools. "So you want a divorce?" She could barely get the words out. She sounded like she was dying. Well, duh. She was.

"I don't know that either. I'll let you know," he said.

Let her know? Let her know? Oh, no.

He looked at her sadly. "God, Tiff. We used to be so happy. What happened?"

Before she could answer he slipped past her and walked down the hall to their bedroom while she stood frozen in place. A moment later he was back with a satchel in hand. "Good-bye, Tiff," he said, and then walked out the door.

Oh, God, oh God, oh God. She suddenly couldn't get her breath. What had she done?

"You shouldn't have bought that stuff on eBay," scolded her conscience as she stood in the doorway crying.

Well, too late. It wasn't like she could return it.

But she could sell it. She didn't need that Juicy Couture bag anyway. She didn't need a lot of things.

One thing she did need was Brian, and there was only one way to get him back. She had to kick her shopping

addiction once and for all. All those things she bought
hadn't filled up the empty places anyway, so there was no
point wasting any more money on them.

It's all about you. Was Brian right? Was it all about
her? Why hadn't she noticed? Why had she been so selfish? And stupid? Why had she bought all this . . . stuff?

She set her jaw, marched to the hall, and scooped up
all her packages. Then she got to work unpacking them,
staging them, and taking pictures. These were all going
up for sale. Well, except the postal scale and the book.
But everything else, and some of the junk she had kicking
around the house, too. She was going to make money hand
over fist any way she could. Before the year was over
those charge cards would be paid off and Brian would want
to come back.

What if he didn't? She burst into tears at the very
thought. He'll come back, she assured herself. And when
he did, he'd find he'd returned to a new woman. That
would be a good deal for both of them, because she sure
didn't like the irresponsible shopaholic she'd become any
more than he did. She wanted the Tiffany she used to be,
the woman who was always happy no matter what, the
Tiffany who didn't hide things under the bed or lie to her
husband.

She'd get her husband back and her life back, and most
important of all, she'd get herself back.

Chapter 18

"Okay, are you going to give me the silent treatment all night?" Michael demanded.

"I might," Jess said, and slammed his plate of leftovers down on the table. She started to leave the kitchen.

"Where are you going? Aren't you eating?"

"I'm not hungry," she called over her shoulder. Simply looking at her husband when he came through the door had made her angry all over again, and the last thing she wanted to do was sit down and enjoy a meal with him. It was going to be a long time before she'd enjoy doing anything with the man. She went to the piano and sat down on the bench.

A moment later he was sitting next to her, perched on the edge. "I know you don't agree with me on this."

She launched into the theme from "The Phantom of the Opera."

"But can't you allow Mikey and me to work this out between us?"

She stopped playing and turned to frown at him. "Not when I'm caught in the middle."

He frowned back. "You're not caught in the middle. This is between us."

"Well, I'm being affected." She played on. She knew Michael was frowning without even looking.

"Jess, we haven't always agreed with each other on how to handle the kids."

It was a diplomatic way of saying he hadn't always liked her parenting methods any more than she had his. That was true. Each of them had blown it as parents any number of times, but together they'd still managed to raise good kids. And they'd had a good relationship with both their children. Until now.

She fingered the piano keys. "Mikey needs to know that you still love him."

"Jess, he knows that."

Jess gave Michael her most penetrating look. "Sometimes you're pretty hard on him."

That wasn't anything new. "Always try your best" was his motto when Mikey played sports, and since Mikey's best had been great that had been no problem. But when he decided he didn't want to play in Little League anymore Michael had not been happy. "Quitters never win and winners never quit," he'd lectured.

Mikey had quit anyway, preferring to play video games with his friends and, when he got older, to tinker on cars.

Dropping out of baseball hadn't been the only bone of contention between father and son. When it came to grades, Mikey's best had never been good enough. "You can get a B in World History. Come on, son, try harder. You don't want to go through life just being average."

As if being average was a crime. A person couldn't be stellar at everything. Maybe a person didn't have to be stellar at anything if he didn't want to be. What was wrong with simply being happy?

"He's never been good enough for you."

"That's not true," Michael protested. "Just because I want him to do well and have a successful life . . ."

"We don't all have the same definition of success," said Jess. "Look at me."

Michael smiled. "I like looking at you."

"I never finished college, I never became a star."

"You're my star," he said, and planted a kiss on her neck.

A kiss on the neck could always start a fire between them, but not tonight. She scooted away. "If you'd just get off his case . . ."

"He'd live at home and sponge off us forever," Michael finished for her.

Jess frowned at him. "Nice thing to say about your only son."

"I'm not going to encourage him to be lazy. He has to learn to take care of himself. If he doesn't, he'll be crippled all his life."

"He'll be emotionally crippled if he thinks his father doesn't love him."

Michael's jaw tightened. "It will be fine," he said, and rose from the piano bench.

"Where are you going?" Jess asked, hoping he'd answer that he was off to call Mikey.

"To watch TV," Michael called over his shoulder.

Jess glared at his retreating back, then brought her hands down on the keys, hitting every minor chord in range, songwriting as she went. *Why do men have to be the way they are? Sometimes I want to hit him with my car. He's making my heart break. I want to drown him in the lake. Oh, yeah.*

She sighed heavily and let her hands fall in her lap. All right. She didn't want to kill her husband. But she wasn't averse to inflicting enough misery to motivate him to make things right with their son and get their lives back to normal.

She returned to her songwriting, going in a new direction. *No sex for Dad. Sad, sad. 'Cause Mamma's mad.*

Mad, mad. And when Mamma ain't happy, ain't nobody happy, especially Daddy.

Not bad, she thought. Maybe she'd finish that song. Then she'd play it for Michael and see what he thought of it. With an evil smile, she went in search of paper and a pencil.

After her fun shopping adventure, Rachel's solitary dinner felt anticlimactic. The novelty of having time to herself had worn off days ago and she felt the absence of her children like a gnawing toothache.

They would be in New York by the end of the week and the grandparents had plans for them for the rest of the month—everything from museums to Broadway musicals . . . and, of course, shopping. Claire was expecting to get an entire new wardrobe out of her visit and was ecstatic. Rachel had to remind herself how good this was for the children and a good deal for her, too. Her daughter would get a new wardrobe and she wouldn't have to pay a cent—a true win-win. Still, she sighed unhappily as she put her scant load of clothes in the dryer. How could Girl Camp compete with shopping in New York? At least David would be ready to come home. Of course, it wouldn't be because he missed his mother. Stuffed in a posh New York apartment, the boy was bound to go through basketball withdrawal.

Rachel sighed. Both her children were growing up so fast. This month was a taste of loneliness to come.

So you'd better build a life for yourself, she thought as she went to her computer to make a blog entry.

Blogging was rather a small building block, but it was something, and Rachel was pleased to discover that she was already getting comments. "I love the idea of making small life changes," wrote one woman. "I'm going to check your blog every day for tips."

Every day? Talk about pressure.

"Instead of getting so much fast food I'm going to make time to cook more meals from scratch," wrote another visitor. "That should save me a bundle."

A third woman wrote, "I kept thinking I needed to make a ton more money to fix my life, but you've got me thinking that what I really need to do is learn to manage what I already have."

Rachel couldn't help but feel warmed by what she read. She'd had a vague idea of helping other people when she wrote her first entry, but to actually see women responding was heady stuff indeed. Maybe she should post a picture of herself in her new bargain clothes.

She paired her new black top with some jeans and slipped on her hot sandals. Checking out her reflection in the bedroom mirror, she liked what she saw. "You diva on a dime, you," she said to her reflection. She grabbed her digital camera and snapped a shot, then looked at the image on the screen. A shot of her taking a picture of herself looked goofy. She needed a photographer.

She called Jess. "Are you guys still eating dinner?" she asked when Jess answered.

"I'm not," Jess said irritably. "What's up?"

Something was obviously up at Jess's house, and it wasn't good. "Is everything okay over there?"

"Not particularly.

"Oh, no."

"Not to worry. What can I do for you?"

"Nothing. Never mind," said Rachel. She remembered Jess's grumpy mood earlier, and the fighting she'd heard the night before. Jess and Michael had the perfect marriage, the perfect family. The sound of raised voices coming from their house had felt unnatural, like aliens had somehow taken over next door. Things obviously still weren't right and Jess didn't need the added aggravation of a high-maintenance neighbor demanding a photo shoot.

"Come on, out with it," Jess commanded.

"It sounds like this isn't a good time. Really, it was nothing," said Rachel.

"If you don't tell me what you want, I'll come over in person and find out."

"Well, I was wondering if I could get you to take a couple of pictures of me in my new bargain wardrobe. I want to put them up on my money blog. But really, it's no big deal," Rachel added, feeling guilty. "We can do it some other time."

"Now is fine," Jess insisted. "I'll be right over."

A moment later she was walking through the front door. "Look at you," she approved, taking in Rachel's outfit. She crooned a line from "You Sexy Thing."

"Yes, I am, aren't I?" Rachel agreed, pleased with herself.

"We should take several shots," said Jess. She looked critically at Rachel. "And we should get Tiffany to come over and fix your hair."

"Oh, my hair is fine," said Rachel with a wave of her hand. "I don't need to take every wife in the neighborhood away from her husband."

"Mine is probably happy you took me," said Jess with a frown.

Rachel laid a hand on her arm. "Okay, spill. What's going on? Are you guys okay?"

Jess scowled. "Michael is being a stubborn jerk and Mikey is staying with a friend. Maybe it's a good thing we don't live on the lake. My husband might have had a sad drowning accident."

"You know you don't mean that," said Rachel.

"Well, not now. But a while ago I was seriously considering it." Jess heaved a sigh. "Men. Can't live with 'em.

Can't drown 'em. We'll work through it," she added. "We always do. But meanwhile, it won't hurt him to stew in solitary for a while. Go ahead and call Tiff, too. Brian's Jeep is gone so that means she's home alone, and you know how much she hates being alone."

"Good point," said Rachel and snagged the phone.

Tiff must have seen her name on the caller ID because she didn't bother with "hello." "Brian's left me," she wailed.

Rachel blinked. "What?"

"He . . . he . . ." The sentence ended in sobs.

"Get over here right now," Rachel commanded. "I'll break out the chocolate."

"What's wrong?" Jess asked, following as Rachel started for the kitchen.

"He left her, the bastard."

"What?"

"What is wrong with that man?" Rachel growled.

"Maybe there's something in the water."

Tiffany was in the house now. They could hear her sobbing her way to the kitchen. Jess went to meet her and returned with her arm around Tiff's shoulder. Rachel stuffed a chocolate in her mouth and led her into the family room and settled her on the sofa. "Okay, what happened?"

Between crying and chewing, Tiffany wasn't able to give an immediate answer.

"I'm sure he's not gone for good," said Jess.

"Why did he leave?" Rachel asked.

Tiffany swallowed. "He found my eBay stuff."

Rachel was confused. "The things you're selling?"

"Nooooo. The things I bought."

Jess and Rachel exchanged looks. So much for getting her spending under control. Tiffany had plugged up one leak in the financial dam only to spring another some-where else.

"My life's a mess," she sobbed. "Brian hates me."

"No he doesn't," said Jess. "He'll be back. He probably needs to cool down. That's all."

"You have got to get yourself under control," said Rachel, and Jess shot her a look that said, *This is hardly the time for a lecture.*

But Tiffany didn't take offense. Instead she sniffed and nodded. "I know. I don't need all this stuff. I really don't. I just need Brian." This started a fresh round of sobbing.

Rachel patted her arm. "That's a real epiphany. Have another chocolate." The phone rang and she picked it up. The number on the screen wasn't one she recognized. "Hello?" she said uncertainly.

"Hi," said a deep voice on the other end of the line. "It's Chad."

Excitement swirled inside her. Tiffany was still sobbing, so she moved out to the patio.

"Is this a bad time?" he asked.

"I have a friend having a crisis, but we're dealing with it."

"Well, I wondered if that dinner offer was still open. I'm coming over to the house to do some work tomorrow."

"Tomorrow will be fine," said Rachel. She'd wear one of her new outfits. "How about around six?"

"That suits me. See you then."

Tomorrow. She had a date tomorrow. She'd barbecue chicken and make a potato salad. They could eat out on the patio. And look at the overgrown grass. Okay, she'd mow the lawn first thing in the morning before it got hot. Speaking of getting hot, what might dinner lead to? It wasn't difficult to envision herself in Chad Alvarez's arms.

The sound of her friend crying brought her back into the present with a jolt. Poor Tiff. Brian was a rat to jump off the sinking ship and leave her to try and bail out alone. What was going on here, anyway? Maybe there really was something wrong with the water here in Heart Lake Estates. Or maybe there was something wrong with the men. Or just men in general?

What kind of trouble was Chad Alvarez hiding in his back pocket?

Chapter 19

By the time Rachel stepped back inside the house Jess had managed to calm Tiffany down from sobs to sniffles and a pile of Kleenex sat in her lap. "I can't blame Brian for leaving me," Tiffany whimpered. "I'd leave me, too."

Still, to up and walk out. It seemed so heartless. Jess found it difficult to match that behavior with the man who had fixed Rachel's minivan for free. "I have to admit, I thought he was one of the good ones." But you never really knew about people, especially males. Even the best of them had faulty mental wiring.

"You're so lucky," Tiffany said to Jess. "You have the perfect man."

"That is an oxymoron," said Jess. She scooped up the tissues and tossed them in Rachel's garbage.

"That's encouraging," said Rachel, taking another chocolate. "Maybe I shouldn't see Chad again."

"Yes, you should," said Jess. "For all you know, he might be one of the good ones."

"I'm beginning to wonder if there are any," said Rachel.

"There are," Jess said. "Hang in there," she told Tiffany. "Things will work out with Brian. He loves you."

This made Tiffany break into fresh tears.

"It'll be okay, Tiff," Rachel said, rubbing her shoulder. "I've got an idea. I got a comedy from Netflix. Let's kick back and watch that. It'll do you good to laugh."

Tiff shook her head and stood. "No, I'm going home. I need to finish listing my stuff. I'm going to make money and pay off those credit cards if it kills me."

Making money, there was a novel idea. The thought of going for it and finding a band to play with tickled the back of Jess's mind. One last time, it was so tempting. Except she was so over the hill.

Over the hill, yes, but she wasn't all the way into the damned valley. Was she?

Tiffany was marching for the door now. "I'm going to prove to Brian that I can do more than spend money."

"I guess I'll watch the movie by myself then," said Rachel. "Unless you want to stay," she said to Jess.

Jess shook her head. "No. I'll take your picture. Then I'd better get back to my not-so-happy home."

So the pity party broke up, and Jess returned home to find that Michael had relocated from the family room to the living room and was now seated at her piano, reading her song-in-progress.

He looked up, a crooked smile on his face. "I guess I'm going to be celibate for a while."

Instead of joining him at the piano, she settled on the couch. "The thought crossed my mind. It's hard to get in the mood when I'm mad at you."

He pressed down a piano key, making the instrument echo a solitary note. "You know our son and I have always settled our differences."

"This was not a difference. This was a shouting match with you doing most of the shouting."

Michael took in a deep breath. "I promise if we haven't heard from him by the end of the week I'll call him. Fair enough?"

Her husband hadn't been fair in the first place, but she nodded.

"Now, how about eating dinner with me?" he asked.

"I don't know. I am right in the middle of writing a song."

He joined her on the couch and slipped an arm around her. "I know it will be a hit with every married woman in America."

"Probably."

"But could you give your man a second chance?" Michael asked humbly.

"Only if my man promises to follow through and make things right with our son by the end of the week," Jess said sternly. "You really hurt him, Michael."

He sighed. "I'll make it right, I promise."

That was one of the things she loved about her husband, he was a man of his word. "Then okay," she said, and they sealed the deal with a kiss. But he was smart enough not to expect more than that, and she didn't offer. Forgiveness was one thing, but wholehearted sex would have been quite another. One thing Jess had learned in her forty-four years on the planet: men were like puppies, and the woman who wanted hers to behave properly only rewarded good behavior.

The following morning, before going to work, Jess got on the computer and checked out several musicians' classified ads sites just for the heck of it. She knew it was a long shot, but she also knew that if she didn't at least try she'd regret it. On one, she found an interesting ad. *Wanted: keyboard player for all-girl band. Classic rock/country. Must be able to sing lead and BGV's.* Background vocals? Yes! She loved singing harmony. *No drugs, no booze, just music,* the ad concluded. That worked fine for Jess. What she wasn't sure would work was her age.

What the heck. She had nothing to lose . . . except
twenty pounds. Knowing it was a long shot, she sent off
an e-mail extolling her talent and then ran to get dressed
for a day of hopping around on mats at the gym.

Gene, the gymnastics instructor, had actually been
working with her and she was looking pretty darned good
mounting the beam now. She could probably work at the
Park Department forever, and that would be okay. She
enjoyed working with the kids.

But the thought of getting to be in a band again was
what really got her blood pumping as she climbed into
the truck. *Please, oh, please, let me find an e-mail when I
get home.* Thinking about the possibility of getting to play
to a crowd again took her mind off the sad fact that she
was not in her little red VW anymore and somewhere a
cute, blond college student was now tooling around in it
with the top down and the radio up.

Miracle of miracles, there was an e-mail waiting for
her when she arrived home, and it was good news. "Yes,
we're still looking for a keyboard player," wrote Amy
Burke. "Our band is called The Red Hots. We're practicing tomorrow night at seven if you want to come jam with
us. Let's see how it works." She gave her address, then
added, "Bring your keyboard."

Jess suddenly felt sick. The Red Hots? She was more
lukewarm. They'd take one look at her and laugh her out
of the room. Her keyboard didn't look any better. It was
an ancient Casio that had been hot stuff when she'd
played in her band. Back when the pterodactyls flew. Did
she want to show up for an audition with that thing in tow?

The answer to that came quickly. So, again, into the
city she went, this time to Gig Land, where she looked at
everything from Casios to Rowlands. She wound up
choosing a Yamaha Motif for a small fortune, reconciling
the cost by getting in touch with her inner Tiffany and

reminding herself it was on sale. She had just saved five hundred dollars.

But look how much she'd spent to save that five hundred!

She chewed her lip as the clerk began ringing up the sale. Okay, this was ridiculous. How fancy a keyboard did she need? In fact, did she really need a new keyboard to go to an audition? It wasn't the instrument; it was the player. A good player could show off her chops on anything. Of course, when the other band girls saw her vintage keyboard they'd fall over laughing and start singing "Hit the Road, Jack." But they could as easily reject her when they saw she wasn't twenty and then she'd have wasted a big chunk of change. She'd make do with what she had and if her equipment wasn't good enough then this wasn't the band for her anyway.

"I've changed my mind," she said.

The clerk's eyebrows shot up. "This is a sweet deal."

"It's only a sweet deal when you've got the money," Jess said, more to herself than him.

"We can set up a payment plan," he offered.

If she got in the band maybe she'd do it. Or maybe she would learn to make do. Now, there was a novel concept. "I'll think about it." Long and hard.

Tiffany had not only listed her garage sale finds on eBay, she'd also listed half the contents of her house. If everything sold she'd have a nice chunk of money for paying down her credit cards, and she'd have a lot less clutter, too. Now that she was on a roll, she wanted to go even faster. Maybe she could run a special on nails and pick up some new customers.

"So, how's the eBay biz going?" Cara asked as they visited during a lull at the salon.

"Great," said Tiffany. "I'll have my charge cards paid off in no time." And Brian back, too, so there was no point in mentioning that he'd moved out. He still loved her and she loved him. This was just . . . what was it? She wasn't sure, but whatever it was it wouldn't last.

She gave two more manicures and a pedicure and then it was time to quit for the day. No more appointments. Time to go home to her empty house.

But first she had to make a quick grocery stop. Not that she had much appetite. She had managed to present a smiling front to everyone who came into the salon, but inside she felt sick. Ginger ale and crackers were about all she could handle. And chocolate.

Maybe she'd grab some chicken, too, because, after all, Brian could decide to come home tonight and she'd have to have something on hand to feed him.

It was a slender thread of hope, but she clung to it for all she was worth as she left Salon H and prepared to cross the street. An older woman was waiting to cross, too, and someone stopped his Jeep to let her go.

His Jeep! Of course, it was Brian. She saw him and he saw her. But he pressed his lips into a thin line and looked the other way.

Mortification set her face on fire and she blinked back angry tears as she hurried across the street. This was the man who had stood in a church filled with family and friends, vowing to love her for the rest of their lives? What happened to "till death us part"? Last time she looked her heart was still beating. When the going got tough he got out. *Thanks a lot, Brian.* She was so not getting that chicken.

She picked up pad Thai from the deli (heck with the stupid ginger ale and crackers) and a bag of mini Hershey bars. She'd go home, have a feast, and check to see how many bids she had on eBay, and she wouldn't give Brian even one teensy-weensy thought. So there.

It was a good thing she'd found out what her husband

was really like before they had a baby. She didn't want to have children with Brian. She didn't want to have a life with Brian. And she sure didn't want to have any bills with Brian. She was so done with him.

To prove to herself that she was serious, when she got home she removed their wedding picture from the dresser in their bedroom. To think she'd gone to sleep the night before looking at that picture and wishing Brian would come back. Well, no more. She stuffed it in the bottom drawer to suffocate under her jeans and shoved the drawer shut. Then she threw herself on the bed and cried.

Chapter 20

Everything was ready for Rachel's dinner with Chad. The chicken had been marinating in teriyaki sauce and the barbecue was fired up. Her potato salad was done and so was the tossed salad, and she had French bread warming in the oven and some cheap white wine cooling in the fridge. She had picked raspberries at her friend Elsa's house and now a freshly baked raspberry pie sat on the counter. The patio table looked pretty with her best dishes and flowers from Jess's garden. Rachel had even broken down and mowed the lawn and it looked beautiful.

So did she. She was wearing her new navy top with her new shorts and sandals, and Tiff would have been proud to see that she was wearing her hair down—no horsetail. The scene was set. All she needed was her male lead.

The doorbell rang, making her pulse jump. There he was. Good grief, she felt like she was fifteen again. She took a deep breath and hurried to the front door.

It was like opening the door on a work of art. In jeans and a simple tee, Chad Alvarez put Michelangelo's David to shame. A perfect body, a perfect face with the most

mesmerizing brown eyes she had ever seen, he looked too
good to be true. She sure hoped he wasn't.

He held out a bottle of white wine. It wasn't the cheap
brand she had chilling in the fridge. "I hope this was a
good guess."

"Perfect," she said, and took the bottle. "Come on out
to the kitchen. I was just about to put the chicken on the
barbecue."

"How about I put it on for you?" he offered.

"Great. Thanks." Here was a pleasant surprise. Aaron
had never been much help in the kitchen. Aaron had never
been much help, period. She'd been so hurt, so angry when
he wanted to wiggle out of his marriage vows. Now, for
the first time, she wondered if her mother really was right
when she said God never closed a door without opening a
window.

Chad slipped out onto the patio to man the barbecue
and Rachel opened the wine and put some brie and crackers on the patio table. She handed him a glass and he
tipped it her direction with a smile. "Here's to a memora-
ble evening."

Her mind immediately played word association. Mem-
orable? Kiss! Very good, said her hormones, and her heart
rate jumped.

"You look nice, by the way," he added.

She looked down at her hot self. "I do, don't I? I found
this outfit at Bargain Boutique."

"You are a smart shopper," he approved.

"I don't know about that," she said, "but a girl's got to do
what a girl's got to do." She shrugged. "Sometimes I think it
would be nice not to have to struggle with money so much."

"Sometimes the struggling makes you appreciate it
all the more when you get it," he said, giving the chicken
a turn.

"There is that." She realized that, while her life was fast becoming an open book, she still didn't know much about him and what he did. "So, do you struggle?"

He smiled. "I work hard. Does that count?"

"I'd say so." Rachel cut a piece of cheese and offered it to him along with a cracker and he popped both in his mouth. "Kind of a tough market around here for selling real estate right now," she observed.

"It's been better."

Having just invested in the house next door and with no renters, his budget had to be tighter than hers. She felt a fresh appreciation for all the effort he'd put into giving her a romantic date.

"Things will turn around," he predicted. "They usually do if you wait long enough."

She thought of her love life and smiled. "I think you could be right."

A few moments later, Chad judged the chicken ready to eat. She brought out a platter and they set it on the table along with the rest of the food. He scored more points by declaring her potato salad the best he'd ever eaten. And he earned her sympathy by admitting that he hadn't come off of the romantic battlefield unscarred. She'd already guessed as much on their date when he'd mentioned having an ex. Even though he brushed over the subject quickly now it wasn't hard to hear the pain. He said he'd been single for several years. Was he still in divorce recovery? Had he had girlfriends since?

"You never wanted to get back on the horse?" she asked.

"You get kicked hard enough and it makes you think twice," he admitted. He set down his wineglass and regarded her. "It would take a very special woman."

"Define *special*."

"The right values, the right heart. I'm not in a hurry, Rachel. Are you?"

After what she'd been through with Aaron? "No."

"But I'd be lying if I said I wasn't attracted to you and that I didn't want to take this relationship further."

It wasn't hard to figure out what he meant by *further*, not with the way he was looking at her. That look in his eye started a sizzle in her that had nothing to do with the hot July evening. Her mouth felt suddenly dry.

He reached for the bottle of wine and poured more into her glass. "How about you, Rachel? What do you want?"

She wanted her prince to come. She wanted to never get hurt again. She wanted to feel loved, protected, and safe. But she didn't tell him all that. She said, "I want you to kiss me."

Amy Burke, the leader of The Red Hots, had given Jess an address in the Shoreline area, which lay south of Heart Lake and north of Seattle. Being directionally challenged, Jess had Mapquested it; thanks to the step-by-step directions, she was sure she'd be able to find the place. She had just loaded her keyboard in the back of the truck when Michael returned home from a late afternoon interview in the city.

She had half hoped to miss him, preferring to leave him a note explaining where she was rather than tell him in person. She was out to land a part-time job that would leave him abandoned on the weekends. Of course, Michael was supportive of everything she did, except he was more supportive of some things than others. She'd been in a band when they first met. She'd joined another band when their kids were small. He'd been a good sport, watching the kids at night while she went off to play, but eventually he'd convinced her that she didn't want to be on a different schedule than the rest of the family, showing up at Saturday morning soccer games looking like a zombie or needing a nap on Sunday afternoons to recharge her batteries. But now it was just the two of them and she didn't want to be convinced out of even auditioning.

She forestalled the inevitable by asking, "How did the interview go?"

"I've had better," he confessed. "I suspect they're going to hire from within." He took in her tight jeans, ribbed black top, and dangly rhinestone earrings, along with her moused hair and freshly painted red toenails peeping out from behind her favorite red flower flip-flops. "Got a hot date?"

"Got a band audition."

His brows drew together. "Band audition? When did this happen? This is the first I've heard of it."

"Well, it might be the last, too. I didn't want to tell you since I may not even be what they're looking for."

"If you're not, they're nuts. But, Jess, I wish you'd talked to me about this."

"What's there to talk about?"

"How about whether I want you to do it or not?"

"Since when do I need your permission to make money?" Of course, this wasn't really about the money. The old Bangles song "If She Knew What He Wanted" came to mind. Only with them it was more a case of if *he* knew what *she* wanted. Except Michael knew. He simply didn't like giving it.

He held up a hand. "You don't have to say it. That sounded controlling."

"A little," she said sarcastically.

"But I remember what happens when you get involved in bands. I'll never see you."

"As of tomorrow you're unemployed. We'll be seeing a lot of each other." Maybe even too much. Probably joining a band couldn't come at a better time.

"I'll be getting another job," Michael said. His tone of voice told her she'd insulted him.

She stepped up to him and rubbed his arm. "I know, Michael. But we don't know when. You could be out of work for months."

"Thanks for the vote of confidence," he said grimly.

"I just want to do my part to help. And as we both know, I don't have a lot of marketable skills."

"Fine," he said grumpily. "Go."

They both knew she was going to, no matter what, but she played along with the charade, kissing him on the cheek and thanking him for being so understanding even though he didn't really understand. People who weren't musicians couldn't.

"But here," he said, letting down the truck's tailgate and pulling out her Casio. "Take the car. You'll use less gas."

"There's lasagna in the oven," she told him as he loaded it in the trunk. Then she kissed him one last time and got in behind the wheel. He watched her, looking resigned. Life was about change. He would adapt.

Maybe he wouldn't have to. Maybe she wouldn't get the gig. Maybe they'd laugh her out of the room. She gripped the steering wheel and swallowed hard.

Jess was glad she'd allowed herself plenty of time to find where the band was practicing since, even with the directions, she'd managed to get lost. But now she was standing with her trusty keyboard and amp at the front door of a split-level house in a middle-class neighborhood. Out-of-control azaleas crouched around the front porch while on the front lawn a sprinkler made a feeble attempt to keep the grass from turning brown under the July sun. An ancient Honda sat in the driveway, blocked in by two other vehicles that Jess guessed belonged to the other band members: an SUV and a Volkswagen bug that triggered a sentimental pang. A boy's bicycle leaned against the garage, evidence that Amy Burke had at least one child.

From somewhere deep inside the house Jess thought she heard the thumping of a bass. She rang the doorbell and the chime started some sort of small dog yapping. Kids, dogs, and a messy front lawn—it reminded Jess of her own life a few years back.

"Killer, stop!" commanded a female voice. The front door opened wide and there stood a pretty thirty-something blonde, holding a Chihuahua. The dog took one look at Jess and started barking all over again. "Oh, stop," said the woman in disgust. "He is wound way too tight," she explained. "You must be Jess."

"That's me," said Jess, trying to inject as much good cheer and youth into her voice as possible.

"I'm Amy. Come on in. Everyone else is down in the basement. Careful you don't trip over the shoes."

Jess maneuvered her equipment through the narrow landing and past a pile of tennis shoes—okay, Amy definitely had more than one child—and down the stairs. She wound up in a huge rec room that housed a battered pool table at one end and a band at the other. She quickly took in her possible future bandmates.

At the drums sat a skinny blonde with the face of an angel who looked like she was barely into her twenties. Her long hair was caught up in a sloppy bun and she was wearing soccer shorts, a baggy T-shirt, and tennis shoes. The bass player stood chatting with her and twiddling her instrument. She didn't look much older than the drummer. Jess took in the stylish clothes, maroon hair, the sleeve tattoo, and the multiple ear piercings and suddenly felt old. These women were too hip, too hot. They'd never want to play with her. She must have been out of her mind to think she could do this.

The bass player smiled at her. It was an open, friendly smile. Maybe she needed glasses and couldn't see that Jess was the only one in this room who was over the hill.

"Well, this is us," said Amy. "You obviously know who I am." She motioned to the drummer. "This is my baby sister, Kit Mason."

The drummer saluted Jess with a twirl of her drumstick and said, "Hi."

"And I'm Melissa," said the bass player.

"You don't even want to know her last name," added Amy. "Her husband's Czech and none of us can pronounce it, not even her." She motioned to a small cooler. "If you get thirsty, we've got Diet Pepsi, Dr Pepper, and Starbucks fraps. That's about as wild as we get. You saw the ad. We don't do drugs and we don't drink when we're playing. Ever," Amy added sternly.

"I'm cool with that," Jess assured her. Did she look like a druggie or something?

"Our last keyboard player forgot to tell us she had a problem," explained Melissa.

Kit snickered and Amy gave her a quelling look. "She fell off the stage. Not cool."

"Don't worry. I think I can manage to stay upright," Jess assured everyone.

Amy nodded. "So, here's us in a nutshell. Melissa just had the big three-oh and a baby. Kit's not married but she has a serious girlfriend."

"That really frustrates all the guys who hit on her," added Melissa.

"And me," Amy concluded, "I'm the fearless leader."

"Bossy old bat," added Melissa. "We call her BOB for short."

Amy pointed a disciplinary finger at her. "Hey, I'm only five years older than you. Watch who you're calling old."

Jess forced a smile and hoped nobody asked her how old she was. If thirty-five was an old bat, Jess was the walking dead.

Amy went on. "I've got two boys in grade school and

they're gonna turn me gray before I'm forty. So, to keep sane, I do the band thing on weekends. We play a couple of clubs in Seattle. Mostly we do the animal clubs."

Eagles, Elks, and Lions—Jess had done her share of them, too. "How did you all get together?" she asked.

"I started the band," said Amy. "I did time in Nashville trying to make it as a songwriter. I finally got tired of starving, came home, and reconnected with my high school sweetheart. But I missed the music. Ya know?"

Boy, did she ever. Jess nodded.

"We met Melissa at Gig Land," Amy continued. "She was looking for a bass and we were looking for a bass player." She looked speculatively at Jess. "You've had some experience, it sounds like."

"About a million years ago," Jess admitted. "But I've missed the music, too. And my husband's been laid off so I decided it was time to jump in again," she finished, then worked up her nerve to add, "One last time, before I'm too old."

Amy gave a snort. "Hey, look at Bonnie Raitt. *American Idol* has got it all wrong. You're never too old if you're good."

"Well, I could be too old to qualify as a Red Hot," said Jess.

"Red hot is how we play," said Kit, hitting a drumroll.

"We can't help it if we look that way, too," added Amy with a grin. Then, all business, she said, "So, let's see what you can do."

With cheeks suddenly warm, Jess broke out her keyboard.

"Whoa, dude, that is a dino," said Kit.

"It is," Jess admitted as she plugged in her amp, "but I think I can still get some sound out of it."

"Well, let's see," said Amy, picking up her electric guitar. "Know any Bangles?"

The Eighties was Jess's prime time. "Uh, yeah," she said with a confident smile.

They launched into "Walk Like an Egyptian."

"Not bad," approved Amy when they'd come to an end. Not bad? That had been a blast. "What else do you do?" asked Jess.

Within a short period of time, they'd tried on everything from "It's Raining Men" and "Girls Just Want to Have Fun" to Carrie Underwood's "Before He Cheats."

"You're good," said Melissa admiringly when they'd finished.

"A hell of a lot better than our last keyboard player," added Kit.

"Anyone was better than our last keyboard player," said Melissa, looking at their fearless leader as if it was her fault.

Amy shrugged. "What can I say? I boo-booed. But not this time," she added. "You can play, girl, and you've got a nice voice. If you want to be a Red Hot you're in. We've got a gig at a club downtown and you can jump in as soon as you feel ready."

"The sooner the better," added Melissa. "We really need keyboards."

She had a chance for one more run. And she'd be bringing in extra money. Oh, yes, she wanted in. Two hours later she left Amy's house buzzing.

Back home, she parked her equipment in the front hall and hurried in to the family room to make her big announcement. Michael looked up from the book he was reading with an expression as far from expectant excitement as a man could get.

She pretended not to notice and struck a pose. "You are looking at the new keyboard player for The Red Hots."

He managed a smile but it didn't reach his eyes. "I'm happy for you."

"Sure you are." She joined him on the couch.

"No, I am. Really," he insisted. "I just wish you didn't feel like you have to do this."

"Michael, I want to do this. One last time." They were empty nesters now and the kids weren't the only ones who needed to fly.

He nodded, chewing on that. "Okay. I'll be your groupie."

She slipped her arms around him. "Thank you for understanding."

He smiled at her. "Who said anything about understanding? I'd like to meet the man who understands women, especially mine."

But her girlfriends understood. Her Friday tennis buddies were delighted and all promised to come hear her. So did Rachel and Tiffany when she told them that evening as they met at Rachel's house to brainstorm cheap craft projects. "We'll have to find a different time to meet since I'll be working Friday nights."

"It's the end of an era," said Rachel with a sigh.

"I suspect your Friday nights will be starting to fill up anyway," teased Jess.

Rachel's self-satisfied smile said it all.

"Just think, we know a star," gushed Tiffany.

"Not really," said Jess. "Musicians are a dime a dozen. But it's going to be fun. I think this group could be good."

"Getting paid for something fun, that rocks," said Tiffany.

"Getting paid for anything rocks," said Jess. "And speaking of money, how are your eBay bids doing?"

Tiffany beamed. "I have bids on everything. So far I'm over two hundred dollars and my bids don't even close until next week."

"You're not going to go crazy and spend that all at garage sales, are you?" worried Rachel.

Tiffany shook her head vehemently. "No way." She dug a twenty-dollar bill and a ten out of her purse and held them up for show and tell. "This is my spending money for tomorrow."

"Good girl," Rachel approved.

"As soon as the money from this week's bids clears I'm transferring it from my PayPal account to my checking and writing a check to pay down my credit cards," Tiffany said with a determined nod. "Then, as soon as my credit cards are paid off, I'm getting a divorce," she added with an angry flash of her eyes.

Oh, no, thought Jess. *What now?* "You don't want to rush into anything," she cautioned.

"Believe me," Rachel added, "divorce is no fun."

"Neither is being married to Brian," Tiffany snapped, and then proceeded to tell them about her husband miseries.

"This can be worked out though," said Jess, trying to be the voice of reason. "Maybe you guys should try counseling."

"We probably can't afford it," Tiffany grumbled.

Rachel's phone rang and Jess said, "If that's a certain hunky Latino, tell him you're busy. And don't say it's us," she added quickly. "It's good for him to think you're in high demand."

Rachel wasn't much of a game player, and after their dinner together the night before it seemed silly and manipulative. She did tell him she was busy, but stood ready to say with whom if he asked.

Surprisingly, he didn't. Maybe because he could hear Jess laughing in the background at something Tiff was saying.

"All night?" he asked.

Knowing how their girl nights went . . . "Yes, probably."

"Well, then how about doing something tomorrow night?"

"What did you have in mind?" As if it mattered.

"Dinner and dancing."

"Dancing sounds great. If you want to come over, I can make dinner," she offered, feeling guilty at the thought of him spending money he didn't have.

"Are you thinking I can't afford a dinner out?" he teased.

"Yes," she said truthfully.

He chuckled. "Don't worry. We won't have to wash dishes. I'll pick you up at six."

"Okay."

"What have you got to wear?" Tiffany asked later as she and Jess and Rachel were poring over recipes for tea and coffee drinks.

Rachel felt mildly panicked. "For going dancing? I don't know, and I've spent my clothing budget for the month."

"I know! Let's go shopping in your closet," suggested Tiffany. "The diva on a dime says sometimes you already have great outfits. You just have to look at stuff with new eyes, pair things up together you normally wouldn't."

"I don't think the diva on a dime has been in this closet," Jess said, once they got there.

It was a little disheartening. Rachel's classic outfits were great for teaching and running errands, but they sure didn't say, "Take me on the dance floor." Instead they primly demanded, "Take me to the PTO meeting."

"Look." Tiffany pulled out the red floral halter top Rachel had gotten at the Bargain Boutique. "How about wearing this and adding that beaded necklace you made last year, the one with the garnets? And you know, I've got the perfect skirt."

"It'll be too short," Rachel predicted.

"And the problem with that is?" Tiffany retorted, and disappeared. She was back five minutes later with a gauzy black skirt in hand. It was definitely short.

"And hot," Jess assured her. "You look great. Now you can go to the ball, Cinderella."

Rachel had a hard time getting to sleep that night. *Cinderella*. Funny that Jess referred to the classic fairy tale. Were women hardwired to want a happy ending, to long for a prince?

Rachel understood the chemistry of attraction. She knew the date and mate buzz eventually wore off. She hadn't expected her marriage to be one long honeymoon, but commitment was another thing. That she had expected. Maybe, in this day and age, expecting commitment was as impractical as longing for the prince.

Here she was, feeling the buzz again, but was it worth the heartbreak that could be waiting for her once the buzz wore off? Chad Alvarez had the whole package: looks, charm, brains. She couldn't help wondering what she'd find when she unwrapped the package further. What kind of heart did he have? It wasn't too late to stop now, before she gave away any more of herself. She could walk away with some great memories and her own heart intact.

But sexual attraction was a powerful drug, and by the time she sat in Chad's souped-up vintage Mustang, riding into the city, she'd lost her desire to get him out of her system. In fact, she was flying high. She had on a perfect dance ensemble thanks to her closet shopping expedition with Tiff and Jess, she was out with a gorgeous man, and she felt sexy.

"You look amazing tonight," Chad told her as the lights of Seattle came into sight.

"Well, you've got me beat," she said. "You look amazing every night."

He chuckled. "I'm beginning to suspect you always say what's on your mind."

"Your suspicions are correct. But you like that. Remember?" she teased.

He nodded. "Yes, I do." He smiled over at her. "I haven't found anything I don't like about you."

"Oh, keep looking. You will," she said lightly.

Aaron had. In fact, one of the things he hadn't liked about her was the fact that she always said what she was thinking. Misty didn't do that. Of course, Misty didn't think, so that helped.

They shot on down the freeway past Seattle, not exiting until they got somewhere south of it. In a little neighborhood in a small town, they pulled up in front of a Mexican restaurant. "They have the best food this side of eastern Washington here," said Chad as they walked in.

Obviously. The place was packed.

But that didn't prevent the pretty Latina hostess from letting out a pleased squeal at the sight of Chad (Well, what woman wouldn't?) and hurrying to give him a hug. "Hermano!"

Hermano. Brother? Rachel found herself staring, wondering if she'd heard correctly.

"This is my sister, Maria," Chad said. "She and her husband own this place. Maria, this is Rachel."

"*Bienvenida,*" said Maria.

"*Gracias,*" said Rachel. "*Agradable encontrarle,*" she added, hoping she was remembering her college Spanish correctly.

This made the woman's face light up. "*¿Usted habla español?*"

"*Poco,*" said Rachel. "Very little."

"Well, we are happy to have you here. Any friend of Chad's is welcome," she added, giving her brother a look that Rachel didn't have trouble translating. Sis was obviously hoping her brother had found Miss Right.

Once they were seated and had ordered drinks, Rachel said, "So you have family on this side of the mountains."

"Only my sister and her husband. My parents and my little brother still live in Yakima."

"How did your sister end up over here?" asked Rachel.

"She married a truck driver from Seattle. They own this restaurant together."

"She has a very traditional name. You don't. What's that about?" Rachel couldn't help asking.

Chad's easy smile tightened. "It was my grandfather's name. My mother picked it in the hopes that it would make up for her marrying a Latino instead of a white guy."

"Oh." This was uncomfortable territory, but Rachel pressed on. "Did it?"

"Nope. My dad had his own landscaping business, but in my grandfather's eyes he was always nothing more than 'the gardener.'"

Rachel found her cheeks warming as she remembered that was exactly what she had thought Chad was when she first saw him.

He saw the blush and managed a half-bitter smile. "Latino guy: gardener or illegal." He shrugged. "Stereotypes happen."

Rachel sighed. "Yes, they do. You forgot another important one though."

He cocked an eyebrow. "Yeah?"

"Hot Latin lover." She blushed a little as she said it, remembering how well he'd demonstrated the truth of that particular perception.

He smiled. "I like that one."

"Me, too," she said shyly, and he reached across the table and held her hand. "Thanks for bringing me here to meet your sister."

"I brought you here because the food's good. And I can get a free meal," he said with a grin.

"No wonder you weren't worried about washing dishes."

"I was only kidding. I'm paying for the meal. It's important for family to help each other. I want to see my sister stay in business."

Their waiter arrived with two margaritas in glasses big enough to swim in. "My God," said Rachel, looking at hers. "If I drink all this, I'll be dancing on my lips. Are you trying to get me drunk so you can seduce me?" she teased.

"Do you really think I need you drunk to do that?" he teased back.

There he sat, looking at her with those gorgeous brown eyes. "Absolutely not."

Later, as he moved her around the dance floor to the rhythms of a hot Latin band, teaching her how to salsa, her skin burning at the touch of his hand, she knew she was going to invest her whole heart in this man. She only hoped it turned out to be a safe investment.

Small Changes,
Big Difference

From Rachel Green's Blog

SMALL CHANGE, BIG DIFFERENCE

Rachel's Money-Saving Tips

Thanks to everyone who has been reading my blog.
I love all the great money saving tips you're sharing
here. You're proving my theory that small changes in
our money habits can make a big difference in our lives.
Here are the latest tips I've come up with. I hope
they help.

• **Pay Less for Services**

Bartering can save you a ton of money. If you have a skill
like cutting hair or cake decorating, you may be able to
trade your services for someone else's. If you have a
vacation home, do a house swap with someone living in
a locale you'd like to visit. If you have small children, trade
childcare services with other mothers in your circle of
friends.

• Pay Less for Your House

Most homeowners wind up paying almost double the cost of their house due to interest. There are two basic ways to knock years off your mortgage payments. Some lenders may not do this, so ask your bank or mortgage company for details. (They'll be sooo happy to talk to you. Not.)

1. Make one extra mortgage payment per year. In other words make thirteen payments instead of twelve. Tell your lender to apply this extra payment toward the principal.
2. Divide your mortgage payment in half and pay that amount twice a month. (For instance, a 30-year mortgage at 5% (fixed rate) on a $300,000 loan would require a monthly payment of about $1600.00; half of that would, obviously, be $800.00, paid twice a month.) This amounts to twenty-four $800 payments per year. With this option, you don't pay any extra to the bank as you do in option number one, but you reduce the number of years you pay your loan. (In banking terms this is called reducing the life of your loan.) You reduce the life of your loan because every $800 payment reduces the principal amount of your loan and thus reduces the amount of interest you ultimately pay. So, how much might you save by doing this? Let's go back to the 30-year mortgage at 5% (fixed rate) on a $300,000 loan with a $1600.00 per month loan payment. Using either method one or two you could save around fifty thousand dollars. You can save a lot more if your mortgage amount and/or your interest rate is higher. Now, that's worth making a call to your friendly lender.

• Pay Less for Your Car

Yes, that new car smell is great, but a new car drops in value the minute you drive it off the lot. Plus you wind up with car payments. For those of you who didn't get in on the Cash For Clunkers program, you can still find a bargain by purchasing your vehicle from a private party. Check online and in your local paper. Always take someone with you who can check major things like engines and brakes.

• Pay Less for Your Food

When you eat out you're not only paying for food. You're paying for ambiance and for someone else to make your chicken parmesan or your turkey sandwich. Neither one is difficult to make, so stay home and do it yourself. If you want to enjoy a treat and support your local restaurant, go out for lunch, which is less expensive. Or meet a friend for dessert and share something decadent. Many restaurants offer great food bargains during happy hour. They make their money on the drinks, so buy one and stop there.

To make the most of eating in, check the weekly in-store specials at your local grocery store and plan your meals around them, including meals that will promptly use up the leftovers. Plan meals ahead for at least a week and always stick to your list when you go into the grocery store. Also, be sure to plant edibles in your flower beds. All right, I admit, I have a black thumb, and I used to hate gardening. But I'm changing my wicked ways because I'm realizing what I grow in my flower beds can supplement what I buy in the grocery store and save me money! Rhubarb tucks in nicely. Rosemary is great in rockeries and you can use it in everything from chicken to biscuits. Blueberry bushes add color and interest . . . and affordable antioxidants.

• Pay Less for Your Fun

Fun doesn't always have to center on spending large amounts of money in theaters or restaurants. Opt for game nights and potlucks with friends. Host a chick poker night. Get together with the girls and learn how to play poker, but don't gamble for money. Gamble for chocolate. A bag of Hershey's Kisses isn't much to spend on an evening out! (I did this the other night with my neighbors. I now know the difference between a full house and a royal flush—as long as I have my cheat sheet next to me. And the good news is, I don't think I even gained a pound in spite of all the chocolate I consumed because I'm sure I laughed off every calorie!)

If you've got cabin fever, check out your community calendar either online or in the paper. You will find plenty of free concerts, movies in the park, and other activities to keep your life interesting and your fun affordable.

Your public library is another great resource. In addition to books, you can also borrow CDs and movies. Public libraries also offer classes and bring in interesting speakers, so check your local branch to see what's happening.

• Pay Less for Everything

Everything goes on sale eventually. What you don't find on sale you can pick up at garage sales. (Just ask my friend Tiffany!) Buy your clothes at 50% off (at least) at the end of each season and store away for the next year. The best time to buy your wardrobe for next winter is the end of January and beginning of February. The best summer bargains can be found in August. (If you want to be instantly current with styles buy one piece of jewelry to update.) Start your Christmas shopping in January and February when stores have their biggest markdowns. Buying ahead, on sale, is also the best way to stock up on birthday presents and hostess gifts. Also keep your eyes out at garage sales for new items you can tuck away to give as wedding and shower presents. Whether you're at a garage sale or in a department store, don't be afraid to dicker. Someone trying to get rid of unwanted clutter will often take less simply to see the junk gone. Stores also need to move merchandise, so ask, especially if you find an item that has a minor flaw, like an article of clothing with a ripped seam. If a clerk doesn't have the authority to give you a markdown, ask to speak with the manager.

The next time you're itching to do some online shopping, check out the Goodwill auction site, which offers all kinds of household goods at secondhand prices. (Great news for all of you who don't have access to good secondhand stores. Goodwill is only a click away!)

Get your facials and manicures at vocational technical schools. (Don't worry, we won't tell Tiffany.) When money is tight, this is a great way to still look good (and feel good) for only pennies. When the money is flowing again, though, remember to support your local businesses and help other women pay their bills.

Don't forget about coupons. These days you can visit any number of online sites and print out coupons for whatever you need.

- **Never Put off Paying Tomorrow What You Can Pay Today**

In other words, pay cash. Not only does this save you from falling into the credit card trap (where you will remain until the end of the world), it helps you remain prudent in your spending. When you pay cash you see your money disappearing before your very eyes. When you whip out the plastic you don't always make the connection between your purchase and your dwindling checking account.

Chapter 21

The Small Change Club was now officially meeting on Saturday afternoons, and this Saturday the three friends were in Tiffany's kitchen, making jam from their freshly picked raspberries.

Tiffany had assured herself several times that she was having a great day. It was actually her birthday. She was now twenty-five.

And separated from her husband and childless. Some happy birthday. She'd gotten a card from her parents, signed by her mom, of course, with a check for fifty dollars enclosed. "Have a wonderful birthday, sweetie," Mom had written.

She always told her mom everything, but so far she hadn't been able to bring herself to make that call, even though she knew she'd get plenty of sympathy. She didn't want sympathy. She wanted her life back. She wanted Brian back, even though he obviously didn't want her. How pathetic was that!

She'd only heard from him once since their not-so-close encounter on the street, and that had been the message he'd left on her voice mail telling her not to worry. He was taking care of paying the mortgage and utilities. There had been no call from him this morning, which was just as well. She couldn't even imagine what they'd say to each other.

Cara and Iris had a cake and balloons for her at the salon the day before, and she'd pretended to be happy, like she was doing now.

"I'm not sure this is saving us any money," Jess observed, pulling the giant pot of bubbling berries, sugar, and pectin from the burner. "Jars and seals and sugar—a jar of jam doesn't cost that much at the store."

"Of course we're saving money," Rachel insisted. "The berries were free. Remember? And we'll reuse a lot of the jars. Plus we've got a start on Christmas."

"I know my son will love getting a little basket of jams," Jess retorted.

"Your mother-in-law will," said Rachel. "Speaking of sons, what's the latest with Mikey?"

Jess smiled. "He and Michael made up, thank God. Michael actually called and apologized to him. He even admitted he'd forgotten how hard it is to hunt for a job.

"So is Mikey moving back?" asked Rachel as they ladled jam into jars.

Jess's smiled faded. "No. He's still staying with his friend." She heaved a sigh. "It's probably just as well. I hate to admit it, but I think maybe we made it too easy for him letting him hang out at home. Mikey seems more motivated now. He's actually going to some temp agencies on Monday. Hopefully, that will work better for him than it did for me."

"With a degree in business, it should," said Rachel. "It looks like life is improving for all of us." Tiffany could tell she was sorry the minute the words were out of her mouth. "I mean financially," she added, looking apologetically at Tiffany. "And speaking of finances, how are your bids going?"

Okay, here was something Tiffany didn't have to pretend to be happy about. "Awesome. I made seven hundred dollars!"

"Whoa," breathed Jess. "What can I sell?"

"What a great way to start whittling down those credit cards," said Rachel. "That is something to celebrate."

It looked like that was all they were celebrating today. Neither of her friends had said anything about her birthday, even though she'd been hinting all week. Tiffany turned back to finish sealing jars.

"Speaking of celebrations," said Rachel, "someone has a birthday today and we have a cake from Sweet Somethings."

"Your favorite," added Jess as Rachel pulled out a pink cardboard cake box from her pantry. "Lemon poppy seed."

"Aw, you remembered. You two are the best." Everyone had remembered except Brian. Well, he'd probably remembered. He just didn't care anymore. She blinked back tears, determined not to ruin her friends' sweet gesture.

Rachel lit the candles. "Okay, Jess, you sing 'Happy Birthday.' I can't carry a tune." Jess obliged and Rachel added, "Make a wish."

Tiffany closed her eyes and wished for all her bills to be paid off. At least it was something she had a hope of making come true.

As soon as she'd blown out the candles, Jess said, "And now, do you want to know what else we're doing to celebrate?"

"There's more?"

"We're going out tonight to hear Jess's band," Rachel announced.

She wouldn't be alone on her birthday. "Awesome."

"Wear your dancing shoes," said Jess as Rachel handed Tiffany a piece of cake.

Tiff took a bite of the cake. The lemon frosting melted in her mouth. Oh, yeah, this was going to be a good birthday after all.

"What are you doing right now?" Chad asked.

Rachel propped her cell phone between her ear and shoulder and walked to her closet to pull out her black top. "I'm getting ready to go hear my friend Jess play with her new band."

"Sounds like you need an escort."

"I have an escort."

"Who? I'll have to beat him up."

"Tiffany."

"So, you'll be out clubbing with your girlfriends?"

"Yes, I will. And dancing and picking up men," she teased. As if any man could compete with the hot moves Chad had showed her on the dance floor.

"Picking up men, huh? Where is this club?"

She told him, pretending she had no suspicion why he asked.

"I think I might have to show up to make sure no one comes along and steals your heart."

"Smart man," she teased. "Actually, I'd love it if you came. I want you to meet my friends."

"I'll see you later, then," he said.

Sure enough, The Red Hots were finishing up their second set when Chad made his way between the tightly packed tables in the dark little hole in the wall to where Rachel and Tiffany sat, nursing drinks. Actually, Rachel was nursing her drink. Tiff was already on her third.

He slipped into a chair next to Rachel and gave her a kiss and Tiffany pointed at him. "Oh, my gosh. It's . . . you."

"Yes, it is," he agreed.

Tiffany's delicately penciled eyebrows took an angry

dip. "I thought this was going to be just the girls," she said to Rachel.

"I wanted to come by and meet Rachel's friends," Chad said smoothly. "Can you make me an honorary girl for the night?"

"I guess," Tiff said grudgingly. "It's my birthday," she informed him. "We're celebrating. I thought it was just the girls," she repeated, and frowned at Rachel.

The cocktail waitress arrived and Chad ordered a Scotch on the rocks.

"No more for me," said Tiffany grumpily. "It's no fun to drink alone."

"So, what are we, chopped liver?" Rachel retorted.

Jess joined them now, eyes shining. "Okay, guys, what do you think?"

"You're great," said Tiffany. "An all-girl band, that's awesome. Who needs men?"

Okay, this was getting embarrassing. "She's having some problems with her husband," Rachel explained to Chad. "She's not usually like this."

"I'm probably going to be like this for the rest of my life," Tiff said, gazing into her glass.

Jess ignored her as if she was a naughty child, instead turning her attention to Chad. "I'm Rachel's neighbor, Jess Sharp."

"I've heard a lot about you. Both of you," Chad added, including Tiffany.

"You'd better not break her heart," warned Tiff. "She already had one man do that, you know. You're all bastards."

"That is an opinion not shared by everyone at this table," said Jess. "Not even Tiffany. Don't let her have any more mudslides," she said to Rachel.

"I don't want any more," Tiffany retorted irritably.

Jess ignored her again, saying to Chad, "I love the new color you painted the house."

"Thanks."

"My husband is the biggest bastard of them all," said Tiffany, and downed the last of her drink.

The cocktail waitress arrived with Chad's drink. He paid and gave her a hefty tip, surprising Rachel. For a man who didn't have any money, Chad Alvarez was a big tipper.

Jess saw her bandmates starting for the stage. "I guess I'd better get back to work," she said, rising. "Thanks for coming, guys."

Chad stood, politely, seeing her on her way.

A moment later the music started again with Jess singing Alicia Keys' "Everything's Gonna Be Alright." "Want to dance?" he asked Rachel.

"Go ahead," said Tiff, her voice dripping with resentment. "Have fun."

"This really wasn't one of my better ideas," Rachel said, once Chad had her in his arms. She looked over to their table. Tiffany was pouting now. Even pouting, she looked cute and a guy in a baseball cap and a Mariner's shirt was already pulling up a chair next to her. "She's not normally like this, really."

"I understand hurt, don't worry. Everybody has to work through their shit in their own way." He planted a kiss behind Rachel's ear, making her shiver.

She understood hurt, too. It turned a woman into a raging river of bitter tears. She didn't want to go there ever again. But where was this relationship taking her? She wished she knew. Then she'd know whether to bail out now or chance the rapids. Chad's arm skimmed her back, heating her skin. Surely, surely this was too right to go wrong.

Tiffany decided to stop being a pill. It was no fun being a pill on your birthday. Better to have fun. Break hearts. She clapped and cheered for Jess. She ordered another drink. And she danced. And danced. And danced. "You know," she told her new number-one fan, taking his hat off and putting it on her head, "Tonight's my birthday and I'm all alone."

"Well, I can change that if you want."

"I don't know what I want anymore," she muttered, punctuating her observation with a hiccup.

"Do you want another drink, birthday girl?"

"No, that's okay," said Rachel, appearing out of nowhere and giving the guy the stink eye. "She's had enough to drink. It's time to go home."

That was easy for Rachel, Tiffany thought as her friend hauled her off. Rachel had a home, with children. All Tiffany had was a house.

And it was dark and uninviting. No Jeep in the driveway, which meant she had no husband waiting to make up. She wished she'd remembered to leave a light on as she fumbled for the front hall light switch. There was something so creepy about an empty, dark house.

Suddenly she realized her house wasn't empty. A solitary figure was coming toward her in the dark.

Chapter 22

With a shriek, Tiffany grabbed for the vase on the hall table. "Get back!"

"It's me," protested Brian.

Now that he was closer she could see that it was, indeed, him. She turned on the light and replaced the vase and let out her breath, willing her heart to settle down. "I thought you were a burglar. What were you doing here in the dark? And where's the Jeep?" Maybe he'd thought sneaking into the house and scaring her to death would be cheaper than divorcing her.

"It broke down halfway here. I walked. I've just been sitting and thinking about what a jerk I've been."

Those were good thoughts. And he walked here to get to her? Her heart melted. "You did?"

"I should have called you, but I wanted to talk to you face to face. Aw, Tiff." He pulled her to him and hugged her. "I'm so sorry. God, I'm a bastard."

His voice broke and that was all it took for her to burst into tears. "I thought you hated me."

He picked her up and carried her to the couch, settling her on his lap. "You should hate me. I'm the one who walked out. It was wrong."

"I don't blame you for wanting to leave me. It's all my fault we're not pregnant. I can't do anything right. I can't even have a baby." Saying it out loud ripped her heart in two. "You don't have to stay with me."

"Tiffy, I don't blame you that we're not pregnant, and I want to be with you whether we have a baby or not."

She looked up at him, searching his eyes to see if he really meant it, and saw only truth there. She started to cry again. "I've been a terrible wife. I'm sorry I spent all that money." *Both times.* "It's just that it . . . oh, I can't explain it. Somehow, filling the house with nice things, finding bargains—it made me feel good about myself. For a while, anyway."

He heaved a big sigh. "We should have gone for counseling."

"We couldn't afford it," she said, her voice watery. Like they hadn't been able to afford fertility treatments. Except if she hadn't spent so much money maybe they could have at least afforded counseling. What a mess she'd made of things. She so wasn't ready to be a parent. She couldn't even fix her own life. What had made her think she could raise a child? This new thought put her in tears all over again.

"Don't cry," urged Brian. "Oh, baby, I'm so sorry." He kissed her and pressed his face to hers. She could feel tears on her cheek but she wasn't sure whose they were. Maybe it didn't matter. He moved her off his lap, then stood and held out his hand. "Come on. Let's go to bed."

Bed, with Brian. That was what she wanted.

The next morning they lay spooned together in bed, talking like they had when their life was problem free. Funny, they still had trouble, but it felt like they were well on their way to fixing their biggest problem.

"I'm sorry I wasn't there to help you celebrate your birthday," he said, and kissed her neck.

"You're here now. That's all I care about," Tiffany said. Coming home and finding Brian had been the best birthday present she could ask for.

"From now on, we need to remember we're in this for the long haul," he said. "We're a team and we have to work together. If you want to buy something—"

"I'm done buying things," she said firmly, cutting him off.

"We still have to live. So if you want to buy something we'll budget for it. We have to learn to stick to a budget, that's all."

"And we have to be patient with each other," she added, turning to face him.

"I can handle that if you can," he agreed, wrapping an arm around her. "I don't want to lose you."

He'd already lost the old, money-wasting Tiffany. She was history now. The new and improved Tiffany was so much better, and she was a keeper.

Tiffany was happy to announce that she and Brian were back together when Jess came in on Monday afternoon to get her nails done.

"I'm glad," said Jess.

For a moment, Tiffany concentrated on the task of turning Jess's fingernails magenta while the music from Cara's favorite rock station and the chatter of the stylists as they cut their clients' hair filled the silence. "I know I messed up. I can't really blame Brian for walking out."

"The important thing is, he came back, and you two are hanging in there."

"No matter what," Tiffany said with determination.

"Does Brian still have his job?" asked Jess, looking at her with sudden concern.

"So far, but he's worried. So I'm going to keep paying off my credit cards as fast as I can and then we'll start putting money in savings for just in case."

"I wish we'd done more of that," Jess confessed. "When you've got it, it's so easy to spend it."

"You had a lot of big expenses," Tiffany said in her friend's defense.

"Some of them we made bigger than we had to." Jess sighed. "You know, my daughter wanted a simple wedding. I'm the one who found ways to turn it into an event."

"Weddings are expensive," offered Tiffany.

"What does your diva on a dime say about them?" countered Jess.

"You don't want to know."

"Oh, well. Too late now anyway. We've given our kids the best we could and I can't really regret that. Anyway, the bad times never last forever. It seems like the one thing I didn't learn was to be prepared for when they come," she added grimly. "I've been pretty damned naïve."

"At least you're doing something now."

Jess sighed. "I am. And I'm cutting back more on my spending." She bit her lip. "And boy, I hate to do this."

Uh-oh, thought Tiffany, feeling suddenly sick. She recognized that guilty expression on Jess's face. She'd seen it on two other women's faces earlier in the day.

"I'm so sorry, Tiff, but one of the things I've got to cut is you."

Of course, Jess had to do what was right for her, Tiffany told herself stoically. Too bad what was right for Jess was bad for Tiffany.

"I hate to be a ratty friend," Jess hurried on, "but until Michael gets a job I can't justify paying someone to do my nails."

"I understand," said Tiffany. "You guys have to be careful."

"So do you, which is why I feel like such a rat."

"Don't," said Tiffany. "I'll be okay. I've still got my eBay business. Anyway, isn't that exactly what you and Rachel and me are trying to do, find ways to save money?"

"It's easier to find them when you don't have to mess up your friend's budget in the process," said Jess. She held up her hands, fingers splayed. "Oh, geez. As usual, I forgot to take out my charge card before you did this. You're going to have to dig it out of my wallet for me."

There would have been a time in Tiffany's not so recent past that merely the sight of another woman's credit card would have filled her with envy and longing. Not today. In fact, not ever again.

Rachel was busy blogging when the doorbell rang. There stood Chad, looking cool in cutoff jeans and a print shirt hanging open over his bare chest, holding two bottles of Mike's Hard Lemonade and looking like he belonged on the cover of one of her romance novels.

He held a bottle out to her. "Happy hour."

She checked her watch. More like dinner hour. Where had the afternoon gone? "Come on in," she said. "Are you hungry?"

"Always."

"I'll make us a chicken salad," she said. "Let me turn off my computer."

"Were you trying to work?" he asked as he followed her to her office.

"No. Just putting some money-saving ideas on my blog."

He leaned against the doorjamb, watching as she typed in her closing remarks. "What kind of tips have you got on there?"

"Come see for yourself," she said.

He walked in and leaned over her shoulder, completely distracting her. Some perfumer should bottle that musky scent of hardworking man and label it *Chad*. "'I am loving my staycation,'" he read. "'So far I've been in a paddleboat on a lake'"—here he stopped to smile at her—"'picked raspberries for jam, and have started drying lavender to make sachets for Christmas presents. My children will be home from visiting with their grandparents in two weeks, and then the fun will really begin because we'll be having Girl Camp, making inexpensive crafts, enjoying a home spa using homemade facial treatments, and watching movies. I can hardly wait.' So your kids are coming home soon."

"Yes," she said, finishing the posting process. She was so ready to have them back, but she couldn't help wondering what that would do to her relationship with Chad. His tone of voice seemed to say, "The party's over."

"I wish I'd had kids," he said as they moved to the kitchen.

"You still could, you know."

He shook his head. "At forty-three?"

"That's not old," protested Rachel. If it was, old age was right around the corner for her. She took her teak salad bowl from the cupboard and salad makings from the fridge.

"No, but it's not exactly young for starting a family," he said. He picked up the lettuce and began tearing it and putting it into the salad bowl. "Anyway, my sister and brother both have a couple of kids. That should be enough to meet my parents' grandchild quota."

Rachel pulled out a cutting board and set to work turning leftover chicken breast into bite-sized pieces. "I don't know. I think when it comes to grandchildren the quota is never filled. Do they wish you were married?" She felt a sizzle on her cheeks the moment the question was out of her mouth. Why was she asking questions that looked like she had a hidden agenda? Probably because she did. She was beginning to have happily-ever-after fantasies that featured Chad as the leading man. Maybe it was just as well she admitted it and he knew it. Then they could come to their senses and stop the madness.

"I think they have mixed feelings. Being good Catholics, they're not happy that I got divorced, but they've come to accept it."

"So, you're not a good Catholic?" Not that it mattered to her. She'd wandered pretty far from her own faith.

"I'd rather be a good person," he said. "It's not that I don't believe in God. I simply don't believe in making yourself crazy when you can't follow all the rules. You try your best and pay the price when you screw up. I screwed up; I paid," he finished with a shrug.

Rachel stopped her cutting. "So, how do you feel about trying again now?"

He set down the lettuce, picked her up, making her squeak in surprise, and set her on the counter. "How do you think I feel?" he asked, his hands still on her waist. Then, before she could answer, he kissed her, pulling her in close to him. She wrapped her legs around his waist and kissed him back and suddenly it was very hot in the kitchen. The lettuce went flying, and so did Rachel. Here was another way to enjoy your staycation. Go at it in the kitchen with a hot man.

They were creating enough steam to roast every vegetable left on the counter and the ones on the floor when the phone rang. Who cared? Rachel raked her fingers through Chad's silky, black hair.

"Mom?" Claire's voice came over the answering machine. "What are you doing? Are you there?"

Rachel scrambled to disentangle herself and get off the counter, sending the salad bowl plummeting to the floor in the process.

"I'll get it," said Chad, making it to the phone in two quick steps. He snagged it and handed it to Rachel.

"Hi honey," she said, straightening her clothes.

"How come it took you so long to answer?" Claire asked.

Rachel felt a blush racing from her neck to her forehead. She bent to help Chad pick up their salad makings, which now lay scattered all over the floor. "I was busy making dinner." He looked at her with a smirk and her face flamed hotter. "Are you having fun?" *She* sure was.

"No," Claire said sullenly. "Grandma makes us go to temple. And I'm sick of museums."

If Rachel hadn't been present at the birth she'd have wondered if this was her daughter. "Oh, honey, do you know how many people would kill to be having a vacation in New York and going to all those museums?"

"I like New York," Claire insisted. "I just don't like museums. They're so boring."

"Well, pretty soon you can come back home and be bored," Rachel assured her. "Where's your brother?"

"He's at a baseball game with Grandpa," said Claire. Her tone of voice implied that watching the Yankees play at Yankee Stadium was as big a drag as hitting the museums.

"So what are you and Grandma doing?"

"Nothing," Claire said in disgust. "She said she's tired."

Rachel couldn't help smiling at that. Having two active children visit for a month had probably seemed like a good idea at the time. "Well, text Bethany or ask Grandma if you can watch TV. That will make up for your boring day. And be a good sport and don't complain about the

museums," she added. "You don't have much time left."
Neither did she. Once the kids were home that would
be the end of wild encounters of the close kind on the
kitchen counter. Maybe it would be the end of everything.
Once her children showed up Chad might not want to
stick around.

"I wish I could come home now," Claire grumbled.

"That would hurt Grandma and Grandpa's feelings."
And Aaron would have a fit. "Try and have a good time.
Okay?"

"Okay," Claire said in resigned tones.

They said their good-byes and the martyr hung up.

"I guess once my kids are back that will be the end of
life as we know it," Rachel couldn't help saying as she set
down the phone.

Chad put an arm around her and drew her to him. "Not
necessarily."

She laid a hand on his chest. "You never really did say.
Do you like children?"

"The ones I know," he answered with a smile that
showed deep dimples.

He started to kiss her but she moved her face away a
little. "Chad, I don't want to take this relationship any
further if there's no chance it can be permanent. Summer
flings are great for Hollywood actresses and jet-setters,
but not me." Wonderful as this all was, she couldn't push
her heart any further toward pain. "If this isn't going anywhere, I want to stop. Right now." Before her hormones
led her over the cliff.

The smile disappeared and so did the dimples. "I'm
not looking to get hurt either, Rachel. You don't strike me
as that kind of woman, and I hope I don't strike you as
that kind of man. I don't know where this is going, but
I'm not here to have fun with you while your kids are
gone and then disappear when they come back."

She nodded. That was fair enough. She knew he couldn't promise her forever right now. Their relationship was still too new. She would have to trust that he was hoping for something permanent, too. She would have to trust, period. She closed her eyes and kissed him.

Chapter 23

"Guess what I got," Tiffany said as soon as Rachel and Jess walked through her front door.

"Gee, let me think," said Rachel. "It's Saturday and you've been hitting garage sales. Sooo, something to sell on eBay?"

"Actually, something for me," said Tiffany. "And Brian is okay with me keeping it cuz he knows I'll save a fortune."

Rachel and Jess exchanged concerned looks. Tiff had been doing a good job of salting away her money, but this was the kind of reasoning that had gotten her in trouble when she was prowling the mall for bargains. Had she finally succeeded in brainwashing Brian?

"All right, now I'm dying to see," said Jess as Tiffany led them out to the kitchen. There, on the counter, sat an espresso maker.

"Ta-dah!" crowed Tiffany.

"That's a pretty big purchase," Rachel observed. Even at a garage sale it couldn't have been cheap.

Tiff frowned at her. "Okay, how much do you think I paid for it?"

"You had to have shot at least fifty dollars on it," said Rachel.

"Well, I didn't. I only paid twenty, which is about the cost of five lattes. Not that I've been buying many," she quickly added.

Jess's mouth dropped. "You got an espresso maker for twenty dollars?"

Tiffany nodded eagerly. "I've always wanted one. And the diva on a dime says this is the smart way to have lattes." She held up a package of coffee grounds. "I got these on the way home. I'm going to make us mochas before we pick blackberries."

Rachel spotted the bottle of coffee syrup. "So you paid another eight for the coffee grounds and probably another ten for the syrup. Now your espresso maker is up to forty dollars."

"It's still cheaper than going to The Coffee Stop all the time," Tiffany insisted. "Now, do you want a latte or not?"

"What the heck," Rachel said with a shrug. "I'll enable you." She picked up the instruction booklet lying on the counter. "Have you figured out how to work this thing?"

"Of course I have," said Tiffany, insulted. She opened the coffee grounds package and dipped in the scoop, then dumped it in the filter holder.

Jess picked up the filter basket. "Don't you need this?"

"I think that's what I put in if I want to make just one cup," said Tiffany.

"Gosh, I don't know," said Rachel, flipping through the instruction booklet.

"Don't look at me," said Jess. "Technology isn't my thing."

"Okay," said Tiff. "It's heating up. This is going to be so great, you guys. Just think, lattes every day for next to nothing." They all stood watching the machine, like kids

in an ice cream shop, waiting for the server to hand them
their cones.

"That light went off," said Jess, pointing.

"That means it's ready," said Tiff.

She pushed a switch and the machine came to life. It
began to hum. Then it sputtered. And then it spat,
launching steaming coffee grounds like missiles. Tiffany
screeched and jumped back. Jess yelped as a blob of coffee hit her sweatshirt. The espresso equivalent of an Uzi,
the machine sprayed coffee on the counter, the floor, and
Tiffany as she gingerly turned it off.

For a moment the three women stood regarding what
had only a moment before been a weapon of mass de-
struction. Then Jess said, "Lucy, I'm home," and they all
began to laugh.

Tiffany picked up the filter basket. "I guess I did need
this."

Jess grabbed a sponge from the sink and began to clean
the mess and Rachel picked up the instruction booklet,
saying, "Okay, let's try this again. This time with safety
goggles."

Another ten minutes and they were enjoying caramel
mochas. "All right," said Rachel, scooping that last bit of
foam out of her mug, "you were right. This is a great investment."

"It's the only thing I've gotten in weeks that I haven't
put up for sale," Tiffany assured her.

"You're doing great," said Jess, "and we're proud of you.
We're all doing great," she added with a decisive nod.

"I'm feeling pretty pleased with us," Rachel said with
a smile. "And just think, after today we'll have more jam
for presents."

"I'm keeping some of this batch for myself," said Jess.
"Anything to help the grocery budget." She downed the
last of her latte and set the mug in the sink. "I may even

keep that blackberry liqueur we're going to make for myself, too. If Michael doesn't have a job by Christmas, I'll drink every drop."

The party atmosphere fled the kitchen. Poor Jess. Heck, poor all of them, thought Rachel. The job offers hadn't exactly been rolling in for her, either, and Brian's job still was tottering on the edge of oblivion. "He'll find something," Rachel assured Jess, not because she believed it but because she wanted to. She had to believe things would improve, for all of them.

"He can't stay unemployed forever," added Tiffany.

Jess heaved a sigh. "That's what you'd think. You know, the only good thing about this is that at least now he understands a little of what it was like for Mikey. There's good news on that front anyway. The temp agency is keeping Mikey busy and he and his friend Dan and another guy are going to get an apartment together in the city."

"So life is good for the kids," said Rachel.

"Thank heaven, because at the rate we're going, we may wind up having to move in with one of them." Jess took her berry-picking bucket from the counter where she'd set it. "Come on. Let's go scrounge up some free food. I have a feeling we're going to need it."

The three friends didn't have far to go on their berry-picking expedition thanks to a patch of berries at the far end of the development, and after two hours of sweat and a good collection of scratches from the stickers, they had harvested a bumper crop of berries. "This should be enough to get half of Heart Lake bombed," said Jess, as they walked home past neat tract mansions with manicured lawns.

"We can freeze them and make the cordial in November," said Rachel. "I think the recipe said it needs six weeks to ferment."

"I say we make some now and sample it. To make sure

it's good enough to give away for Christmas," said Jess with a grin.

"Good idea," agreed Tiffany.

"We still need enough berries to make jam," cautioned Rachel.

Tiffany sighed. "I think we're going to have to come back and pick more. Gosh, who knew it was so much work to save money? No wonder hardly anyone ever does."

"But think of the fun we're having while we work," Rachel reminded her.

Tiffany looked at her scratched hands. "Yeah, fun."

It was fun, Rachel wrote later in her blog, conveniently forgetting to mention the heat and the scratches from the stickers. *It's hard to describe how rewarding it feels to work together to help each other survive. This is what our grandmothers and great-grandmothers did when they canned together and had quilting bees. They reaped a double bonus: the work got done and they kept their friendships strong. I'm beginning to think our grandmothers and great-grandmothers were onto something.*

Rachel finished typing and sat back, to recheck her grammar and spelling. Good enough, she decided. Chad was taking her to his sister's restaurant for dinner and another salsa dancing lesson. After that, she would change back from swinging single woman to mom. She could hardly wait to see her children again, but she had to admit she was going to miss the everyday freedom she'd been enjoying. For a few weeks she'd had a great buzz going and it had helped her cope with the looming specter of a financially uncertain school year. The irritants that were Aaron and Misty had been happily missing from her life and she had lived in a romantic bubble.

She went upstairs and ran a bath, adding her favorite bath melt. After tonight the bubble would probably burst, but, like Scarlett O'Hara, she'd think about that tomorrow.

Rachel's last ride in the bubble was perfect. Chad had arrived bearing a single red rose. Amazing how much the man could accomplish on little money—so much more than Aaron had ever managed on probably twice the income. Chad's sister Maria had been delighted to see her again and kept them supplied with complimentary margaritas. And dancing with Chad had gotten Rachel hotter than a chili pepper.

Remembering his steamy kisses was enough to heat her up all over again as she drove to Sea-Tac Airport to fetch the children on Sunday.

Once she was at the luggage claim and saw them all thoughts of romance were obliterated by a strong maternal takeover. Her babies were back!

David bounded up to her all smiles and energy. He'd grown at least an inch, she was sure of it. Even Claire was smiling. She had changed, too. Claire had a new haircut.

"Look at you," said Rachel, running a hand through her daughter's hair. "Don't you look all New York?"

"Grandma bought me new clothes for school, too," said Claire.

"Your reward for going to the museums," said Rachel, and her daughter made a face. The unsporting half of Rachel wanted to make a face, too. So much for getting a new haircut as part of Girl Camp. Her mother-in-law had stolen her thunder. But, Rachel reminded herself, she should be happy her children had grandparents who could afford to spoil them. Her own mother certainly couldn't. And neither could she. *So, it's a good thing,* she told herself, channeling Martha Stewart.

"I'm starving," announced David.

The stomach with legs had returned. Rachel tousled

his hair. "I figured you would be, which is why we're going to get hamburgers before we go home." It was a far cry from the restaurants where her children had been eating in the Big Apple, she knew.

Fortunately for Rachel, her children hadn't outgrown the stage where burgers were bliss. "All right!" said David. Even Claire was still smiling.

All through the meal the children regaled her with tales of their adventures in New York. She listened and said all the right things, but behind her positive façade, resentment grew. The children had spent a month living the high life thanks to Aaron and his parents. Now that they were back with her it was going to be burgers and budgets once more. It was unfair. Aaron and his gang got to spend money on fun like there was no tomorrow. Rachel had no guarantee of a tomorrow and could hardly spend a dime.

"Are we still doing Girl Camp?" Claire asked as the minivan sped down the freeway toward home.

"Do you still want to do it?" asked Rachel.

"Well, yeah," said Claire in a voice that implied if her mother thought otherwise she was beyond stupid.

"Then we are," said Rachel, and tried not to think about how pathetically her Girl Camp activities would stack up next to New York and Disneyland.

On her side of the minivan, Claire was already madly texting, probably to Bethany. "Can Bethany spend the night tonight?"

"Sure. Why not?" *Let the games begin.* "And I guess if Bethany is spending the night we'd better stop by the store and stock up on essentials like ice cream," Rachel added.

"And chips?" asked David hopefully.

"And chips."

They not only got ice cream and chips at the store, Rachel also wound up with candy, refrigerated cookie dough, microwave popcorn, and the makings for Belgian waffles in her grocery cart. *What are you doing?* she asked herself as she wheeled her unnecessary purchases to the checkout. As if she didn't know. She was spending money out of guilt. Again. And trying to buy her children's affection. Stupid.

"We are not going to make a habit out of this," she said firmly, and both Claire and David nodded solemnly. It went without saying that they didn't really believe her. She didn't really believe herself.

She thought of Tiffany's buying binges. Every time it seemed Tiff had rationalized her behavior, then followed that with a vow to do better next time. Now she was doing the same thing. She bought different things and for different reasons, but where was her control? A whole month of being careful with her money and look what she did within two hours of getting her children back! She looked in the cart. The goodies sat there, mocking her. This was celebration overload.

She stopped, right in the middle of the aisle. "Okay, guys. We have to make a decision."

"About what else to get?" asked David.

Rachel shook her head. "No. About what to put back. Sorry, but I just totaled what we've spent so far and we really can't go this much over our food budget. Two things have to go. You two decide."

"Mom." Claire looked at Rachel as if her last brain cell had died.

Rachel's diet had been relatively spartan with her children gone. Watching what she spent on food was as important now that they were back. Even more so, in fact, because she had to make sure they ate well. She motioned to the goodies in the cart. "This is the kind of overload that sinks ships. So, before ours sinks, I want you two to figure out what we're going to toss. Okay? Pretend we're in shark-infested waters in a rubber boat with a big leak and we're going down fast. We have to make it to the island. What's going?"

David shrugged and grabbed for the ice cream, but Claire reached out a hand and stopped him. "No, not that. If we keep the ice cream we can have shakes." She stood a moment, studying the contents of the cart. "Popcorn will last longer than chips."

David frowned. "I like chips."

"Then let's put back the cookies and the candy," suggested Claire. "We can make cookies, right?" she said to Rachel.

"Absolutely. In fact, that's on our list of activities for the week."

Claire and David looked at each other, considering, then David scooped the candy and the cookie dough out of the cart and trotted off to put them back.

"Good choices," Rachel said, and hugged her daughter. "You will be an amazing money manager someday."

Claire showed her appreciation for her mother's compliment by making a face. But she had a perfectly good time that evening consuming popcorn and chocolate shakes and playing Crazy Eights with her family and her best friend. Someday her daughter would look back and savor this moment, Rachel assured herself. She knew she would.

The following day Girl Camp was in full swing, starting with Belgian waffles for breakfast and followed by egg yolk facials. Lunch was lemonade and egg salad sandwiches dressed up with fancy shapes prepared by Rachel and served by David, who agreed to be a waiter in exchange for his very own batch of peanut butter cookies. And in the afternoon Rachel taught them some basic salsa steps.

"Wow, Mom. When did you learn to salsa dance?" asked Claire in amazement.

"A friend taught me," Rachel said with a smile.

"That was so fun," Bethany enthused when her mother came to pick her up. "What are we doing tomorrow?"

"Beading, and after lunch Tiffany's coming over to give you manicures and pedicures."

"Wow," breathed Bethany.

"You're setting the bar pretty high," teased Bethany's mom.

No, setting the bar high was a month-long stay in New York, thought Rachel.

But as the week rolled by, Claire and Bethany enthused over every activity she came up with for them. Of course, every day included some kind of girly spa thing, and a craft of some sort. Three days Jess met them at the tennis courts as soon as she was done teaching gymnastics and gave both the girls and David tennis lessons. The highlight of the camp was on Friday. David, not wanting to dress up, ate early and escaped to shoot baskets while the girls enjoyed a gala dinner of hamburger stroganoff and biscuits that they had made themselves. They finished with the strawberries they had dipped in chocolate and sparkling cider served in Rachel's good champagne glasses.

"So, a toast," Rachel proposed after she'd poured sparkling cider all around. "To being a girl."

"And to my mom," added Claire. "She's awesome."

It was all Rachel could do not to cry as they all clinked glasses. She grabbed her camera and held it at arm's length, capturing three smiling faces—two young, fresh, and hopeful, and one not so fresh, but hopeful all the same.

Dressed to the hilt in the fancy clothes they'd found at the Goodwill, the girls paraded to the living room to finish the strawberries and enjoy a teen chick flick. Rachel watched them with a smile. Girl Camp was a success. She'd expended a little money and a lot of effort and what she had right now was priceless.

The movie was half over when Chad showed up at the front door, holding a pizza box. "I was in the neighborhood and thought I'd stop by and see how Girl Camp went."

Rachel noticed that her son was already coming their way, the smell of pizza luring him like the Pied Piper's pipe. "Hi," he said.

"Hi," said Chad, and introduced himself, offering a hand for David to shake, which, well-mannered child that he was, he did.

"What kind of pizza is that?" asked David.

"Four-cheese," answered Chad.

"Awesome," said David, following him into the house.

The girls weren't above taking a break from their movie to snag some pizza, so Rachel made casual introductions as they got glasses from the cupboard and hunted down plates. She found herself feeling oddly embarrassed, like she'd been caught doing something naughty. She had nothing to be ashamed of, she reminded herself. She wasn't the one who had split up the family. Still, it somehow seemed unfaithful to the cause of motherhood for her to have found a boyfriend in her children's absence. What if they didn't like him? (*They* meaning Claire, since David's affections could easily be bought with a pizza.)

The girls wandered back to the family room to watch TV and David joined them, sprawling on the floor.

"Would you like to go out on the patio?" Rachel suggested after she'd handed Chad a glass of lemonade.

"Sure," he said, giving her an intimate smile.

As she followed him out she heard Bethany ask Claire in a low voice, "Is that like your mom's new boyfriend?"

"I guess," said Claire.

"He's sooo cute."

"He's okay."

Rachel was happy to settle for okay. Okay was a good place to begin. In fact, it was a perfect place since she had no idea what kind of ending her story was moving toward.

Chapter 24

By mid-August Chad had found renters for his house and Rachel had new neighbors. David was in Michael Jordan heaven because he suddenly had two boys right next door who lived to shoot hoops. Their mother, frazzled from juggling a part-time job with raising two active sons and a preschool daughter, was happy to sign the boys up to attend basketball camp with David.

It was nice to have neighbors, but Rachel found herself half wishing the house next door was still empty and in need of repair. Now there was no reason for Chad to stay in Heart Lake. Except her, and was she really a good enough reason? "I suppose you'll be moving on to build your real estate empire," she said when he called her later that week.

"Not yet," he said. "I've got the place on the lake for as long as I want."

Ah, yes, the mysterious friend's house. Much as she and Chad had been hanging out together, he'd never taken her there.

"Nice friend." A nasty thought flickered in Rachel's mind. What if the friend was a woman? Was that why

Chad hadn't ever invited her over, because he was playing two women at once?

"Yeah, he is."

He. The nasty little thought vanished with a satisfying poof. But Rachel was still left wondering why Chad hadn't invited her over.

She imagined the place to be one of the little cabins left over from the days when the lake was an undiscovered summer getaway, nestled in among the trees, hiding from the finer homes that had been built in the last fifteen years. Maybe his humble living quarters embarrassed him. Maybe he was embarrassed by his circumstances in general. All their dates had been fun yet inexpensive. They had done everything from the occasional dinner at his sister's restaurant to bicycling around the lake or meeting for coffee at the Sweet Somethings bakery, and, of course, he had been at her place often enough. Maybe she'd have to come right out and ask him about that. She should probably come right out and ask him about his finances. Period. He was always so vague about his business, preferring to keep their conversations centered on movies or books, her life, or just life in general, making it obvious that he didn't want to share.

But times were tough for lots of people. If he was in the process of rebuilding his life, he could certainly admit it to her. She understood about rebuilding, and she didn't care how much money he made. She'd learned from her experience with Aaron that the size of a man's bank account was far less important than the size of his heart. And if this relationship was going to keep going, they had to be honest with each other.

When he called to invite her family to the North County fair, she accepted, but said bluntly, "Only if we pay our own way in. County fairs can get expensive."

"Don't worry," he assured her. "I can afford it."

"Can you?" she countered.

"If I couldn't I wouldn't have asked you."

"Okay," she said doubtfully. Male pride was a dangerous thing.

She let him pay their way in, but once they hit the midway she sent David and Claire to buy ride tickets with their allowance money.

"Actually," said Chad, holding up a hand to stop them, "I'm picking up the tab for the day." He gave both kids a twenty-dollar bill.

"Cool," said David.

"Thanks," said Claire, smiling around her new braces.

Rachel didn't say anything. Instead, she stood bug-eyed while her children darted to the ticket booth.

Chad cocked an eyebrow at her. "Why are you looking so surprised?"

"Because that's a lot of money."

He smiled and put an arm around her. "It's okay to splurge once in a while. And I figure since this is the first time I've gone out with you and your kids I should make a good impression."

"In other words, buy their affection?" teased Rachel.

"Why not?"

"Because it's not necessary. You didn't need to buy mine," said Rachel.

"That's one of the things I love about you," he said, and gave her a kiss that sent her insides whirling. "I suspect your kids are a harder sell," he added. "Anyway, you can't go to the fair and not go on the rides. Come on," he said, steering her toward the ticket booth. "Let's get some tickets for us. I'm sure you want to ride the Ferris wheel."

"And go through the fun house," Rachel decided.

"And the roller coaster."

"Not so much."

He gave her a squeeze. "It'll be okay. I'll hold onto you so you don't fly out."

"What if we both fly out?"

"Then I'll pull out my Superman cape and take us to safety," he said with a grin and gave her another kiss, and she found herself believing he could probably do just that.

She loved following Claire and David through the fun house, maneuvering over shifting floors and standing next to Chad in front of mirrors that distorted their reflections. Riding the Ferris wheel felt like living a scene from one of her romance novels as she felt herself whisked up, up, and around, cuddled next to Chad. As they dangled at the top of the wheel with the fairgrounds spread out in all its country glory around them and, in the distance, the Cascade Mountains, still wearing a snowy shawl, he pulled her close to him and kissed her.

Eyes closed, she murmured, "That was perfect. Every girl should get kissed at the top of a Ferris wheel."

"Especially this one," he said, and kissed her again.

But as they sat in back of Claire and David on the roller coaster, *clack-clack*ing their way up the track, she experienced a very different feeling. "I hate these things," she muttered, grabbing the bar in front of her. Anything could happen on a roller coaster.

Up and down, whipping around corners at breakneck speed, if something broke, if somehow the little train of cars disconnected from the track . . .

Chad gave her shoulders a squeeze. "Rides like this are only an illusion. You're probably in more danger when you're driving your car."

Rachel barely had time to retort, "I don't drive like this," before they plummeted. Then all she could do was grit her teeth and hang on for dear life. When the ride finally ended, she walked away on shaky legs.

"Let's go again," said David, bouncing in front of her, grinning.

"I am never going on that thing again. Let's go look at the pigs."

"Aw, Mom. We still have tickets left," David protested.

"How about we let them finish up and I'll buy you a scone?" suggested Chad.

Much to her children's delight, she let him distract her with a simple biscuit wrapped around jam. She was so easy.

Later he bought her children hamburgers and cotton candy, and then he took them all to a concert featuring a popular country band. By the time they drove back to Heart Lake in his Mustang to the sound of soft rock on the radio it was dark. David was snoring in the back seat, Claire was texting, and Rachel was thinking how family-like this moment felt.

She could see this man as part of their family, could envision them driving home from similar outings, unspoken contentment hanging in the air. Was that where they were going with this relationship? She hoped so.

The next week Rachel convinced the children that it would be a great idea to pick blackberries to add to her stockpile in the freezer.

"I'll make you a pie," she promised.

That had been all it took to send David looking for a pot. Claire went with a little less enthusiasm, but she went.

As they stood at the edge of the berry patch, filling their pots with fat, juicy berries, the morning sun warming their backs, Claire casually asked, "So is Chad your boyfriend?"

There, indeed, was the question of the day. "What would you think if he was?"

Claire gave a one-shouldered shrug. "It'd be okay, I guess."

David, who had already lured Chad into shooting baskets with him on several occasions, added, "He's cool."

"Anyway, Daddy's got Misty," said Claire. "You should have someone."

Rachel found herself pleasantly surprised. Very magnanimous. And she couldn't have said it better.

"I'm going over to Sam's for a minute. He wants help timing his carburetor," Brian said, giving Tiffany a kiss on the cheek.

"Have fun," she said, logging onto her eBay account as he wandered off. He'd be at the neighbor's getting greasy for the rest of the day. But that was okay because she had things to do herself. After finishing up she'd be off to Jess's house for her weekly finance pep talk. She could hardly wait to share how well her business was doing.

Up popped her list of current bids. Good. Everything was selling and the bids on several items had gone up. And it was only Saturday. By tomorrow she'd be raking in the money, which was a good thing, considering the fact that her number of nail clients had dropped. They'd be okay though. Come fall her first charge card would be paid off. Then she only had one more to go. Maybe, if she worked really hard and if Brian didn't lose his job, by next summer they could afford a project car for him.

She was logging off when her phone rang. It was her mother, calling for her weekly check-in. Tiffany happily picked up and told her all about her latest moneymaking triumphs.

"Your father will be so pleased," said Mom. "Now I have some news for you. Cressie's pregnant."

Her baby sister was pregnant? Cressie had only been married a year. How was that possible?

This would be a good time to say something. "Oh, wow. I'm happy for her," said Tiffany. She was. She'd run right out and buy a present to prove it.

"It would be nice if you could call her. I think she was a little hesitant to tell you for fear of making you feel bad."

"I can't feel bad that we're going to have a new baby in the family," Tiffany said as much to herself as her mother.

"That's what I told Cressie."

Tiffany felt like her throat was closing up, but she said, "I'll call her. Tell her I'll have a baby shower for her."

"You could tell her yourself," suggested Mom.

"I will. But right now I have to go. I'm late for my money club."

Tiffany managed to say the proper good-byes and I-love-you's, but by the time she hung up she was close to hyperventilating. "You'll have a niece," she told herself. "That's awesome." She'd be a supportive sister and a fab aunt. Obviously, the universe thought she'd be a much better aunt than a mother. The universe was right, of course. She'd already decided she wasn't ready for motherhood so there was no reason to feel sorry for herself. And she was happy for her sister. Happy.

"Where's Tiff?" asked Rachel as she and Jess settled on Jess's deck with their iced tea. "I thought she'd be over here already, bragging about her garage sale finds."

Jess checked the wall clock. Tiff was her usual fifteen minutes late. "I'll call her." The second Tiffany answered the phone Jess could tell she'd been crying. "Oh, no. What's happened? Did Brian lose his job?"

"No. Everything's fine," Tiffany insisted, her voice watery.

"I can tell. You'd better get over here right away. We've

got iced tea and Rachel brought day-old donuts from the bakery."

"Actually, I have to go run an errand."

Jess covered the mouthpiece. "She says she has to run an errand," she reported to Rachel. "She's been crying."

"Keep her talking," said Rachel, and took off.

"We could run errands with you," Jess suggested. "You know, save on gas."

"That's okay," said Tiffany. "I'll catch up with you guys next week."

Jess was still scrambling around for a way to keep her talking when Tiffany hung up.

Tiffany had her purse and was at the door when Rachel walked through it.

"What's going on?" Rachel demanded. Her eyes narrowed at the sight of Tiffany's purse. "Were you going shopping?"

"Just to get a baby present." How could she not get a baby present? She had to get a baby present. Right now. And . . . who knew what else? "My sister's pregnant, and I'm so happy for her," Tiff added, blinking furiously to keep back the tears.

Rachel's angry teacher expression melted away. "Aw, come here, you," she said and gathered Tiffany into a hug.

"I'm happy for her. I really am," Tiffany insisted, tears making her voice uneven.

"I know you are," said Rachel, patting her back.

"I hate myself for being jealous. What kind of horrible woman gets jealous cuz her own sister is pregnant?"

"You wouldn't be human if you weren't a little green-eyed," Rachel assured her. "Come on over to Jess's and have a donut."

"I should get a present," insisted Tiffany. She had to show Cressie how happy she was for her.

"Uh, no. Not in your condition you shouldn't. You'll go on a spending spree."

Tiffany pulled away and rubbed her face.

"Her baby's not due for months, right?"

Tiffany bit her lip and nodded.

Rachel gave a knowing nod. "So, come January we'll go to the children's department together and get something awesome on sale. Okay?"

Tiffany took a deep breath. "Okay."

"Now, do you need to call her?"

"I can't. I'll cry and she'll think I'm not happy for her."

"No, you won't," Rachel said sternly. "Because you're going to be thinking that soon it will be your turn."

It was impossible to go there. Tiffany's throat closed up and she shook her head.

"You'll be thinking how much fun you're going to have spoiling your niece. Or nephew. Sleepovers, movies—if it's a boy, Brian can teach him how to work on cars. If it's a girl, you can give her pedicures. You're going to have so much fun. And none of the expense. Or the gray hairs." Rachel looked her in the eye to see if she was getting through.

Tiffany nodded.

"Come on, get the phone," urged Rachel.

Tiffany fetched the phone and dialed. The line started ringing and her heart sped up.

Her sister answered. "Tiff, did Mommy tell you?"

"Yeah, she did. I'm so happy for you," said Tiffany, and even as the words came out of her mouth she realized she was.

"Did Mommy tell you I want you to be the baby's god-mother?"

"A godmother?" Tiffany breathed.

"We're not sure yet what we're having, but we had the ultrasound and we think it might be a girl."

"A girl." Tiffany had always wanted a girl. Girls were so much fun. "Perfect."

"So, will you?"

Maybe a godmother was all she'd ever be, but so what? She'd be the best godmother in the entire world. "Of course," Tiffany said.

"I'm so excited," gushed Cressie.

"Me, too," Tiffany said, assuring them both. "I'm going to throw you an awesome baby shower. And names! You'll need to start thinking about names. I'll get you a baby name book. And I can help you set up a nursery."

"You're the best sister ever," gushed Cressie. "My child is going to be so lucky to have you for a godmother."

They exchanged I-love-you's and I'll-call-you's and then Tiffany hung up. "Wow, I'm going to be a godmother," she said to Rachel.

Rachel nodded solemnly. "It's a huge honor. People don't ask just anyone to be a godmother, you know."

Tiffany nodded, internalizing that. The main reason she'd wanted to be a mother was so she could have a child to love, a little someone to give herself to. She could give herself to her sister's baby. Cressie would share the love.

"You'll be a great godmother," Rachel predicted. "Come on. Let's go tell Jess the good news."

Tiffany followed her friend out the door, tossing her purse on a nearby chair as she left the house. She wouldn't be needing it.

Chapter 25

"Back-to-school shopping season is almost here," moaned Rachel, accepting a latte from Tiffany as the three women settled in at Tiffany's house for their weekly session. The era of the spitting espresso machine was behind them and Tiff had become a true barista. Rachel took a sip of her latte and sighed. "Taste bud heaven."

"It's my latest invention: white chocolate and caramel," said Tiff.

"You were so right to keep that espresso maker," said Rachel. Hey, she could admit when she was wrong.

Tiff beamed. "I'm good."

"I thought Grandma had come through with the clothes," said Jess, bringing them back to the subject of back-to-school spending.

"Only for Claire. So I have David to outfit, plus we have to get all the usual school supplies."

"I remember that," said Jess. "It adds up in a hurry. Have you budgeted how much you're going to spend?"

"Yes, but let me tell you, I'm finding it scary to budget when the income flow is so low."

"No jobs on the horizon?" asked Jess.

Rachel shook her head sadly. "I biked over to the school

district office again yesterday and I checked the Web site this morning. Nothing."

"If you need help, I'm sure I could come up with a few dollars," offered Jess.

As if she had any extra money. "I'll be okay," said Rachel. "At least I've got some kids lined up to tutor. That plus subbing should get me through for a while."

"I bet Chad would help you if you really needed it," said Tiffany.

"The king of the cheap date? I don't think so. Anyway, I wouldn't ask him. It wouldn't be right."

"I don't see why not. After all, he did spend a fortune taking you guys to the fair," argued Tiffany.

"And I suspect he paid for it big time." Rachel shook her head. "No, I'd rather depend on myself than a man, anyway. That way I know I have someone I really can count on."

"He seems pretty dependable so far," said Jess. "Did I see him out there mowing your lawn this morning?"

Rachel grinned. "We bartered."

"Yeah?" Jess's eyes took on a lascivious twinkle, making Rachel's cheeks turn pink. "What did you barter?"

"I'm making him dinner tonight," said Rachel.

Jess took a thoughtful drink of her latte. "Do you have any idea how much longer he's going to be hanging out at his friend's cabin?"

Good question. So far Chad showed no signs of leaving. "I don't know."

"Do you think he doesn't have any other place to go?" asked Tiffany. "I mean maybe all he has is this rental house. Maybe he's barely making it."

Hearing someone else voice her suspicion was a little unnerving. "I don't know," said Rachel. Every time the subject of jobs and money came up Chad stayed vague.

Jess frowned. "Is this getting serious between you two?"

"I . . . don't know."

"How do you feel about him?" Jess persisted.

"That I do know. I can't imagine my life without him."

"Can he afford you?" asked Tiff bluntly.

"He's not penniless. He has the rental house, and I know he sells real estate."

"Did he ever tell you who he works for?" asked Jess.

"Well, no. But I never asked," Rachel said. "I know he goes to the city a lot." She saw Tiffany and Jess exchange worried looks. "He's not a scammer if that's what you're thinking." He couldn't be. She'd met his sister, for crying out loud.

"It just seems odd that he's so secretive," said Jess.

"Maybe he's really rich," said Tiffany. "And he doesn't want you to know cuz he wants to be sure you like him for him."

"A man who's kind, hot, *and* rich? Do they ever make them that way?" asked Rachel.

"I wouldn't get your hopes up," Jess agreed. "He's probably just uncomfortable talking about money. A lot of people are."

"Well, I guess when the time's right he'll show me his balance sheet," Rachel said with a shrug. "Right now we're just dating."

She wanted it to be more in the worst kind of way, but she wasn't going to push for more. She wasn't in a hurry anyway, she told herself. There was no need to rush. She'd been there, done that. Anyway, she had plenty of other good things in her life to keep her busy, she reminded herself.

And as school approached, she got busier, signing the kids up for their activities, meeting the students she'd be tutoring and their parents, and blogging.

Her site was starting to get a lot of hits and she was fast learning that it took a quite a bit of effort to find new helpful information and money management tips and post them. But it made her feel good to know she was helping other women who were struggling with financial challenges.

"Who knows? Maybe you can find a way to make this pay," said Jess when the subject of the blog came up again.

They were sitting on the public dock, helping Rachel celebrate the first day of school and enjoying the unusually warm fall day.

"I don't know how I'd do that," said Rachel, gazing out at a couple of ducks crossing the lake.

"You could let people advertise on your site," suggested Tiffany.

Rachel dipped a foot in the cool water. "Gosh, I wouldn't know where to begin."

Tiffany snapped her fingers. "You could write a book!"

"A book?"

"Why not?" said Tiffany. "You're putting up all these tips and stuff. Turn 'em into a book. How hard can it be?"

"I'm no expert."

"I don't know that you have to be an expert," Jess said.

Tiffany gave a lock of blonde hair a thoughtful twirl. "You could talk about how we started our club and what we've learned so far and all the things we're doing to save money."

"The neighborhood school clothes swap you hosted last week is a great example," added Jess.

Rachel couldn't help smiling at that. Even Claire, who had returned from New York determined to be picky, had come away with a treasured outfit.

"There are all kinds of online sites for self-publishing now," Jess continued, warming to the subject.

"It's a thought," said Rachel. "Speaking of saving money, Chad and I were hiking on Green Mountain with the kids last weekend. The huckleberries are almost ready to pick."

Tiffany stopped twirling her hair. "That's where the bears are, isn't it?"

"Lions and tigers and bears. Oh, my!" teased Jess.

"Nothing's going to get us," Rachel assured Tiffany. "If we see a bear, Jess and I will throw ourselves in front of you."

"That'll only work if we see one before it sees us," Tiffany retorted with a frown.

"I can go any day next week," said Jess, ignoring her. "I'm done at the gym so my mornings are free. And my income's been slashed in half, so the more free food I get the better."

"Does Michael have any leads?" Tiffany asked, bringing up the subject Rachel had been afraid to touch.

Jess shook her head sadly and stared into her mug. "I need another mocha."

Tiffany grabbed her thermos and Rachel put an arm around Jess. "He'll find something."

Jess's normally sunny expression was dark. "We never dreamed it would take this long. His severance money is disappearing and our medical runs out the end of the year. If only we'd had a chunk of money in savings. We'd still be unemployed, but at least we'd have a cushion. I tell you, sometimes I feel like a walking example of what not to do."

"Things will turn around. You'll see," Tiffany said, and freshened their mugs with more of her latest latte creation. "Look at us. Things are starting to pick up in Planning and Development. Brian says that means things are probably going to start picking up all over."

Jess heaved a shaky sigh. "Sorry. I guess it's all starting to get to me. Michael isn't sleeping well. He tosses and turns half the night."

Which meant that Jess probably wasn't sleeping well either. For the first time, Rachel saw beyond the makeup to the circles under her friend's teary eyes. "Something will happen to turn things around, I just know it." Actually, she didn't know it, but surely wanting it badly enough for her friend counted nearly as much.

"I don't know how to help him," Jess confessed. "Other than trying to be positive and cut corners at every turn." Her shoulders slumped. "My father was right. I should have finished college. At least I could have been a music teacher."

"Yes, because teaching is such a steady profession," Rachel said with a frown.

"I wish there was something we could do to help," said Tiffany.

"You just did." Jess grabbed a napkin and blew her nose. "Just being able to talk helps. Thanks for listening."

"Hey, you should put this in your book, too," Tiffany said to Rachel as if writing a book was a settled matter. "Having a money support group with your friends is about more than money. It's the only way to get through hard stuff."

"That's for sure," said Jess.

They were right, thought Rachel. Brainstorming ideas for making extra income, working together to save money, and encouraging each other hadn't necessarily kept the wolf from the door, but it was helping them all feel like they could face him if he got in.

"Speaking of doing things with friends," said Jess, "when do we want to go huckleberry-picking?"

Tiffany's smiled dropped. "I need another muffin."

"I don't know about this," said Tiffany as Rachel pulled her minivan into the parking lot at the foot of Green Mountain on a Friday morning.

"No bears are going to get us," Rachel assured her for the third time since they'd gotten into the car. "Too many people come here to hike and mountain bike. The bears make themselves scarce."

"The only time you have to worry is when you come up on one with her cub," put in Jess.

"Well, how do you know we won't find some mother and her baby out for a stroll?" Tiffany fretted. "Don't bears love berries?"

"Instead of thinking about bears, think about that wild huckleberry jam we're going to be making for our families and friends and the pies and the huckleberry pancakes we'll get to eat," suggested Rachel. "And think of the money we'll save."

"If we live," Tiffany muttered, but she grabbed her pan and the big Tupperware bowl Rachel had brought and got out of the van.

The parking lot at the head of the hiking trails was old and rutted. At one end a large map mounted behind glass and posted under a rustic little cedar roof showed hikers where to find various trails among the fir and alder and bushes. The women didn't have to follow the main trail very far before spotting the berry bushes. The things branched out on all sides.

"Wow," breathed Jess, taking it all in. "It's a berry goldmine. Free food, here I come." And with that she left the beaten trail and charged into the thick of the bushes. Rachel took her Tupperware bowl and followed after.

Tiffany lingered on the trail and began to pick the more sparse offering from a nearby bush.

"You have to blaze a new trail to find the bushes that haven't been picked," Rachel told her.

Tiffany took a tentative step.

"Oh, come on, will you?" Rachel said in disgust. "Nothing's going to get you. Do you see any bears?"

"Of course not," snapped Tiffany. "They sneak up on you."

"No, they don't. That's lions and there are no lions here."

"I've heard there are cougars though," Jess said.

Thank you, Jess. Rachel frowned at her, then said to Tiffany, "Get out here and quit being such a weenie."

Tiffany scowled and marched through the underbrush to join them. "Okay, fine. But if we get eaten, don't blame me."

"At least we'll all go together," quipped Jess. "And think of the free food we're getting." She started singing, "Food, Glorious Food" from *Oliver!* which distracted Tiffany enough to help her get into the spirit of the adventure and start picking.

Ten minutes later, though, Tiff had a fresh observation. "These berries are so small. It's going to take forever to fill up my pail."

"Good things take time," Rachel said.

That shut her up for a few more minutes. Meanwhile, Jess had slowly wandered off. "Where's Jess?" Tiff asked, panicked.

Rachel looked around and frowned. "I thought we decided we were going to stick together. Jess!"

"Over here," came Jess's disembodied voice. "I've hit the mother lode."

"Come on," Rachel said, starting off in search of Jess.

"We're getting farther from the trail," protested Tiffany.

"We won't lose it."

"How do you know? Did you bring a compass?"

"We're heading straight one direction. To get back all we have to do is turn and retrace our steps," Rachel said patiently. Honestly, what did Tiff think she was, an idiot?

"This is not a good idea," Tiffany whimpered, following behind.

A second later Rachel heard an "oomph" followed by

the snapping of twigs. This was quickly followed by an emphatic "shit!" She turned to see Tiffany picking herself up and looking like a thundercloud. "What happened?" As if she couldn't tell. Actually, she was surprised she hadn't been the first one to go down.

"I tripped over a branch." Tiffany picked up her pail, which was now empty. "And I spilled my berries," she groaned.

"Oh, well. You didn't have that many anyway," Rachel informed her.

"Thanks."

"Are you two coming?" Jess called.

"We're on our way," Rachel called back.

"I don't see why we have to go so far into the woods," Tiffany complained behind her.

Rachel turned and frowned at her. "Because that's part of the adventure. Come on, now. Try to make this fun, will you?"

"All right, all right. I hope my mother-in-law appreciates her Christmas present. That's all I've got to say."

"Homemade blackberry and huckleberry jams and syrups? She'll think you're a saint."

"That would be a change."

Now Jess was in sight. She held up her big soup pot and tipped it so Rachel could see how many berries she'd already gotten. The pan was already a quarter filled.

"Wow, you've made great progress," Rachel praised her.

"I'd made progress, too, till I fell," Tiffany grumbled.

"You fell?" Jess asked.

She had enough concern in her voice to encourage Tiffany to display her scratched arms. "Look at this."

"Well, that's no fun," said Jess.

"Don't give her sympathy," Rachel said in disgust. "You'll just enable her."

Tiff tossed her head and marched to a bush on the other side of Jess.

Rachel and Jess looked at each other and laughed.

"What's so funny?" Tiffany demanded.

"You," said Rachel. "You'd think, the way you're behaving, that we dragged you to the ends of the earth. I swear, I feel like I've got Claire with me."

"Well, you did drag us to the ends of the earth," Tiffany snapped.

"At least you're with your friends," Jess said comfortingly.

"That will make me feel so much better when we're getting torn limb from limb," said Tiffany, grabbing a branch and pulling a handful of berries off of it.

"Listen," said Rachel. "You hear that?"

"What?" Tiffany looked over her shoulder.

"Voices," teased Jess in sepulchral tones. "We are not alone."

"People are hiking up the trail," said Rachel. "See? You're not really in the wilds."

"Wild enough," grumbled Tiffany, but she gamely kept picking.

Oh, well, thought Rachel, *we can't all be nature girls.*

But as Tiffany's pot began to fill with berries she got more into the spirit of the outing and even strayed as far as three feet away from Rachel's side. Progress, indeed.

It was a perfect September day, and the morning sun fell warmly on Rachel's shoulders, lulling her into a sense of peacefulness. The air smelled so fresh! She took a deep breath, filling her lungs. So what if she was on a shoestring budget? The point was, she was living, really living. She was in love and her children were healthy and she had her friends. And saving money was becoming an adventure.

She was so busy musing on the wonderful turn her life had taken that she didn't hear the crashing in the underbrush until Tiffany screeched.

"Bear!" cried Tiffany. She threw her pot over her shoulder and bolted, starting a female stampede.

She pushed into Jess and Jess's big pot of berries went flying as well. Jess didn't stop to mourn. Her eyes were the size of CDs as Tiffany swept her forward. The two of them collided with Rachel, who was still taking in the whole drama—the screaming friends, the lost harvest, the black shape bounding toward them. Down they all went like the Three Stooges in drag.

Tiffany scrambled up, heedless of the branches scratching at her, still screaming like a banshee, and bolted off in a direction that Rachel was sure wouldn't lead them back to the trail. Jess hauled Rachel up and was ready to follow.

Too late. The animal was upon them. It burst forth from the underbrush and Rachel's heart stopped. Jess let out a shriek.

And the big, slobbery, overjoyed black lab jumped up on Jess, ready to play, and knocked her back down on top of a huckleberry bush.

"Moose!" called a male voice.

"Moose," muttered Rachel. "That is not a bear." She reached down and hauled Jess back to her feet.

"Oh, my God," panted Jess. "I almost had a heart attack."

Now two young guys wearing jeans and University of Washington Huskies sweatshirts came running up. "Sorry," said the one wearing glasses. "Did he scare you?"

"Well, our friend is still running," said Jess.

The spectacled guy grabbed the dog by the collar and snapped a leash on it. "Sorry. He saw a squirrel."

"Just so he didn't see a bear," said Jess. "We'd better go find Tiff," she said to Rachel.

After apologizing again and helping the women find their now empty pans, the invaders moved off, and Rachel and Jess went in search of Tiffany.

"Tiff! It wasn't a bear," called Rachel.

"I don't care," Tiffany's voice echoed back to them. "I'm done."

They exchanged glances. "I guess we are, too," Rachel said with a sigh.

"Let's stay a little longer and see if we can recoup our losses," Jess suggested. "She'll wait at the van."

Jess was right. It would be stupid to abort the mission simply because one of them was a wimp. "Hey Tiff, wait at the van," Rachel called. "We'll be there in a little bit."

"Fine. Don't blame me if you get eaten," Tiffany called back. "And just for the record, neither one of you jumped in front of me and the bear like you said you would."

Jess rolled her eyes.

"I'm not sharing my berries with her," Rachel said as they started picking again. "She who doesn't work doesn't eat."

"You're a mean one, Mrs. Grinch," crooned Jess.

"That's right, and proud of it," Rachel said with a smile.

They picked on for another forty minutes with no sign of a bear. Or a dog. Or any human life. It was now afternoon and Rachel realized she was beginning to overheat. "My tongue feels like cotton," she said. "I guess we should have brought some water."

"Probably," agreed Jess. "But then we'd have to go potty out here in the woods and I'm not a potty in the woods kind of girl. Come to think of it, neither is Tiff. And I just realized, she's locked out of your van."

"Yes, but there's a restroom at the trail head."

"She'll have to be really desperate to use it," said Jess. "But no more talk of restrooms. This is giving my bladder ideas."

Come to think of it, Rachel was feeling the need of the restroom. "We'd better head back," she decided. "I want to make sure I'm home in plenty of time to beat the school bus."

"I think we've got enough berries for a few gift jars anyway," said Jess. Rachel started in the direction of the trail.

"Wait a minute," said Jess. "Where are you going?"

"To the trail?"

"Well, it's not that way."

"Yes, it is."

Jess pointed in a different direction. "We need to go that way."

"That's not going to take us there," Rachel insisted. "I'm positive."

Jess shrugged. "All right. Have it your way."

"Trust me," said Rachel. "I know what I'm doing." Twenty minutes later, she said, "All right. We're lost."

"Great," said Jess irritably. "Now I really do have to go to the bathroom."

"I'm sorry," Rachel said humbly. "I don't know how I could have gotten turned around."

"It probably happened when we were running from the dog," said Jess.

YOU were running from the dog, thought Rachel, but she wisely kept her mouth shut. No sense pointing that out. If she did, Jess might feel the need to point out that she was the one who had gotten them lost. "So, what way do you think we should go?"

Jess shook her head and looked around. All they could see for miles were baby pines, scrubby alders, rhododendrons, and huckleberry bushes. "Your guess is as good as mine."

Rachel heaved a sigh. "Let's try this way."

So, off they went. This way didn't work any better than that way had.

"God help me. I'm going to have to go to the bathroom in the woods," groaned Jess.

"Just so we don't wind up having to sleep in the woods," said Rachel.

"Don't even joke about things like that," Jess said with a shudder. "I have a gig tonight."

And Rachel had to be home for her children. She checked her watch. At the rate she was going she'd be lucky to get home in time to make dinner let alone be there for them when they got out of school. And she had a student coming for a tutoring session at five. Never mind getting back by five. Would they get back at all? She was hot from hiking and dying of thirst and Jess was probably ready to kill her.

She suddenly wanted to cry. "I'm such a big know-it-all. I should have listened to you." Why did she always think she was right even when she was wrong?

Jess gave her a hug. "You're not a know-it-all. You're a teacher, a born leader, and we love you for it."

"Does that mean that if we are stranded out here and never found that you won't eat me?"

Jess grinned. "I don't like to make rash promises. Come on, let's try going this direction."

"I should have brought a compass," Rachel moaned, falling in step behind Jess. What kind of teacher went into the woods without a compass? One who hadn't meant to stray so far from the trail or run from a bear that turned out to be a dog. Oh, well, live and learn. Hopefully.

Another ten minutes of walking didn't seem to bring them any closer.

"Now what?" Rachel asked Jess.

"Scream for help?"

Of course. Why hadn't she thought of that? "Great idea." Tiff was at the van. They could follow the sound of her voice and find their way back.

"Tiffany!" they both screamed.

No answer.

They looked at each other. Rachel saw her own panic reflected in Jess's eyes.

"Tiffany! Tiffany!"

Maybe a bear got her. "Tiffany!" Rachel screeched.

Finally a faint voice echoed back. "Rachel?"

"We're lost," called Rachel. "Keep hollering."

It was a moment before they heard anything, but then they heard her again. "Stay put. I'm coming in."

"No!" they both screamed.

"It's okay," Tiff's disembodied voice assured them.

Rachel collapsed on a stump and hugged her pot of berries. "We're doomed."

"Tiff, just stay put," called Jess, "or we'll all be lost."

"No, we won't," hollered Tiffany.

Jess fell onto another stump. "I don't believe this." She heaved a sigh. "And now I'm going to have to suffer a fate worse than death." She set down her pot and wandered off between the clumps of bushes.

"Where are you going?" cried Rachel in a panic.

"Nature calls," Jess said over her shoulder. A moment later she disappeared behind a shield of rhododendrons and huckleberry bushes.

Rachel heaved a sigh and hugged her pot. They weren't that far from civilization. Someone would find them. Someday.

Jess was emerging from her sylvan restroom, her face a picture of disgust when they heard a crashing in the underbrush. Rachel jumped up, clutching her pan like treasure, her heart racing. Another moment and a black, four-legged form bounded into sight. Moose.

A moment later the two college boys appeared, followed by Tiffany. Saved. They were saved!

"I brought help," said Tiffany.

"Thank God," said Jess, coming up behind Rachel. "We've been wandering for hours. Why didn't you answer when we first called?" she demanded of Tiffany.

Tiffany blushed. "Well, it was so nice and warm. I stretched out on the hood of a car and fell asleep. These guys actually heard you." She smiled at one of the rescuers. From the way he was looking back at her, Rachel suspected he would have carried her into the woods on his shoulders if she'd asked him to. "Good thing they woke me up," she added.

"We knew right where to find you," said the one with glasses. "Didn't we, Moose?"

The dog wagged its tail and barked.

"Just so you know how to get us out of here," said Rachel.

"No prob," said their bespectacled hero. "Come on, Moose." The dog bounded off into the huckleberry bushes and the humans followed at a more sedate pace. Moose's daddy pointed to Jess's pot. "That's a pretty good haul. What are you gonna do with all those?"

"Make jam," said Jess. "If you give me your address, I'll save a jar for you."

"Sweet. My name's Ted, by the way. This is Mark."

As they made their way to the parking lot it quickly became apparent that Tiffany had already told the guys all their names and pretty much shared their entire life stories.

"Your blog sounds awesome," Ted said to Rachel. "I'm gonna have my girlfriend check it out."

It took them less than fifteen minutes to hike back to

the parking lot . . . and the restroom, which Rachel used as soon as she had thanked their rescuers.

Ted and Jess were exchanging information when she rejoined the group. "Here's my number and my dad's e-mail," he said to Jess. "He's in HR at Microsoft. You should have your son give him a call."

"How cool is that?" crowed Tiffany as they waved good-bye to Ted and Mark.

"Very cool," admitted Jess.

Even more cool, thought Rachel as she checked her watch, was the fact that it looked like she'd actually make it home in plenty of time to meet her children when they got off the bus.

"I can hardly wait to go home and drink a gallon of ice water," said Jess once they were back in the minivan.

"I just hope we're done picking berries for the year," Tiffany said from the backseat.

Picking? Who had been doing most of the picking? In fact, who was responsible for the fact that they'd lost their first harvest and had to start picking again? That was it. Berries be damned. Rachel was going to bean Tiff with her pot. She glared at Tiff's reflection in the rearview mirror.

"Don't do it," said Jess, reading her mind. "We have no place to hide the body."

Tiffany looked from one to the other, irritated and perplexed. "What?"

"Never mind. Just be glad we're letting you live another day," said Rachel. But she'd be doing it without any of their precious huckleberries.

Chapter 26

"Great last set," Amy told the band as she unhooked herself from her guitar.

The party was over for another weekend and the remaining hangers-on at the club where The Red Hots were playing were tipping down the last of their drinks and putting on their coats, ready to face the rainy fall night. Jess looked beyond the dance floor to the far end of the room where the bar was situated and saw the bartender busily scooping up glasses. She'd forgotten how much she loved this life—the way the band fed off the crowd and then one another, the fun of watching people dance, the high of making harmonies. Too bad a girl couldn't really make a living doing this.

"We rocked this place," agreed Kit. "That piano lick you played on Amy's new song was dope," she told Jess.

"Thanks," Jess said with a smile.

"Are you coming to Denny's?" asked Amy.

"Not tonight. Some of us have a long commute to work, you know. Even going straight home it'll be another hour before I'm in bed."

"You need to leave the burbs," said Kit in disgust. "That's for old people."

"Compared to you guys I am old," said Jess.

"Tell that to the college bum who was hitting on you every time we went on break," teased Amy. "You're only as old as you act, and that puts me at nineteen."

Jess smiled and shook her head as she lowered her keyboard into its case. If she didn't get some sleep, she'd be a zombie all day on Sunday.

Jess got some sleep, but she was still a zombie on Sunday. She'd read somewhere once that a person got her best sleep before midnight. If that was the case she hadn't been getting any good sleep on the weekends for quite a while. She stumbled out of bed and made her drowsy way to the kitchen around ten, following the aroma of coffee like a bloodhound on the scent.

Michael was already up and parked at the kitchen table, checking out the newspaper want ads. "How'd it go last night?" he asked as she shuffled to the coffeepot.

"We rocked the house, of course," she said and poured a mug of caffeine. Strong, black coffee—the weekend warrior's friend.

He laid the paper on the table and regarded her. "What would you think about moving?"

She almost choked on her coffee. "Ohio?"

He shook his head. "Nope. That ship already sailed."

She heard the discouragement in his voice. Michael had been so sure he'd find something right away. So far, he'd been both stoical and positive, but she sometimes wondered how much longer he could keep up that front. "Then where?" She walked over to the table to check out the paper. "Did you find a job someplace?"

He shook his head. "Not yet."

"Then I don't understand. Where do you want to move?"

"My mom was hoping maybe we'd move in with her."

Move to Seattle and live with her mother-in-law? Jess blinked. "When did this happen?" Not that she had anything against her mother-in-law. Myra was great. But to up and leave their house and move back in with a parent at their age felt a little extreme.

"We were talking last night," Michael said. "The house and yard are getting to be too much for her."

No surprise there. Michael's widowed mother suffered from arthritis, and wasn't in the best condition to maintain a two-story, three-bedroom house with a good-sized yard. She'd surrendered the yard to a yard service a year ago. Now she was ready to surrender her home to another woman?

It was hard to imagine, almost as hard as it was for Jess to imagine herself living in that house on Magnolia with its décor that was caught in a time warp and its seventy-something neighbors. She couldn't. Not that she had anything against pink bathrooms, powder blue carpet, and crystal chandeliers. They just weren't her. And her neighbors here were her best friends.

Of course, the idea of going bankrupt wasn't exactly appealing either. Could she be happy living with her mother-in-law? She tried picturing family holiday gatherings and stockings hanging in front of the brick fireplace.

"I know you don't want to move," Michael said gently. "But I don't know what the future holds. I'm thinking it might not be a bad idea to see if we can sell this place."

Or sell her mother-in-law's place and move her to Heart Lake. Of course there was one minor flaw in that plan. Myra wouldn't want to move. Jess couldn't blame her. She didn't want to move, either. "You could find a job tomorrow," she protested. "And then we'd have moved for nothing."

"Jess, I don't know how long it will be before I get another job," he said. It was depressing to hear him talk this way, to see the sober expression on his face. "Remember, our COBRA runs out at the end of the year."

Jess swallowed hard.

"I don't want to wait until we're completely broke to put a plan B in place."

It was her fault they even had to worry about a plan B. She'd been the one who balked at moving to Ohio. If she'd been a sport and sucked it up they wouldn't be in this position now.

She took a swallow of coffee, willing her brain to think of the right thing to say. "I hate that house." This had not been the right thing to say. How had she let it slip out?

Michael's face fell, but he nodded gamely. "Well, I wasn't sure how you'd feel."

But he'd suspected. She laid a hand on his arm. "I love your mom. You know that. But that's her home. It would never be mine. I'd feel like the world's oldest teenager living there, camping out in the middle of all her things."

"She said you could redecorate."

"That wouldn't be fair to her. She loves the place just like it is."

Michael nodded, tight-lipped and stoical, and returned his gaze to the newspaper.

Michael didn't want to move any more than she did, she was sure of it. He loved this house and was happy here with his neighborhood buddies. To suggest such a drastic measure, he had to be desperate.

Jess spent the next two days weighing her options. Which was better, being a bankrupt woman with a house in foreclosure or a noble daughter-in-law? When she looked at it that way, noble daughter-in-law suddenly didn't look so bad. She loved her mother-in-law. And she liked brick fireplaces. The kids would love being at Grandma's for Christmas.

Once you say it you can't take it back, she reminded

herself. She thought of the fun times she'd had with Jess and Tiffany and swallowed hard.

Seattle wasn't all that far away. She could still come back to Heart Lake to visit. Maybe, once Michael's fortunes improved, they could buy a summer cabin on the lake.

"Let's put the house up for sale and see what happens," she finally said.

That had been the right thing to say, obviously. Her husband not only looked relieved, he also smiled gratefully at her. "I know you don't want to leave your friends."

"It's not like I won't ever see them again," she said, both to Michael and herself. "We have to be responsible. We'll make it work," she added, hoping she was right.

Monday night Laney Brown from Lakeside Realty came over to check out the house and assure them that she would, indeed, get it sold. Next thing Jess knew Laney had a six-month exclusive listing and was pounding a For Sale sign into their front lawn.

She'd barely left when both Rachel and Tiffany were at the front door, wanting to know what was going on. Jess burst into tears and they led her over to Rachel's house for a strong dose of chocolate.

Rachel was crying, too, before she even had the Hershey's Kisses out of hiding. "I can't believe this. Where are you going?"

"To live with my mother-in-law."

"Eeew," said Tiffany, grabbing for the candy bag.

"It's okay." Jess sniffed. "I like my mother-in-law. But I hate her house, and I don't want to leave you guys."

"At least you're only moving to Seattle," said Tiffany. "We'll still get together."

"It won't be the same as having her next door," said Rachel, passing around a Kleenex box.

If there was one thing Jess had learned in her forty-four

years on the planet, it was that things never stayed the same, no matter how much you wanted them to. "We'll just have to make sure we meet on a regular basis. I can still come up for our Saturday meetings."

"And you haven't moved yet," added Rachel.

"Maybe it won't sell," said Tiffany hopefully. "Except you need it to, don't you?"

"Yes, unless Michael miraculously gets a job."

"Then let's hope for a miracle," said Rachel.

A miracle happened all right. The house sold in two weeks.

"I hate this," said Tiffany when Jess returned for a complimentary farewell manicure.

So did Jess. She had missed coming to the salon, missed the sounds of Cara's favorite rock station, the camaraderie of the women, the crazy smells. Right now Cara had Maude Schuller in her chair and was in the process of giving her a perm, injecting the air with the strong smell of permanent wave solution. Iris was between customers and sampling one of the freshly baked oatmeal cookies Maude had brought in.

Ironic, thought Jess, *now we're out from under mortgage payments and I can afford to come to Tiff again I won't be living here.* Well, she'd still come up to Heart Lake and have Tiff do her nails. She was still going to meet with her friends and do crafts anyway. She'd make a day of it.

"Well," said Jess, "it won't be as much fun as us all living on the same block, but at least we still all live in the same state. Hopefully, none of us will move far away."

"Not me," said Tiff, applying blood red polish to Jess's nails. "I'm going to stay in Heart Lake forever."

"You never know," said Jess. "I thought I was, too. But a girl's gotta do what a girl's gotta do. And in my case that meant moving. We probably should have sucked it up and

SMALL CHANGE 265

taken the job in Ohio, but oh, well. At least Michael's not so stressed now."

"If you ask me," said Cara as she squirted solution on Maude's roller-clad head, "a girl's gotta be crazy to move in with her mother-in-law."

"For us this is a win-win," said Jess. Myra was grateful for the help and they'd have money in the bank. Plus she would be closer to most of the clubs where the band played. Why, then, did she want to cry?

You don't have to live there forever, she told herself. It would just feel like it.

'Tis the Season
to Be Frugal

From Rachel Green's Blog

SMALL CHANGE, BIG DIFFERENCE

Frugal Gifts from the Kitchen

The holidays are right around the corner, but I'll be ready. Remember that lavender I dried? I made sachets with it and they turned out fabulous. Every woman I know is getting one for Christmas this year. In fact, almost everyone on my holiday list this year is getting a present homemade with love. I'm proud of what my friends and I have done and I'm excited to share.

All this gift-making has gotten me thinking. Why do we tend to believe the best gifts are things we buy? What propaganda! Sometimes the nicest gifts are the ones that involve time and effort and lots of heart. (I'm predicting our Small Change Club goody baskets are going to be the most popular presents under the tree! Oh, and by the way, we picked up the baskets at garage sales. ☺)

Now, in keeping with the spirit of this blog, here is an

early present for all of you: our recipes. I hope you enjoy them!

BLACKBERRY CORDIAL

Ingredients:
  4 quarts crushed berries
  4 cups granulated sugar
  1 fifth Vodka

Directions:
Mix the above ingredients and place in a glass container. Stir daily. Strain after six weeks and bottle. Can fill six to eight bottles depending on what size bottles you use. (Hint: you can use old liquor bottles, but glass salad dressing bottles work great, too!)

BLACKBERRY SYRUP

Ingredients:
  4 cups pureed blackberries
  2 cups granulated sugar

Directions:
Put pureed berries through sieve to remove seeds. Put in large pan and bring to a boil. Add sugar. Boil and stir two minutes. Remove from heat and skim off foam. Pour into pint jars, seal, and process in a water bath for ten minutes. Makes approximately three pints.

NOTE: If you want to, you can make a double or triple batch. Raspberries, blueberries, and huckleberries also make great syrup.

FRIENDSHIP TEA

Ingredients:
    1 cup instant tea
    1 18 oz. jar orange juice mix such as Tang
    ½ teaspoon cloves
    ½ teaspoon cinnamon
    ½ cup granulated sugar

Directions:
Mix together and store in a large plastic container. If giving as gifts, double the recipe and pour into quart- or pint-size canning jars, then top with a fancy fabric lid.

Note: When making tea, add 1 to 2 spoonfuls to each cup of boiling water.

CAFÉ VIENESE

Ingredients:
    ½ cup instant chocolate drink like Nestle's Quik
    ½ cup granulated sugar
    ½ cup powdered cream
    1 teaspoon cinnamon
    ½ teaspoon nutmeg

Directions:
Mix the above. Makes one eight-ounce can. (You can easily double or triple this recipe and give it as hostess gifts. Note: Use 2 to 3 spoonfuls of mix for a cup of coffee.)

Okay, that's about all I have time to post. The Small Change Club is about to start and we have a lot to do!

Chapter 27

It was Thanksgiving weekend, and the three friends had gathered at Rachel's house to start preparing their holiday gifts.

"Gosh, I miss this place," Jess sighed as she stood at Rachel's sink, bottling the liqueur they'd made from the blackberries they picked over the summer. The women had been scrounging and saving salad dressing bottles all fall and now a variety of sizes sat on the kitchen counter next to Jess, waiting to get filled with either berry syrup or liqueur.

"It's not the same without you," said Tiffany, who was busy decorating their gift bottles with curling ribbon. "The new neighbors are so not fun."

"Maybe they need time to settle in," Jess suggested.

"They're settled all right," said Rachel with a frown. She wiped a dribble of liqueur off a bottle and set it on the table. "I told you how Mrs. Wellton called to complain about the noise when we were having our Halloween party, didn't I? It wasn't even ten yet. Fine neighbor. Did I complain when her stupid cockapoo dug up my strawberry plants?"

"You'd better take her some syrup for Christmas," said Jess.

"Can I lace it with drain cleaner first?" cracked Rachel. "This is all your fault for leaving us, you know."

"Well, I'm paying for it," said Jess with a smile that looked forced. "I have to use a pink bathroom."

"I think pink accessories are pretty," said Tiffany.

"This isn't just accessories. Everything's pink: tiles, tub, shower curtain, even the toilet paper. It's like taking a bath inside a Pepto Bismol bottle."

"If I lived with my mother-in-law I'd have to take Pepto-Bismol every day," said Tiffany, wrinkling her nose.

"My mother-in-law is great, and she loves to cook, which is a good deal for me. The hardest part is Michael's not having found a job yet."

"That's tough," Rachel agreed. Boy, did she feel his pain.

"I know it frustrates him," said Jess, "but he's trying to keep a positive attitude. Thank God at least Mikey is working full time. Who knew getting lost in the woods would turn out to be such a good thing?"

"A good thing would be you moving back," said Rachel.

"Maybe we will someday. Who knows?"

"I wish you were going to be here for Christmas," said Tiff. "It's not gonna feel right without your Christmas open house."

"I guess you'll have to carry on the tradition," Jess told her. "We'll come. Speaking of holidays," she said, turning an inquisitive eye on Rachel. "How was your Thanksgiving with Chad's sister and her family?"

Now, there was something nice to dwell on. "Perfect. Let me tell you, they know how to celebrate. Chad's sister says any excuse for a party and any reason to be thankful works for her." Thinking back, the day was a swirl of laughter, music, and spicy food. She'd enjoyed the jalapeño-spiked cornbread and turkey mole, the fried ice cream to go with the pumpkin pie. With the warm welcome, the games, and impromptu dancing she had felt right at home. Surprisingly, so had her children. She could still see Claire and David in the middle of the living room, rocking out to Latina singer Belinda.

"Christmas is coming. I bet you'll get a ring," predicted Tiffany.

"If he can afford one," teased Jess.

"He bought another rental house, so I guess business is picking up," said Rachel.

"So, he's actually telling you something about his balance sheet? That's a good sign," said Jess.

Everything about the way the life she was building with Chad was a good thing. She had yet to meet his parents, but she was sure that was coming soon. He had already talked about taking her to eastern Washington for a visit in the spring. They'd even discussed driving down to California to visit her mother. If that didn't hint at happily-ever-after she was going to give away her romance novels.

"You know this is the first time in forever that I haven't been at the mall doing the Thanksgiving weekend sales," said Tiffany, putting ribbon around the last bottle of liqueur.

Tiff had been doing so well with her budget and was close to paying off her first credit card. Rachel exchanged a concerned look with Jess.

Tiff caught it. "Don't worry. I don't really miss it. Of course, I'd have saved a lot by shopping today."

That was the kind of attitude that had gotten her in trouble in the first place.

"But I saved so much more doing all this with you guys," she added with a grin. "I'm so proud of us."

Jess smiled. "Me, too. We're all doing what we have to do and it's paying off. We just have to remember that this Christmas."

"Anyway, Christmas isn't about stuff. It's about being with the people you care about and making memories," said Tiff.

"So, we're going to have a nice, simple holiday this year and make lots of new memories," Rachel concluded as she and Claire and David enjoyed their Sunday night treat of popcorn and chocolate shakes.

Somehow, the atmosphere in Rachel's kitchen wasn't as glowing as it had been the day before with Jess and Tiffany.

"Does this mean we're not going to the *Nutcracker*?" asked Claire with a frown.

"I don't want to go to that again," said David, making a face. "That's girl stuff."

"That is not girl stuff," Rachel corrected him. "It's culture. And no, I'm afraid not." They'd made a tradition of going into the city and spending the night, eating at a nice restaurant, and then enjoying the Pacific Northwest Ballet's performance of the beloved masterpiece. Last year Rachel had managed to take the kids in for lunch and a matinee performance and that had been fine with Claire. This year even that was more money than she could justify spending considering her unsteady income.

"But we always go," Claire protested.

Looking at her daughter's unhappy face, Rachel waged an inner battle between guilt and responsibility. For a moment she was tempted to charge it, find a way to pay for it later. But that would be guilt spending and she was past that. Wasn't she?

Absolutely. "I'm sorry, sweetie," Rachel said. "I can't afford it this year. You know I'd take you if I could."

"It's so not fair," Claire said, scowling.

"I know," Rachel agreed, nobly resisting the urge to remind her daughter that life wasn't fair.

"Okay, fine," Claire said in her best snotty voice. "I didn't want to go anyway." She shoved away from the table, leaving her shake half finished.

"Hey, are you going to eat that?" David called after her.

"No."

He gleefully pulled his sister's glass to him, leaving the women to sort out their problems.

Rachel started to go after her daughter and then changed her mind. What was the point in chasing Claire to her room and promising something she couldn't afford to give. So instead she decided to blog. She typed in her title: "'Tis the Season to Be Frugal," and then let the words flow.

You should not feel guilty for being financially responsible, she concluded. Now, there was something every mother in America needed to hear this time of year. It was very true, very wise.

Very depressing. There had to be some way she could take her daughter to the *Nutcracker.* She began to poke around online. After a few minutes she'd found the perfect solution. Coeur de Danse, Heart Lake's dance studio, was putting it on, and for what they were charging she could afford to do both the *Nutcracker* and the Christmas tea special that Sweet Somethings was running through December.

She left her computer in search of Claire.

Her knock on her daughter's door only brought a tearfully dramatic "I don't want to talk."

"Not even if I told you I found a way for us to go to the *Nutcracker*?" Rachel asked and waited for the thunder of happy feet.

Sure enough. A moment later the door swung open.

There stood her daughter, tears still on her cheeks, eyes full of excitement. "Really?"

"Almost really."

The brows knit.

"We can't go in to the city, but I can take you to a local performance and we can do Christmas tea at Sweet Somethings. That's the best I can manage this year. Are you good with that?"

Claire's face lit up. "Yesss!" She threw her arms around Rachel's neck and hugged her. "Thanks, Mommy."

"You're welcome," Rachel said, hugging her back.

Claire pulled away, biting her lip and looking at their feet. "I'm sorry I wasn't very nice."

Rachel raised her daughter's chin so they could look each other in the eye. "You weren't, and I understand you were disappointed. But sometimes we can't get what we want. I'm doing the best I can for all of us. I hope you know that."

Claire nodded.

"Good." Rachel hugged her again. "We'll have a good time. In fact we'll have a great time."

"We will," Claire agreed.

And they did. Claire loved the tea at Sweet Somethings, consuming every cookie on the three-tiered cookie plate and eating both Rachel's scone and hers, leaving it to Rachel to consume the cucumber tea sandwiches. The *Nutcracker* performance was amateur, but Claire didn't seem to care. In fact, as they left the Heart Lake High auditorium where it had been performed, she asked, "Could I take dance lessons?"

"I think dance lessons would be great. Tell Daddy. I bet he'd love to see you up on that stage," Rachel said, giving her daughter a hug. There. Aaron liked lavishing gifts on the kids. He could pay for the dance lessons and she'd come to the performances.

Later, Rachel wrote triumphantly in her blog: *I have concluded that there are always frugal alternatives to favorite activities. You just have to look for them.*

That, she decided, would make a good subject for a chapter in her book.

So would chronicling the various triumphs of the Small Change Club. And Tiffany would deserve special praise.

She was literally dancing when she met Rachel and Jess at her front door. "I paid off my first credit card!"

With squeals and laughter, the three women managed a group hug that turned Tiff's entryway into a mosh pit.

"Come on out to the kitchen," said Tiff. "Brian's got champagne for us."

They followed Tiffany to her kitchen to find Brian standing at the counter, uncorking a bottle of modestly priced champagne. Nearby sat a small plate of truffles from the Chocolate Bar. "So how great is my girl?" he greeted Rachel and Jess.

"She rocks the house," said Jess.

The champagne cork came out with a pop, making Tiffany jump and then giggle. "Brian got us the chocolates, too."

"I figured you deserve to celebrate," he said, pouring champagne into the first glass. He produced an intimate smile for Tiffany. "I'm really proud of you, Tiffy baby," he said, and handed her the glass. She took it with pink cheeks, and he handed glasses to Rachel and Jess. "She used every cent she's earned to pay off that card," he bragged. As if her two best friends didn't know. "So, a toast," he said. "To my wife, who's paid off a fortune and is priceless."

"To Tiffany," echoed Rachel and Jess.

"And to my great friends, who helped me stay on track," added Tiff with a smile. "By this time next year the other one will be gone and we'll be debt free." Looking at

Brian, she added, "I'm never letting myself get in a mess like that again. It is so not worth it."

"I guess it's not bad to have a card to fall back on for emergencies," said Jess.

"But Brian and I have decided it's better to have money in savings," said Tiffany with the zealous enthusiasm of a new convert. "That way we can earn interest instead of pay it."

Rachel helped herself to a truffle. "What I have in savings right now wouldn't even earn me enough interest to buy one of these. But slow and steady wins the race. Hmmm. I think I'll put that in my book."

"So, are you really gonna write one?" asked Tiff.

"Why not? You never know. Maybe I'll become the next Suze Orman."

"Between Jess and her band and you and your book, one of you guys is bound to get famous," Tiffany predicted.

"From your lips to God's ears," said Rachel. "Never mind the fame, though. I'll take the money," she added with a grin.

Ten minutes later Brian took off for the gym, leaving the women to enjoy working on their latest craft. "Okay, I've got six garage sale teacups for our teacup candles," said Rachel. "Did you bring the votive candles?" she asked Jess.

Jess held up a little bag from Vern's. "Got 'em. And I brought my glue gun."

"Then let's get to work while I'm still awake," said Jess. "I tell you, I can't stay up till two in the morning anymore and then get up at the crack of dawn."

"This is the crack of dawn?" teased Rachel.

"It was when I got up," Jess retorted.

"That's the price you pay for being a hot band chick," Rachel informed her.

"Speaking of my band, who's going to come hear us play on New Year's Eve? I need to reserve space at the band table."

"We are," said Tiffany.

"Count me in, too," said Rachel.

"And Chad?"

"Hopefully." Who knew? He'd already warned her he'd be over at his parents' for Christmas.

She'd been disappointed when she learned Chad wouldn't be around. Secretly, she'd been hoping for a ring, which, of course, was utterly stupid since they'd only been seeing each other a few months. She was in no hurry, Rachel reminded herself. There was no need to rush into anything.

Still, the night he came by the house before leaving town with a small gift box for her, she couldn't help thinking *ring*. Naturally, she had something for him, too—a bottle of her blackberry liqueur and a picture she'd taken of him in the fall when they'd gone mushrooming, which she'd framed.

He seemed genuinely pleased, pulling her to him and giving her a thank you kiss. "I like it."

"Do you really? I know it's not a very expensive present."

"It's better than an expensive present because it's from you."

"And I have some friendship tea for you to give your parents from me."

"They'll love it," he said and gave her a little squeeze. "Open your present."

She pulled off the wrapping paper and opened the box to find a pair of pink pearl earrings. "They're beautiful," she said. *It's not a ring.* "I hope you didn't spend too much." *I wish you'd bought a ring.*

"Do you like them?"

Well, of course, they were gorgeous. "I love them."
They're not a ring.

And so what if they weren't? Did she need a ring to be
happy? Did she need a man to be happy, for that matter?
Really, she had to stop operating her life under the influence of romance novels. "Thank you," she murmured.

"And don't make any plans for New Year's Eve," he
added.

Because then she'd get a ring? Oh, stop, she told herself firmly. "I already did. I told Jess I'd come hear her
band play. Want to join me?"

"Okay, but how about dinner first?"

"I think I could swing it."

He nodded, pleased with the deal. "We'll make it a
night to remember."

What did that mean, dinner and a ring?

It means a new year, Rachel told herself firmly. And
she was going to make it good no matter what happened
on New Year's Eve.

Chapter 28

The three friends had their own holiday celebration right before Christmas at Tiffany's house, turning a potluck lunch into a competition to see who could come up with the most inexpensive and tasty dish. Rachel won, hands down, with her potato soup. Tiffany came in second with pasta dressed up with Italian dressing, black olives, and drained canned tomatoes—cheaper than using fresh ones, she bragged. Jess knew she wouldn't even be in the running, so she brought a tossed salad.

"Not a salad in a bag though," she said. She knew she would never be the queen of the kitchen, but she was making progress and learning important kitchen truths her mother had tried to teach her years before, one of which was that it didn't take much more time to tear up lettuce and cut tomatoes than it did to dump something from a bag into a bowl. Shortcuts weren't always that much shorter. And to think it had only taken her until her forties to make that discovery!

"I say we call it a three-way tie," said Rachel.

"Oh, we have to have a winner," protested Tiffany. "I have a prize."

"Then give it to Rachel," said Jess. "That soup was the bomb, and it's hard to get cheaper than potatoes."

The prize was a small envelope filled with grocery store coupons. "All right," crowed Rachel. "I'm rich!"

Gifts, too, were bargain goodies selected with care. Jess was thrilled with the Cyndi Lauper poster Tiffany had picked up at a garage sale. "Girls just wanna have fun, right?" said Tiffany.

"That's always been my motto," said Jess, and hugged her. "Thank you so much! Now, you two, open yours."

They did and found twin pink glass piggy banks.

"This is so cute!" cried Tiff.

"Somehow, I thought it was fitting," Jess said. "Oh, and I have something else for both of you." She produced two rolled scrolls of printer paper tied with red curling ribbon.

"What's this, a proclamation?" teased Rachel.

"It's our holiday theme song," said Jess.

Tiffany had her scroll unwrapped. "Sing to 'Jingle Bells,'" she read.

"Okay, sing it for us," said Rachel, opening hers.

"We can all sing it together," Jess said. She counted them down and they chorused:

Dashing through the store
Everywhere I see
Merchandise on sale,
And it's calling me, "Buy, buy, buy!"
But they're only things
They can't make memories
So I'll spend less and give more
To my family. Yeah!
Jingling coins, jingling coins, I am going to save
Lots of money by not spending all of them today.

Jingling coins, jingling coins, I'm careful how I spend
That way I will have a merry Christmas in the end.

"That is a perfect holiday theme song for us," Rachel said
when they were finished. "I'm putting it up on my blog."

The fun, silly gifts went on: a book Tiffany had found
at a garage sale for Rachel on how to test her man's IQ, a
flower ring made of sequins for Jess along with a children's cookbook Rachel had picked up at the Goodwill as
well as a used book full of inexpensive crafts for Tiffany.
The big present of the day was for Rachel from Jess and
Tiffany.

Rachel pulled out the gift card for a haircut at Salon H
and almost cried. "Hey, you two. We're supposed to be
exchanging inexpensive presents."

"It didn't cost that much," Tiffany assured her. "I bartered with Cara. Anyway, we figured you needed a new
look to go with your new man."

"Speaking of your new man, did he give you anything
for Christmas before vanishing to eastern Washington?"
prompted Jess.

"Pearl earrings," said Rachel.

"Can a ring be far behind?" Jess teased.

Rachel's shrug was nonchalant and, Jess suspected,
totally fake. "Who knows? Meanwhile, we're enjoying
being together."

Okay, maybe Rachel was perfectly happy to drift
along indefinitely with no commitment. It wasn't Jess's
idea of a wise way to run a relationship, but in light of
past hurts she could understand the need to take their
time. Love was such a gamble. Heck, life was a gamble.

Lately, it looked like Jess and Michael had gambled and
lost. Reduced from never having to worry about money to

living with her mother-in-law. Boy, had her fortunes changed in a hurry.

You love your mother-in-law, Jess reminded herself on a regular basis. But loving her mother-in-law and loving living with her were two different things. Women were never designed to share a house together, Jess concluded.

Myra did some things on a regular basis that were beginning to get to Jess. Every time Jess sat down at the piano, Myra thought of something she needed. "Oh, dear, would you mind getting the hamburger out to thaw. I forgot to do it." . . . "I hate to ask, but would it be too much trouble for you to run to the post office for me? I'm completely out of stamps and I want to get this letter out today." . . . "I love to hear you play the piano." . . . "I'm sorry to trouble you, Jess, but I'm getting a bit of a headache. Would you please get me an aspirin and a drink of water." . . . "Would you mind playing something a little softer?"

Pretty soon Jess got the message. Her piano wasn't welcome in the house. They'd had to rearrange the furniture to make room for it and Myra had insisted she didn't mind. Myra needed to revisit that attitude. The piano wasn't the only thing that wasn't particularly welcome. With the exception of her bedroom set, Jess's furniture was in storage, along with her pictures and knickknacks and even her dishes. "I simply don't know where we'd put them," Myra lamented.

Equally annoying were Myra's repeated requests for Jess to do all of the household cleaning. "Could you do the dusting this morning? My back is killing me." Or, "You know how it hurts my hips to lean over the tub, dear."

You'll be old, too, Jess reminded herself as she trudged to the bathroom on Christmas Eve day, cleanser in hand. Except Myra wasn't that old, and Jess was beginning to suspect that bad health had been a ruse. First it had been a ruse to help her son and allow him to save face. Now it was becoming a ruse to turn her daughter-in-law into a cleaning service to replace the woman she'd fired the week before Jess and Michael moved in.

"If you don't kick this bad attitude you're going to get nothing but a lump of coal for Christmas," Jess warned herself. She began to hum "Deck the Halls."

By the time she was finished with the song she felt better. It was the season to be jolly and that was exactly what she was going to do. She and her husband had a place to live and no mortgage payments. Michael didn't have a job yet, but a new year was right around the corner. Things could be a heck of a lot worse.

When Mikey and Erica and her new husband arrived on Christmas day, their arms filled with festively wrapped presents, Jess saw firsthand how rich she was. Her children loved her and were happy to be with her. They were all well and safe, and they were about to enjoy a holiday feast. Did it get any better than that?

She and Michael had warned the kids that this would be a budget Christmas, and they'd kept their word, limiting the presents to a gift card for each one tucked into a gift basket filled with their mother's homemade goodies.

"Wow, Mom. You really made all this?" asked Erica, looking at Jess in amazement.

"Living proof that jam doesn't always come from the store."

"I used to make all my own jam," put in Myra, managing a bit of motherly one-upsmanship. "But I must admit, I never tasted anything as good as that huckleberry jam you gave me," she added, beaming at Jess. "We had some this morning for breakfast," she told Erica.

Okay, Myra might just live to see the new year.

"And so prettily wrapped. You always had a flair for

that sort of thing," Myra added, helping Jess remember why she did, indeed, love her mother-in-law.

Even though Jess had encouraged the kids to save their pennies and not get carried away, they hadn't listened. Oh, there were the token inexpensive trinkets, like a trophy from Mikey to Jess proclaiming her the world's best boss. For Michael he'd found something called The Perfect Employee doll, which Mikey said came in both a boy and girl version. Michael's doll was a man in a three-piece suit, wearing a big smile and a very brown nose. When Michael pulled the cord, his new toy spouted comments like "There is no 'I' in team" and "I'm all over it, boss" and "I don't want a bonus. I'm just happy to work here." He also gave his father a bottle of champagne. "To celebrate when you get a job," Mikey explained.

"Thanks, son," Michael said. "That was really thoughtful," he added, and his voice broke. He got up and hugged his son, clapping him on the back.

For a moment, shock hung over the room as the children processed seeing their father so emotional. Then Erica handed Jess a large box. "Here, Mom. Open this next. It's from Mikey and me."

Jess opened the box to find another smaller one inside, also wrapped. She couldn't help smiling. She'd pulled this gag on Erica more than a few times over the years.

"How does it feel?" taunted Erica.

"I'll let you know when I get to the last box," Jess retorted. "All I can say right now is you learned this trick from a darned clever woman."

Three boxes later she was down to a small checkbook-sized box. She opened it and found, nestled inside some tissue paper, a gas card. Jess looked up, surprised.

"So you can go see your girlfriends at the lake," Erica explained.

Jess burst into tears.

"Told you she'd love it," Erica said to Mikey.

No, what she loved was her children.

The surprises kept coming. Even though she and Michael had made a pact not to get each other presents, he'd sneaked off and gotten something anyway. "Michael," she gasped, as she opened the jewelry box and saw a heart-shaped necklace ringed with little diamonds.

"Don't worry, I didn't pay a lot for it."

Jess frowned at him. "That's not the point."

"Well, you can't take it back because the pawnbroker said no returns."

"You got Mom a necklace at a pawn shop?" squeaked Erica.

"Well, I never," said Myra in disgust. "Really, Michael!"

Jess smiled as she put it on. "I think it was a great idea. Don't be surprised if this ends up on Rachel's blog."

The biggest present of all came inside an oversized Christmas card from Myra to Jess. Jess pulled out an estimate for a bathroom remodel from Seattle Bath. "What?"

"All you have to do is pick the colors," Myra said with a smile.

She'd said Jess could redecorate, but Jess had never believed she really meant it. Considering how much Myra loved her pink bathroom, this was the ultimate sacrifice.

In addition to the card, Myra had written Jess a note on her favorite floral stationery.

Dear daughter,

 I have always loved you and you have always been a blessing. But never more so than these last few months. I can only imagine how hard it has been to leave the home you loved so much and move into another woman's house, but you did it all without complaint.

Jess could feel her cheeks heating and tears pooling in her eyes. She blinked hard and read on.

I can only hope that someday you get a daughter-in-law who is as good to you as you have been to me.

Jess was crying in earnest by the time she finished. It had been a miserable year with the money worries and having to leave her home. But it had also brought unexpected blessings, like an opportunity to live her rocker chick dream and a chance to make precious memories with Myra. She hugged her mother-in-law and sent up a quick prayer of thanks for allowing her to become such a rich woman.

Chapter 29

"Do you like my outfit for New Year's Eve?" Tiffany asked, twirling in front of Brian.

He turned aside from his computer game to take in her backless black dress and silver heels with an appreciative eye. "Oh, yeah."

"Want to know where I got it?"

Wariness flitted across his face. "I don't know. Do I?"

"Yes, you do. I went shopping." Brian opened his mouth to remind her about their budget pact but she cut him off. "I went shopping in Cara's closet."

Now he was really looking appreciative. "No shit?"

"No shit," she assured him. "And Cara's wearing my dress from last year. Am I good or what?"

"Yes, you are," he agreed. "Come here, you." She came and perched on his lap and he took a nibble of her neck. "I like it even better when you're bad."

She was just starting to show him how bad she could be when the phone rang.

"Let it ring," said Brian, running a hand up her thigh.

"It might be important," she insisted, and picked up.

"What is it?" demanded Brian, taking in her shocked expression.

Only the call of a lifetime.

"You never told me where you were taking me for dinner," Rachel said after Chad had gotten her settled into his vintage Mustang. She hoped she wasn't overdressed. She'd dug out some black velvet pants she'd had forever and teamed them up with her slinky black top and some rhinestone jewelry Jess had loaned her. Considering the number of inexpensive dates she and Chad had enjoyed, it wouldn't have surprised her if they'd wound up at Crazy Eric's eating hamburgers. That would be fine with her. When she was with Chad she was never aware of her surroundings for long anyway.

"I'm taking you someplace I hope you'll like," he said. Instead of heading for the freeway he turned the car toward Lake Way.

So, somewhere in town? The Two Turtledoves? The Family Inn? She hoped he'd chosen The Family Inn. The prices were reasonable, and Ty Howell, who was both chef and half owner of the place, had done a wonderful job of revamping the old restaurant's menu. Two Turtledoves would be way too spendy.

But Chad bypassed both restaurants, instead driving them to the less developed side of the lake. "I thought you might like to see my place," he said.

"Oh, you mean where you've been staying."

He gave her a cryptic smile and nodded.

As they drove, she could catch glimpses of the lake hidden among the trees, the lights from the houses around it reflected on its surface. She'd often driven by the lake with a jealous eye, wishing she could live on it. Not likely, even if she had the money. A few wooded spots remained and some charming, old family cabins, but most of the waterfront was developed now, and lake-front houses rarely came up for sale. Once people got their hands on one they didn't want to sell.

Chad turned down a private gravel road, hidden among fir, alder, and general forest tangle.

"Secluded," Rachel observed.

He looked at her. "Is that a good thing or a bad thing?"

"It depends on who your neighbors are, I guess." She had liked her house, but she'd loved the camaraderie of the neighborhood thanks to Tiff and Jess. Now, with her grumpy new neighbors, not so much.

"I actually have nice neighbors," Chad said, "but I like the fact that we can't see into each other's places."

"Oh, you get used to it," said Rachel, thinking about all the fun she'd had running back and forth from her house to Jess's.

"You miss your next door neighbor, huh?"

"There's an understatement," said Rachel. "The new neighbors are enough to make me wish I lived someplace like this." The road ended, leaving them in front of a two-story cedar home. It wasn't huge, but it was no cabin, ei-ther. She looked at Chad in surprise. "This is your idea of a cabin?"

He shrugged. "It's only three bedrooms. But it's got a great deck."

He took her in through the back door and they passed through a combination mudroom-laundry room, then down a hall past a couple of doors which, she assumed, led to bedrooms. The master bedroom was probably on the second story to take advantage of the view. She caught a whiff of something spicy, probably their dinner, as she followed him through a den area complete with leather couch and chairs and a flat panel TV. Then they were in a huge great room that housed a state of the art kitchen, dining area, and living room. Floor to ceiling windows framed a view of the lake. A fire burned in the wood stove in the corner of the room, casting a romantic glow on the hardwood floors and the furniture. The sofa and two chairs were sage microfilter, big, and comfortable looking.

"Wow," Rachel breathed. "Some cabin. I can't believe your friend has let you stay here so long."

"We're tight," said Chad, moving to where he had champagne chilling in an ice bucket next to the table, which was set for two and decorated with a vase holding a single red rose.

Rachel followed him over, taking it all in as he opened the bottle. The dishes were Fiestaware, the colors tastefully mix 'n' match. "You are definitely in touch with your inner Martha Stewart," she observed.

"Don't let that stuff fool you," he said, popping the cork. "My sister picked out the dishes for me."

"She has good taste." Judging from the way he'd spiffed up the house next door, so did Chad. Odd, though, that he'd had to bring his own dishes to stay in a friend's furnished house.

Before Rachel could say anything he was handing her a glass of champagne. He touched his glass to Rachel's. "Here's to the new year."

"To the new year," Rachel echoed, and they drank, watching each other over the rims of their glasses. She couldn't help but wonder what the coming year held. Surely, with a romantic beginning like this, it had to be something wonderful.

He took her hand and led her over to the couch. Once they were settled, he took the champagne glass from her hand and set it on the coffee table. Her heart began to flutter in anticipation. Here came the first something wonderful.

"Rachel, I've got something I need to tell you."

His serious tone of voice erased her happy glow and her heart plummeted to her stomach. It was the night Aaron told her he'd found someone else all over again. Dinner. He'd taken her out to dinner and told her right there in the Two Turtledoves so she couldn't make a public scene. She'd gotten dressed up and farmed out the kids, just like tonight. *Rachel, I've got something to tell you.* Her lips suddenly felt dry. This is not the same scenario, she told herself firmly. Not even remotely.

"You need to know a few things about me."

"What, you're a serial killer?" she joked.

He smiled and shook his head. "I haven't been entirely honest with you, but before I shared more of my life I wanted to be sure of what we were building together."

That didn't sound like the prelude to a breakup. "You're sure now?"

"I'm sure enough to tell you that this place doesn't belong to a friend," he said. "It belongs to me."

This gorgeous lake house? How was that possible? He was broke. "You?" she stammered.

"I was hoping you'd like it enough to want to move in," he continued.

"Move in? With the kids?" she said stupidly, still reeling from mental whiplash.

"I figure you're a package deal," he said with a smile. "Do you think they'd like living on the lake?" Now he was reaching into the pocket of his sports coat. Out came a little box.

This time she knew it wasn't earrings. Her shocked gaze flew from the box to his face.

He was looking at her with love and hope. He handed it to her and she opened it with trembling hands.

There it was, the diamond ring she'd been dreaming of.

"Will you marry me?"

Say yes! "There's still so much we don't know about each other." Or rather, there was so much she didn't know about him. How did he come to be living in this lovely house on the lake? "I thought you were poor, like me."

He grazed her cheek with his fingers. "I was, once."

"So you own this house and . . . more?" This was too weird. The cheap dates, the secretiveness—it made no sense.

"Actually, I own several rentals. I have one in Richland, where I lived before I bought this place and moved up here, the house in Renton where my sister lives, a condo in Seattle that I'm renting out, and, of course, the one next to you. I'm far from poor, Rachel."

She blinked. She was sitting on a couch with Prince Charming and staring at a gorgeous diamond solitaire. She opened her mouth to say, "Yes, I'll marry you." Instead, she said, "When you told me you were in real estate I thought you meant you were a Realtor, that you sold it."

"I do. I buy, too."

"Why didn't you tell me?"

"Did it matter? Did you need to know I was rich?"

He was rich. Tiffany's words from months ago popped into Rachel's mind. *Maybe he's really rich and he doesn't want you to know cuz he wants to be sure you like him for him.* Tiff had nailed it. "I get it. We were doing a princess and the pea thing. You were testing me to see whether or not I'm a gold digger." Which meant he'd questioned her character. She left the couch and went to stand in front of the window while excitement over Chad's proposal fought with her sense of outrage. The lake stretched out beyond the deck and the small yard, a length of dark mystery. "I don't know what to say, what to think."

He was behind her now, his hands on her shoulders. He turned her to face him. "Come back to the couch. Let me tell you a story."

She let him lead her back to the couch. She perched on the opposite end, facing him, and waited. There, between them, sat the ring, still in its box. Of course, she wanted to put it on, wanted to say, "Yes, I'll marry you." It was silly to smart over the fact that he hadn't been more forthcoming with her. He'd been being cautious. So what? She'd felt cautious at first, too.

But she had told him everything about herself. And he hadn't trusted her. She frowned. "So, once upon a time there was a young prince named Chad."

"Who fell hard for a girl he met in college," Chad finished. He suddenly became fascinated by the sight of the flames dancing behind the glass in the wood stove. "He was quiet, a little shy. She was beautiful and had so much personality, so much life. Every day with her was like a party. He worked hard to give her everything she wanted." Chad's expression turned sour. "The harder he worked the more she wanted, but he kept trying, thinking if he could become as rich as Bill Gates then maybe she'd finally be happy." Chad fell silent.

"And when he became as rich as Bill Gates?" Rachel prompted.

Chad turned and looked at Rachel now. "I didn't. But I had a good chunk and she took half when she left me for another man."

His pain, so like hers, burned into Rachel's heart, consuming her feelings of hurt pride over the fact that he hadn't confided in her sooner. "I'm sorry," she said softly.

Chad shrugged like it didn't matter anymore. "I should have learned from that but I didn't. Chita was the first, Monica was the second. We never married but we were together for almost eight years before it dawned on me that if I lost everything she'd be gone in a heartbeat. I haven't had a serious relationship since . . . until you." Now his expression pleaded for Rachel's understanding.

"I had two strikes against me. I wanted to make sure that you wouldn't be the third. I wanted to find a woman who cares more about people than things, a woman who wants to be with me for what we can be together, not what we can buy together. I'm hoping I've found her."

Rachel took the ring out of the box. She picked up his hand, turned it palm up, and dropped the ring in it. "What do you think?" she asked, and held out her left hand for him to slip the ring on her finger.

His smile split his face. "I think I found her."

And there, in the glow of the firelight, Rachel experienced a fairy tale moment where she was kissed by her prince and offered the world.

They finally came up for air and, drinking more champagne, they talked. And talked. And talked.

When he finally remembered to offer her dinner, she found she didn't have much appetite. The only thing she was hungry for was Chad.

"Where's Rachel?" wondered Tiffany, looking around the club. Some revelers were dancing; others were sitting at tables, wearing funny hats. All were drinking. "If she doesn't get here pretty soon she's going to miss midnight."

"And our big news," Brian added, taking Tiff's hand and kissing it.

Jess and the band were on break and she was sitting opposite them, nursing a soft drink. "You can tell me," she said.

"I want you both to be here," said Tiffany.

"Well, while we're waiting, I have some fun news," Jess said. "Guess where The Red Hots are going to be playing in February."

"Las Vegas," joked Brian.

"Better," said Jess. "Heart Lake. So you guys can take turns putting me up on the weekends."

"Oh, my gosh, that will be so fun," said Tiffany.

"Hey, here comes Rachel with her boyfriend," said Brian, pointing toward the door.

Rachel still hadn't gotten in for her hot new hairstyle and she was wearing the same velvet pants Jess had seen her in for the last three holidays, but she still looked elegant, the rhinestone jewelry Jess had loaned her making her outfit look more classic than recycled. In fact, she looked well beyond elegant. Rachel had the glow of a woman in love.

"What's that I see on her finger?" Tiff said, pointing. "Oh, my gosh!" she cried, and jumped up from the table, plowing her way through the crowd to hug Rachel.

"It looks like everyone has news tonight," said Jess with a smile.

Sure enough, Rachel had a ring with a fat diamond to show off. For a man on a budget, Chad had certainly done well. Sudden concern slipped into Jess's mind. Where had this guy gotten the money to buy that bit of bling? Was he in debt up to his eyeballs? Had they talked about money at all yet?

Of course, this wasn't the moment to ask those questions, so Jess smiled and hugged Rachel and said how happy she was for her.

"Have you set a date?" asked Tiff after the men had been introduced and they were all seated at the table.

"We're thinking June." Rachel smiled at Chad and he smiled back—an intimate exchange that left out everyone else in the room. If ever a couple was madly in love it was these two.

"Let me do the music for the wedding," Jess offered.

"We can do the flowers for you, too," offered Tiff. "Oooh, and we can make the invitations ourselves. We'll do a diva on a dime wedding."

Rachel shot a look in Chad's direction, which Jess found hard to interpret. "I don't think we want a big wedding."

"Well, you still have to have flowers," said Tiffany.

"And music," added Jess.

"And friends, which means you'll need invitations," Tiffany said.

Rachel laughed. "Okay, you've convinced me. We'll do a diva on a dime wedding. And I'll blog about it."

"Just so you don't blog about the honeymoon," said Chad as he signaled for the cocktail waitress.

"This calls for champagne," said Brian as she arrived.

"I've got it," Chad assured him, and ordered a bottle of champagne that Jess knew Brian sure couldn't afford. Big spender.

"While we're sharing good news, Brian and I have some," said Tiffany. She was practically bouncing in her seat.

"You're having a baby," guessed Jess. Hardly difficult in light of how they'd been acting.

Brian grinned and Tiff nodded eagerly.

"Oh, Tiff, that's wonderful," cried Rachel, and hugged her. "When?"

"Next month."

"Next . . . what?"

"We're adopting," Brian explained. "Tiff has an uncle who's a doctor. He has a patient about to give birth and she's decided at the last minute that she doesn't want to keep the baby. We're doing a private adoption."

"My parents are helping us with the bill," said Tiffany. "As a reward for handling my money so well these past months," she added proudly.

"When did all this happen?" asked Jess, wondering how Tiffany had managed to keep quiet about it.

"Today," said Tiff. "Well, the girl made the final decision

today. We've been talking all week. I told her we didn't
have a ton of money but she said she didn't care. She
could tell we had heart."

"So do you know if it's a boy or a girl?" asked Rachel.

"It's a girl," said Tiffany. "And guess what we're going
to name her? Grace."

"I love that name," said Rachel.

Tiffany smiled at Brian with tears in her eyes. He took
her hand and held it. "It seemed like the perfect name.
Cuz that's what I've been given a lot of lately, especially
from my husband."

The champagne arrived and Jess proposed a toast. "To
my friends, who are both getting what they so richly deserve. Happy New Year."

"Happy New Year," everyone echoed.

As she drank her champagne, Jess found herself wishing she still lived in the old neighborhood so she could
play grandma and babysit for Tiff. She gave a mental
shrug and reminded herself that it could be worse. She
could live clear across the country.

Of course, she could still wind up living far away if
Michael didn't find something in the area. She took another drink of champagne. Borrowing trouble was not an
option, especially on the eve of a new year.

It was mid-afternoon on January first when Rachel's children came home from their sleepovers. She found herself
more nervous than she'd ever been in her life as she set a
plate of the last of the holiday cookies on the kitchen table. Her engagement ring was burning a hole in her jeans.
She hadn't had the courage to wear it today, didn't want to
answer any questions until Chad was here with her. What
she was going to do if her children didn't like the idea of
her marrying Chad, she had no idea.

She thought back to when Aaron started his new life

with Misty. He sure hadn't bothered to ask Claire and David what they thought. Well, there was a parenting model she wanted to follow. Not.

The doorbell rang and she jumped. There's no reason to be nervous, she told herself as she let Chad in. Why wouldn't her children be as excited as she was?

He smiled and gave her a fortifying kiss after he came through the front door. "Where are the kids?"

In their rooms, putting away their things. "Claire, David," she called. "Come down here. We've got company." She lowered her voice. "I am terrified."

"No need to be," he said, and took her hand.

First they heard the thunder of feet on the stairs. Then Claire and David came into view.

"Oh, hi, Chad," said Claire. Her tone of voice asked, *This is your idea of company?*

They'd done everything with him from mushroom-hunting to playing board games. He probably didn't qualify as company anymore. Rachel hoped he qualified as family.

"Hey, Chad, wanna shoot hoops?" David asked eagerly.

"Maybe later," Rachel said. "Come out to the kitchen, you two. We need to talk about something." The kids plopped down at the table and Rachel got down glasses for milk to go with the cookies.

Claire eyed her mother as she poured milk. "Is something going on?"

"You could say that," said Rachel. How hard was it to come right out and say . . .

"Your mother and I are getting married," said Chad, taking the whole decision of how to do this out of her hands.

David grinned and snatched a cookie. "Cool."

Claire looked at her mother, her eyes big. "Really?"

"We want to," said Rachel. "Are you okay with that?"

Claire's brow furrowed and she started fiddling with her braces. "Um, where will we live?"

"How about on the lake?" said Chad.

Claire's body language changed instantly. She sat up. "On the lake? For real?"

"Awesome!" cried David. "Do you have a boat? Can we water-ski?"

"Probably," said Chad.

That clinched it. Rachel's offspring looked at each other like two lottery winners who couldn't believe their good fortune.

They weren't the only ones. Neither could their mother. "Pinch me," she said to Chad later that day, after he came in from playing basketball with David and the neighbors.

Chad took the glass of water she'd poured for him and looked appreciatively at her backside. "I could do that."

She slipped her arms around his neck. "I never thought I'd fall in love again. I never thought I'd find anyone." *I never thought anyone would want me.*

"That makes two of us," he said, and kissed her.

"I still can't believe it," Rachel said to Jess later that week as they talked on the phone. "I feel like any minute now I'm going to wake up and be back in the real world of scrimping and pinching pennies."

"I guess you won't have to do that anymore," said Jess.

"Not so much, but Chad is definitely the millionaire next door and I'll still be on a budget."

"But a heck of a lot bigger one than you had before," said Jess. "And to think I was worried about him not having any money."

"I'd marry him even if he didn't," said Rachel.

"I know you would. But I bet you're finding it just as easy to love a rich man," Jess teased. "Now, for the most

important question: where are you going for your honeymoon?"

"We haven't decided for sure, but it's looking like the
Caribbean."

Jess began to croon the Beach Boys' "Kokomo." "Need
someone to carry your suitcase? Oh, that's right. It's your
honeymoon. Clothing optional. You may need to remind
Tiff of that. She'll want to help you shop for an entire
trousseau."

"I have a feeling she's going to be too busy with
her new baby to worry about my trousseau," Rachel predicted.

Sure enough. Every time Rachel talked to Tiffany it
was baby, baby, baby. Tiffany had already signed herself
and Brian up for parenting classes. Amazingly, Tiff hadn't
gone overboard with spending though. She had found
bargains online and on eBay to round out what her friends
had given her at the impromptu baby shower Cara hosted
at the salon.

"I can't believe it. Grace comes in two weeks," said
Tiff, as she showed Rachel the finished nursery. Of course,
all the trimmings were pink and white, and the room
looked fit for a princess. Tiff's smile slipped a little. "Do
you think I'll make a good mother?" she asked in a small
voice.

"Of course you will," Rachel assured her. "You're fun
and kind. You'll be great."

"Do you think I'm selfish?"

"If you are, don't worry. The baby will beat it out of
you," Rachel said.

"No, seriously. Do you?"

"No more than any of the rest of us," said Rachel. She
gave Tiff a hug, saying, "Trust me. You'll be a great
mother."

Tiff sighed happily. "Here I was so miserable last year

and now this year we're going to have a baby. Gosh, things sure can change in a hurry."

They sure could. Rachel could hardly believe she wasn't dreaming. If she was, it was the busiest dream she'd ever had. There was so much to decide and plan and do. And every day included Chad, which made every day wonderful, no matter how routine.

January was coming to a close and she was getting her teaching materials ready for an afternoon of tutoring when he stopped by. "I know you're trying to get ready," he said, "but I wanted to drop off some papers for you." He held out a fat, legal-sized envelope.

"Oh, what's this?" She opened it and slid out the papers.

"Just a formality," he assured her. "You don't have to sign it right now. Take your time. Read it over."

She began to skim the first page. Phrases started jumping out at her. *Each party has separate property, the nature and extent of which is fully disclosed in the statements of assets and liabilities . . . Thereafter, each of the parties shall separately retain all rights in the property he or she now owns . . . each party hereby waives, releases, and relinquishes any and all right, title, or interest whatsoever . . .*

Rachel looked up, shocked. "This is a prenup."

Chad's dark skin couldn't hide the guilty flush. "Yes, but like I said, it's only a formality."

A cold chill swept over Rachel. She slowly slid the legal document back into the envelope. "No, it's more than that." She remembered all her doubts when she'd first met Chad, all her fears that she'd get hurt. Now that it was happening it was so much worse than she'd ever imagined.

He looked pained. "Rachel, it's a safeguard, that's all. Please don't make this into more than it is."

Inside she wanted to scream, throw the envelope with his precious safeguard at him. "I know exactly what this is. It's proof that you don't trust me."

"Rachel," he cajoled.

He moved to take her in his arms—always a good negotiating position for a handsome man—but she backed away.

He looked pained by her refusal to let him kiss her stupid. "This has nothing to do with you. It's standard operating procedure when there's money involved. It's simply a legal document, like a marriage license."

"Not quite," said Rachel. "A marriage license proves to the world that we're committed. This proves to the world that you don't trust me. I understand why you have trust issues. You've been hurt. But so have I. Remember?"

He threw up his hands in frustration. "So, if you understand, why are you making a big deal out of this? If we're going to be together for the rest of our lives, what does it matter if you sign a simple document?"

"If we're going to be together for the rest of our lives, what does it matter if I don't?" she countered. "I have to sign this for you to marry me, don't I?"

His hesitation gave Rachel her answer.

She could feel tears building up, but she kept her voice level. "I guess we don't know each other as well as we thought, because if we did you wouldn't be here with this. I loved you when I thought you had nothing." Her voice broke. It made her look weak and stupid, but she couldn't help it.

"Rachel, don't."

She longed to hear him say, "Never mind. You're right, I'm being paranoid," but the words didn't come.

She could feel her heart cracking under the crushing weight of her broken dreams. "You may have a big bank account but this is the only asset I have," she said, putting a hand over her heart. "I was willing to give it to you without any safeguards, without any protection at all. I was willing to put everything I have on the line for this relationship. You're clearly not willing to do that. It's like you already have one foot out the door."

"That's not it at all," he insisted. "This is . . ."

"Insurance?" she finished for him. "I guess in this day and age you need insurance. But I can't go there." She pulled the ring from her finger and dropped it in the envelope, then pushed it at him, forcing him to take it. "I'm sorry. I can't do this," she managed.

The doorbell rang and she opened the door to find her first student standing on the porch. Her storybook romance had just been destroyed and now she had to go to work.

Good thing she hadn't quit her day job, such as it was, she thought bitterly. "Good-bye, Chad," she said.

"We'll talk later," he insisted.

She shook her head. "No, I'm afraid we won't." What would be the point?

Chapter 30

"Where's Chad?" David asked at dinner.

Rachel hadn't had time to process what had happened to her. How was she supposed to explain to her children? She took the coward's way out. "He had some things to do."

That satisfied David, but Claire was a little more observant. Taking in Rachel's red eyes from her secret premeal crying jag and her distracted air, Claire asked, "Did you guys have a fight?"

"No," Rachel lied, forcing her lips to smile. "Everything's fine."

"Then where's your ring?"

The ring. Rachel stared at her bare finger. It didn't look right. Funny how quickly she'd gotten used to seeing that diamond on her left hand. "We've decided to wait a little." Another lie.

David frowned. "Does that mean we don't get to live at the lake?"

"That means I don't know," Rachel said, keeping her voice level. "It's better to wait and be sure." After a reasonable interval, she'd tell the children that she'd changed her mind.

"Does that mean he's not even coming over?" David demanded.

"For the time being."

David scowled and gave the mashed potatoes on his plate an angry shove. A moment later he pushed his chair away from the table and stalked off.

"David!" Rachel called after him, her voice sharp.

"He's mad, Mom," said Claire, stating the obvious. "He liked Chad."

"Well, so did I," Rachel snapped. Now Claire was looking hurt. "I'm sorry," Rachel said. She could feel an ache starting around her temples. Maybe after dinner she'd just go to her room and cry for about three hours.

Claire got up, but instead of marching out of the kitchen like her brother, she came around to where Rachel sat and draped her arms around Rachel's neck. "I'm sorry, Mommy," she murmured. "I bet you guys will make up."

She put on a brave front and gave her daughter's arm a pat and said, "You never know."

There was another lie. The chasm between Chad and her was too great to cross, and that horrible knowledge kept her crying into her pillow late into the night.

"Well, good riddance, then," said Jess, as the three friends sat in Tiffany's living room taking turns holding the baby.

Little Grace was a perfect. With her blonde fuzz and rosebud lips she promised to grow up to be as pretty as her mother. Who at the moment was wearing what all well-dressed new mothers wore: dark circles under the eyes, neglected hair, and a towel draped over one shoulder. She gave Grace a kiss on the top of her head, and then took the little pink bundle to the nursery to lay her down for her nap.

"I can't blame him for being leery," Rachel said to Jess.

"Not after getting taken by two women. Once burned, twice shy. Or, in this case, twice burned." She couldn't blame him, but she found she couldn't quite forgive him, either. He'd called twice since she returned his ring, but she'd refused to talk to him.

"Still, if you can't start out a marriage with trust you're in trouble. I think that increases the odds that you'll fail," said Jess.

"I don't have to worry about that now," Rachel said bitterly, setting aside her mug of coffee. "I failed before I even started. You know what's really bad? I still want him."

Jess moved to the couch where Rachel was sitting and hugged her. "I'm so sorry."

Sorry didn't even begin to cover it, Rachel thought as the lump in her throat grew to unbearable proportions.

A moment later Tiff was at her other side, holding out a box of tissues. "Things will work out. I know they will."

Of course, Tiff was only trying to be helpful. But of all the inane, inaccurate, impossible things to say . . . "No, they won't." Rachel glared at her friend, just to make sure Tiff got the message. *No false cheer wanted.* Tiffany pulled out a tissue and handed it over and Rachel snatched it and blew her nose.

"You don't know that," said Tiffany, refusing to get the message. "If you guys really love each other, one of you will make the first move."

"Then, it will have to be him," said Rachel. "I already passed his damned princess and the pea test."

Tiff's brows knit. "What test was that?"

"The going out all those months and loving him even when I thought he was poor. I mean, if that didn't prove I wasn't after his money, I don't know what would."

"Signing the prenup," said Tiff.

Rachel yanked another tissue out of the box. "Are you delirious? Why would I do that?"

"Cuz you don't care about money and you love him," said Tiff.

"You're right. I don't and I do and he should know that."

"He probably does in his heart," said Tiff. "I guess he just wants reassurance. You said yourself that you weren't out for his money. So, why not sign the stupid thing?"

"Why ask her to sign it in the first place?" argued Jess. "If he trusts her, he shouldn't need her to sign a piece of paper."

"But if she loves him maybe she should be willing to do whatever it takes to prove it," said Tiff, refusing to back down. "How bad do you want him?" she asked Rachel.

There was the most important question of all. Rachel thought about it long after she left Tiffany's house. She took it to bed with her that night and tossed and turned with it. She carried it around with her the next week and a half as she filled in for sick teachers, tutored, did laundry, made meals, and helped her children with their homework. What if she did sign that agreement? She'd really only be telling Chad he could keep his toys. And what if she and Chad married and things didn't work out? She'd be back to doing exactly what she was doing now. She'd be fine. She didn't need his money.

But she did need his love. Ever since she'd given him back his ring and his precious insurance policy she had been walking around with a big hole in her heart. A perfect man was hard to find. Heck, impossible. Chad wasn't perfect, but he was as close as she'd ever come. If she wanted him she was going to have to overlook his fear and insecurity.

Valentine's Day was right around the corner by the time she finally went online. It didn't take her long to find some free prenup forms. She printed one out, filled in what she could, and signed it. Then she put it in a manila envelope along with an invitation to join her on that special day at The Last Resort to hear Jess's band play. As she left the post office to go sub at Heart Lake Elementary she had a dark moment of doubt. What man would ask this sort of thing of a woman? What kind of love was so selfish?

She could only answer her questions with more questions. When a man asked this sort of thing of a woman, did he act because he was selfish or because he was wounded? And did she have it in her to heal him?

She hoped she did. In fact, she was sure she did. She was smiling by the time she pulled into the school parking lot.

"You look happy," said her friend Elsa, when Rachel walked into the teacher's lounge. "Does it have anything to do with that good looking man I saw you with at Christmas?"

"It could," Rachel said with a smile. Yes, it could.

Rachel hoped she would hear from Chad before Valentine's Day, that he'd rush over the minute he got the prenup and put the ring back on her finger. But he didn't rush over. And he didn't call.

As Valentine's Day drew nearer, she got more nervous, so nervous in fact that she actually finally went in to Salon H and had Cara cut and dye her hair. She even went to Bargain Boutique and bought a new dress: basic black, with beading. But still no word from Chad.

"You *are* coming to hear the band tomorrow, right?" Jess asked her the day before.

"I'm coming," she said. It was her last hope. She had to be there.

Valentine's night she stood in front of her mirror, assessing herself. She half wished her kids were home to assure her that she did, indeed, look wonderful, but they were both at friends' houses. So that left only her.

"You look great," she told herself as she slipped on the silver cuff bracelet Jess had bought for her in July. "And you'll have fun tonight, no matter what."

Who was she kidding? If Chad ignored her invitation and didn't show, she was going to throw herself in the lake.

"Not funny," she scolded her reflection. Then she grabbed her purse and left the house to meet her fate, whatever it might be.

The Last Resort was the closest thing Heart Lake had to a club, and it was hopping. The air was thick with the scent of every perfume and cologne known to man. Twenty- and thirty-somethings crowded along the bar, all dressed to kill, and couples and foursomes sat at the small tables, laughing and leaning in close, trying to talk over the band. The little dance floor was packed with Valentine lovers and The Red Hots were in great form, keeping the dancers happy with Aerosmith's "I Don't Wanna Miss a Thing." Jess looked like a superstar in her tight leather pants and red sequined top.

Rachel could only hope that, before the night was over, she'd be with Chad, among the swaying couples, laying a foundation for a future of love and trust. She spotted Tiff and Brian and Michael all dressed to the nines and holding down a table near the dance floor and wove her way through the crowd.

The music wound down as Rachel took her seat. "Hi," Tiff greeted her. "I was beginning to think you'd never get here."

Rachel checked her watch. "It's only nine. The band just went on, didn't they?"

"Well, yeah," Tiff admitted. Then added, "But we can't stay all night."

Brian smiled indulgently at her. "The baby will be fine. She's with my mom."

Tiff didn't say anything to that. Instead, she took a sip of her drink.

Rachel couldn't help smiling. She remembered those new-mother nerves. It had probably taken every ounce of Brian's persuasive power to get Tiff to come out. "What are you drinking?" she asked.

"Coke."

"Just Coke?"

"I don't want to drink too much and have a hangover. Anyway, booze knocks me out. I want to be able to hear when Grace wakes up for her feeding."

"You're such a good mother," Brian told her, and they kissed.

And Rachel felt ridiculously, insanely jealous. She looked around the room, but saw no sign of Chad. Disappointment settled over her like a cloak.

Now the cocktail waitress was at her side. "Let me buy you a drink, Rachel," Michael offered. "What would you like?"

Arsenic, she thought, but she ordered a Chocolate Kiss martini.

Chocolate Kiss martinis were highly overrated. So were love songs, and it looked like the band was going to play every romantic rock song ever written.

The night would have been perfect if Rachel hadn't been alone, if she had hope that she wouldn't wind up alone forever. But nothing was perfect. It had been almost forty-five minutes now and there was still no sign of Chad. He obviously wasn't coming.

"I'm going to go, you guys," she said to the others.

Tiffany looked panicked. "No. You can't leave. We're . . . not done. Jess wants to join us when the band goes on break."

Who knew how long it would be before they took their break?

"Don't go," Michael added. "Jess'll be disappointed if you don't stay long enough to say hi."

Rachel resigned herself to her fate and took another sip of her martini. This had been such a stupid idea.

The band ended the song and launched into a new one, more upbeat. It sounded old and funky and vaguely familiar.

The crowd didn't care. They were already boogying. It took Rachel a minute to realize Jess was singing the old Beatles song "Can't Buy Me Love."

The song was half over when Rachel knew she had really had enough. In fact, if she stayed any longer she was going to have a complete nervous breakdown. She'd call Jess tomorrow and tell her the band had been great. "I really need to go," she told Michael. "Tell Jess I'm sorry. I don't feel good." No lie. She was sick at heart. She plucked her jacket off the back of her chair and picked up her purse.

Tiff grabbed her arm and looked at her with narrowed eyes. "Don't. Leave."

The song came to a screaming halt and the crowd on the dance floor clapped and hooted. Jess spoke into the microphone. "Happy Valentine's Day, Heart Lake."

More hooting and clapping.

Yeah, happy, thought Rachel. Here she sat pinned to her chair by someone who was supposed to be her good friend, while the damned gremlin rubbed it in her face that she was a Cupid reject.

"We have someone tonight who has a special delivery to make and a special song request," Jess continued. "Where's Rachel Green?"

"Here," called Tiffany, waving an arm while keeping one hand on Rachel.

Rachel felt a million eyes on her and her face caught on fire. What was going on? She hadn't requested any song.

"Okay," said Jess. "There she is. Go get her."

And suddenly, there came Chad, weaving his way among the tables to catcalls and clapping, a manila envelope in his hand. Rachel's heart went into overdrive.

He stopped in front of her and opened the envelope. Down drifted a shower of torn paper. He smiled down at her. "You were right. We don't need this." He pulled her engagement ring from his pocket and held it up questioningly.

Rachel could feel tears spilling from her eyes. She put a disbelieving hand to her mouth. Was this really happening?

"Take it," called a female voice from the crowd.

Her heart was going to burst, she was sure. She held out her hand and he slipped the ring on her finger, then he pulled her to him and kissed her while it seemed like all of Heart Lake applauded their approval.

"Okay, you two," said Jess. "This song's for you, so you'd better get out on the dance floor while there's still room."

The band played Metallica's "Nothing Else Matters" and Chad pulled Rachel to him. She was hardly aware of other couples drifting onto the dance floor to join them. "I didn't hear from you. I thought . . ."

"I was gone. I went to see my family and get my head screwed on straight. They can hardly wait to meet you, by the way."

So they were on again, just like that. "Chad, are you sure?"

"I should be asking you that," he said. "I'm sorry I hurt you. I'm a fool. If I can't trust you, then there's no one in this whole world I can trust. I love you." And to prove it, he kissed her.

She kissed him back and gave the gremlin the boot. For good. God bless those romance writers.

The song ended and the band went on break.

Tiffany was practically gloating when Rachel and Chad returned to the table. "So, I guess you're staying after all?" she teased.

Chad squeezed Rachel's hand and she smiled at him. "Yes, I guess I am. And I suppose you were in on this," she said to Tiff.

"I recruited their help," Chad admitted.

Tiff beamed. "I'm good."

Now Jess had joined them. "It looks like we need to make a toast." "Did you order the champagne?" she asked Michael.

Right on cue their cocktail waitress arrived with the glasses. After everyone had taken one, Michael raised his and said, "To love."

"And to second chances," added Tiffany. "Everybody needs at least one."

"And to the third time," said Chad. "It really is the charm."

Small Change, Big Difference

It had been nearly a year since Tiffany, Rachel, and Jess altered their financial lifestyles. To celebrate, Jess had baked a cake. "From scratch, no less," she'd bragged. It was a little on the dry side, but Rachel and Tiffany had praised her for her efforts.

Now they sat at Rachel's kitchen table among bits of ribbon, stamping supplies, and card stock, addressing the last of the homemade wedding invitations. This year a wedding, next year they'd be making invitations to celebrate a graduation. Jess was back in school finishing up her music degree.

Baby Grace sat on a blanket in the family room, laughing as Claire and her friend Bethany entertained her with the new toys Tiffany had snagged at a garage sale. Yells and hoots drifted in through the open kitchen window from outside, where Chad was playing half-court basketball with David and the neighbor boys.

"That's the last one," said Jess, slipping an invitation into the envelope.

"It's funny, isn't it? Here you are marrying a millionaire and we're sending out homemade invites," Tiffany observed.

"That's how people with money keep their money," said Jess. "They're careful with it. And let me tell you, we've learned our lesson. The savings account is growing. Slowly," she added, "but slow is better than not at all. And if Michael's executive temp job turns into something full time we'll really be able to grow our rainy-day fund."

"And maybe move back?" Tiff asked hopefully.

"I think I'm stuck in Seattle for a while," said Jess with a resigned shrug. "But at least I'm not stuck in a Pepto-Bismol bathroom. And I'm not worried about how we're going to make the mortgage payment."

Tiffany shook her head. "I can't believe how different my life is now from last year."

"I need to do an anniversary blog post," Rachel decided.

"And put it at the end of your book," Jess advised.

Rachel grabbed a piece of paper and a pencil from her kitchen junk drawer. "So, what do we want to say?"

"Happy anniversary to us," declared Tiffany.

Rachel smiled. "That's great, but I'd like to add a little more content. Have you two got any great advice for my readers?"

"Just because you buy something on sale it doesn't mean you're saving money," said Tiffany with a decisive nod. "Oh, and things won't make you happy."

Rachel smiled. "I love that." She looked expectantly at Jess. "Got anything to add?"

"Budgets are our friends. And *save* is not a four-letter word."

"And how about you?" asked Tiff. "What are you going to say?"

"You know, I'm going to have to think about that."

Much later, after her friends had gone home and Chad and the kids were busy making his mother's recipe for enchiladas, Rachel sat at her computer, reading what she'd just written for her blog.

I have come to realize three important facts of life this last year.

1. Cinderella can keep Prince Charming. A good man's love is all any woman needs to make her feel like a princess.
2. The only person who can fix your life is you.
3. Small changes can make a big difference.

And that about summed it up.